Priya Popat

Josie's Upturned World

from dumped to daring

Gem Write Publishing

First Edition: September 2019

ISBN: 978-1-9162115-0-6

Cover and Formatting: Streetlight Graphics

Seek the wisdom that will untie your knot
Seek the path that demands your whole being
Leave that which is not, but appears to be
Seek that which is, but is not apparent

-Rumi

The above quote was chosen by Joshna, my long lost, but not forgotten friend. I dedicate this book to you & to my friend for many years, Sandra. Both of you have a special place in my heart.

Book One
Four Fiancés & A Funeral

Chapter One
Dumpsville

A WISE MAN NAMED LAO-TZU ONCE said that a journey of a thousand miles begins with a single step. So why did it feel like I had travelled thousands of miles, barefoot and bleeding, only to discover that I hadn't moved at all? My single steps only led me into dead-end jobs and disastrous relationships.

Here I was again. In Dumpsville. Worse still, dumped by (supposedly) Nice Niles, nearly forty, fiancé number. 4. Not the best way to start a new year. The year I turned thirty. I had always imagined that I would be married, with a baby on the way by now. I patted my stomach. No, that was most likely the result of too much Christmas turkey and yule log. Most definitely *not* a baby.

I dragged myself up the five flights of stairs. Trust Dame to have a bloody top floor flat with an out-of-order lift. (The engineer had been round to 'fix it' six times in the last three months). As soon as I got inside the flat, I took huge deep breaths to fill my lungs and collapsed on the sofa.

'Someone's had a good seeing to!' Dame flounced into the room, winking and grinning at me.

I squeezed my eyes tightly shut, hoping against all hope that this had just been a bad dream. The cutting pain in my chest told me otherwise. I opened my eyes to find Dame standing in front of me wearing an obscenely bright t-shirt bearing the words: *'young, dumb and full of cum,'* aka Simon Pegg in the film 'How to lose friends and alienate people.' His beam threatened to split his face in half.

'Guess who called?'

'Was it Ni … Niles?' I replied, my heart drumming erratically.

'No, *not* Niles.' Dame rolled his eyes. 'George. Dishy doctor, better than Clooney. The one with the *very* impressive bedside manner.'

'Oh him!' I said, trying to inject some level of enthusiasm in my voice. The A&E doctor who had treated Dame's uncle with appendicitis a few months back. The one he had been stalking ever since, skulking outside the hospital and hanging out at the local bar in the hope of seeing him again. It had worked. They had exchanged numbers and a slobbery kiss on a drunken night out.

'Anyway, I've invited him to come dine with me, so you know … if you could disappear for a bit ….'

'Don't worry about me, I'll be nursing a bottle of vodka in my room,' I replied morosely.

'Oh Josie, not *again.'* He slowly shook his head, while hugging me to within an inch of my life. I sniffed loudly into his fluorescent t-shirt.

'I know just what you need,' he said, getting up. 'A big

knob of Belgian chocolate Haagan Daas and one very large spoon.'

'Sprinkled with Niles' crushed nuts,' I called out, noting how frequently Dame worked the word *knob* into conversations. He couldn't help it, he was knob-obsessed and I was, it had to be said, attracted predominately to ... well ... knobs.

He hurried back with the tub of ice-cream and a full bottle of red wine.

'Just mind you don't get any on the sofa.'

'I've just been bloody dumped,' I spluttered, 'and all you can think about is your sodding sofa?'

'Well, I have just had it upholstered ...' he trailed off, seeing my scowl. Honestly, sometimes Dame had all the sensitivity of a sledgehammer.

'Go on, what's happened this time?' he asked, licking his chocolatey spoon.

'We were enjoying what I thought was a cosy romantic meal at 'La Dolce Vita' when he suddenly got all weird and twitchy, like he'd just had a suppository inserted or something. Then he said 'It really pains me to say this but...' and that was it. I just wanted to put my fingers in my ears and sing La La La really loudly, because I knew exactly what was coming next.' I paused, trying not to break down.

He squeezed my hand, encouraging me to continue.

'Dame, the bottom line is: he has no intention of getting married. He would rather go deep-sea diving and explore new continents. I mean, that's just so fucking random, even for Niles.'

Dame suppressed a snigger.

'I explained that it was possible to travel the world, dive *and* be married, but he had this determined look on his stupid face and said the flights were already booked. I didn't even think to ask where he was going. Now he won't pick up his phone or answer his door.' I buried my head in my hands. 'It just doesn't make any sense.'

A tiny part of me actually admired the fact that he was out there, having adventures and living his life. I just wish it hadn't been at my expense.

'Being dumped for deep sea diving. That's a first! Are you sure it's not muff-diving he's doing?'

I gave Dame a dirty look which he chose to ignore.

'And all this coming from a couple's counsellor?' he scoffed. 'That probably makes him more screwed up than the rest of us.'

'You've not liked *any* of my boyfriends' I said, flatly.

'Well darling, if you are going to pick the ones with such glaring defects ....'

'Dame!' I hissed.

'OK, I'm sorry. Let's look at this objectively,' he said, handing me the bottle of wine. 'You start dating someone. Within days you're officially going out together, within weeks you're engaged, and then about six months into the relationship you get dumped. I'm no therapist but there seems to be a bit of a pattern here, wouldn't you say?'

'I was with Geoff for seven and a half months,' I replied, somewhat mutinously.

'Geoff? You mean that 9ft goof who gave you gonorrhea?'

'He was 7ft 2 inches and he did not give me gonorrhea. It was all cleared up by the time we got intimate.'

'What about Domineering Dan, Selfish Stewart and now Not-so-Nice Niles?'

My eyes burned. I know having four fiancés was highly

unusual, and maybe even a little bit peculiar. Especially for someone under thirty. But I hadn't planned it this way. I didn't collect men the same way some people collect shoes or bags. NO. I wanted a forever-man. For once in my life, I didn't want to feel like the kid with her nose pressed up against a frosted window, looking into a world of happy families yet feeling so intensely alone. Because that's exactly how I'd felt since Dad had left us.

'Maybe I'm wrong about Niles?' Dame's voice brought me back to the present moment. 'Maybe he just needs some space and he'll come crawling back to you with his tail between his legs. But in the meantime, you are *so* getting on with your life. Just look at you,' he said, grabbing my hand and pulling me off the sofa in true Gok Wan style. He spun me round to face the ornate silver mirror hanging above the fireplace.

'You are truly beautiful, girlfriend - inside and out.'

'I'm bootiful!' I slurred, imitating Bernard Matthews talking about a prize turkey while holding the wine bottle high above my head.

'No, really look ...' encouraged Dame. I squinted at the mirror. I had a smooth olive complexion, sparkling jade green eyes and long dark glossy hair, pulled up loosely in a chignon, with wispy strands falling onto my face. I was quite pretty, I suppose. Not devastatingly gorgeous like some women I knew, but attractive and approachable. At least that's what I got told by the men I dated, all of whom seemed totally smitten to begin with. Calling me constantly, buying me gifts and generally behaving as if I were 'The One.' Right up until they dumped me, that is.

Maybe it was because I was a nasty cow really. Hadn't I recently barked (or should that be mooed?) at my neighbour downstairs, dear 87-year-old Pru Morel, all because she had blocked my descent down the staircase when I was late for meeting Niles. Being pre-menstrual and therefore extremely grouchy at the time was no excuse. At least Niles didn't think so.

I linked arms with the blond, angelic-looking boy standing by my side, always with a mischievous twinkle in his eye.

I sighed deeply. 'Why couldn't you have been straight? We'd be married with triplets by now.'

'Steady on love,' he said, looking faintly nauseated at the prospect. 'Would have made my parents happy though,' he added sadly. But then he quickly poked me in the ribs. 'May as well open another bottle.'

'But what about George?' I asked, remembering Dame's hot date with the dishy doctor.

'He'll just have to come over another night. I'll call to cancel. Let him know what it feels like to chase me for a change.'

'Damian Hart, you are a diamond,' I said, hugging him appreciatively.

'Well, I don't want to sound big-headed but I get told that every time. Anyway, stop being such a soppy tart,' he said, slapping my arse.

***

I had moved into Dame's flat near Clapham three weeks ago. Not something I could ever have afforded on my own, but Dame's parents were minted. They had bought him this two-bedroom flat as a reward for obtaining a first-class degree in Accountancy and Finance from the London School of Economics. He said he did the degree just to please them, as compensation for 'turning out' gay. I think that despite their disapproving manner they were secretly proud of Dame for having the courage to be himself, and for being immensely bright. Not that they would ever have admitted it to him, of course.

I just about managed to scrape a third in my Business and Finance degree, and was now working as an Information Assistant in an art gallery in Pimlico, not a million miles away from the Tate Britain but nowhere near as impressive in size or collections. I didn't have much of an aptitude for finance or even the slightest interest in the business world, just a vague ambition of wanting to work in an office full of powerful and attractive men in designer suits. Which hadn't materialised thus far: the closest I got to hot men in suits was commuting on the London Underground. My mum was just relieved and grateful that I had made it out of university with any sort of qualification to my name at all.

That was where I first met Dame. We shared some classes and during one lecture, when I had almost chewed my fingers off from extreme boredom, he swaggered in late and slid into the seat next to me.

'Did I miss much?' he whispered, his full red lips so close to my skin that I felt a ripple of heat run right though me.

'Don't think so, wasn't paying much attention,' I mumbled, now having lost all ability to concentrate on fiscal affairs.

'My name's Hart, Damien Hart,' he said, sounding more Bond than Bond himself.

I fancied the pants off him from the minute I met him and assumed the feeling was mutual. We had great banter, laughed at each other's sick jokes and shared similar interests such as drinking, dancing and eating cold pizza. We seemed to be the perfect couple in every way. Except that he was gay, of course, and I was the last to realise. I forgave him for finding a boyfriend and began a manhunt of my own. Dame was witness to that.

Gregarious gym-honed Geoff was the first. I honestly didn't think I'd get a look in, what with him dating a bevy of popular, attractive girls. Maybe I appealed to him because I wasn't throwing myself at him like all the other girls? Looking back, I'd say that he was quite insecure. He sought my advice on everything, from what clothes suited his muscular frame to what he should do with his life. He spent all his free time with me, taking me out to new fancy places. Naturally I was flattered. No girl had ever seemed that important to him, or lasted longer than two weeks. When he proposed after three months it felt like we were meant to be. Things were going great and we were happy. At least I thought so, until he started becoming irritable and moody, handing in coursework late, failing exams. Rather than talk to me, he chose to blame me for the way things were going in his life - and dumped me.

Feeling miserable and vulnerable after that, Dame dragged me out as often as he could. I made the most of the 10-shots-for-£10 nights at a little bar called 'The Swinging Hippy.' That's where I met Dan, who fixed on me with his glittering green eyes, looking straight past Dame. 'I love a girl who can handle her drink, fancy another round?' was the first thing he said to me, looking deeply impressed after watching me sink my tenth shot in a row.

'Sure,' I'd slurred, swaying slightly while giving him what I had considered to be a seductive smile.

'I think she's had enough,' Dame had interrupted. 'No, I'm fine Dame, honestly. We'll share our shots,' I'd hiccupped.

Dan had led me to a couple's booth where we demolished our shots then snogged until our lips felt numb.

'Let's meet tomorrow, I want to get drunk on you, no alcohol required,' he'd whispered in my ear. Something exploded inside of me: joy, desire. Dan made me feel deliriously happy and for the next six weeks he showered me with compliments, affection and numerous gifts. When he proposed, I said yes instantly. I was in love.

'Have you lost your flaming marbles?' was Dame's response to our engagement. Dan also had a habit of deciding everything. From where we'd eat to what movie we'd watch, to which friends I hung out with. 'Can't you see what he's like?' But it was like I was under a spell, addicted to the many highs we had until it all came crashing down. Dan decided to dump me because he thought I wasn't committed enough. That if I really loved him, I wouldn't have chosen to celebrate my best friend Dame's birthday on the same day that he'd had a bad day and needed me at home. Nothing changed his mind. Once Dan decided that was it, that *was* it.

I kind of went off the rails after that, and had a brief dalliance with Professor Waltman, Dame's Economics tutor. He wasn't my tutor so I convinced myself that it was ok, except that he hadn't quite been telling the truth when he said he was separated from his wife. Yet even more heartache. No wonder I couldn't concentrate on my studies, I was an emotional mess. More of a mess than I had ever admitted to anyone. I'd felt as if my life was completely unravelling and I kept a bottle of vodka under my pillow to help me through the lonely nights and dark places I sometimes found myself in. Anxious thoughts slithered around in my head, like a nest of snakes. Would I ever fit in? Find love? Belong to someone?

Dame had been there each and every time to pick up the pieces and put me back together again. I had other friends at university, but none like Dame.

Eight years later Dame was still my fabulous, flamboyant friend and now he was my flatmate-extraordinaire. He also charged a very reasonable rent and only watched sports on TV to scrutinise fit men in their shorts. The only downside to sharing a flat with him was that Dame was very neat, bordering on obsessive-compulsive. Whilst I wasn't exactly slovenly, I could be a bit scatty. I often left the jar off the peanut butter or forgot to close kitchen cupboards. This drove Dame so potty that he nicknamed me 'Scatty Batty'. I nicknamed him 'Sweaty Betty' as he always got so hot and feverish about housework, making it seem like an assault course that needed conquering. Even on a good day he could be found with a feather duster in his hand, flicking away my loose cookie crumbs.

Still, I had nothing to complain about. I had finally left home after twenty-nine years of living with my mum and younger brother, Ant. A lovely spacious Hertfordshire home where I had a large airy bedroom and all the comforts I could imagine. But I always felt a bit out of place there. My mum had been dead-set against me moving in with Dame.

'Josie darling,' she drawled, 'you know I only want what's best for you.' She took a long slow drag on her cigarette, sucking in her cheeks purposefully, thinking herself to be a potent combination of elegant and sophisticated, yet tough and authoritative somehow, like Joan Collins in Dynasty. She was 80s mad and still lived in the 80s if her striking black and white skirt suit with big brass buttons, enormous shoulder pads and matching hat were anything to go by.

'There's no way you are going to attract your soul-mate if

you shack up with that queer boy.' I had known him more than eight years and she still referred to him as 'that queer boy'. 'Being a fag hag won't do you any favours,' she said flicking her hair. My mum could be so obnoxious at times. Living here at home certainly hadn't done me any favours, I wanted to shout back at her.

My mum continued talking. 'After all, when I left home it was to move in with your father ..., she tailed off suddenly, scuttling into the bathroom saying something about fixing her hair, but I could hear her sobbing through the walls.

Thankfully that didn't happen too often anymore. Dad left home when I was five. Mum said he was a work-hard, play-hard 'boy,' pretending to be a man. He was eight years younger than Mum and hadn't really been prepared for the responsibilities of parenthood. The weird thing is, even though my memories were fuzzy, I remembered him as being the doting dad, loving and full of cuddles. I saw a suitcase by his side one morning. Mum said that he was going on a little holiday, but he never returned. Ant was only five months old. He had left us. Mum shut down after that, saying that it was normal for partners to leave sometimes. Normal. It felt anything but normal.

What if she was wrong and he hadn't chosen to leave us but had been abducted? What if his body turned up floating in a river somewhere? My young mind had conjured up all sorts of sinister imaginings. I found it hard to accept that he had willingly left us. And then the postcards arrived. 'I'm sorry.' That was the first one. At least we knew he was alive. Over the years more postcards arrived alluding to the fact that he had had some kind of mental breakdown and was trying to sort himself out. Birthday cards arrived too, showing that he was thinking of us. There was never a return address though. It had near enough broken my heart that he was struggling. Why couldn't he let us help him? Or was it just a big cover up for the fact he had willingly chosen to dump mum and his kids for someone else? Another family perhaps? Although I had moved on with my own life, the void was still there, never shrinking, never filling itself up.

My most vivid memory of my dad had to be on my fifth birthday. I still remember feeling big and important as I stood on a chair in my floral party frock, looking around at the sea of smiling faces. My mum and dad, aunts, uncles, cousins and lots of friends. Everyone sang Happy Birthday to me and I was thrilled and excited when Dad lifted me up, twirling me around the room, calling me his 'little dancing queen'. Even when Ant came along I still felt like I was his Number One. He put five orange smarties in my hand. 'Because I know orange is your favourite,' he'd smiled, 'and next year you'll have six, then seven, then eight ….' He blew raspberries on my stomach and made me laugh so hard. That was my best birthday ever.

***

I had been lamenting my problems for the last two hours. I only got like this when I was really drunk, or in other words when I had drunk more than a large glass of wine. Gone were the days when I could sink my drinks in a matter of minutes.

'… and then there was Professor Waltman.' Dame interrupted me. 'I don't think you ever told me what really happened with him?'

I shifted uncomfortably in my seat, lighting up another cigarette. I hardly ever smoked, and never smoked in public

- unless you counted my stress-induced chain smoking in our last year of university.

Dame frowned, his forehead wrinkling. 'Did you do it?'

'Do what?' I said, exhaling slowly, trying to blow smoke rings out of my mouth but ending up choking instead.

'Send those photos to his wife?'

'You mean those sex photos?' I was getting the hang of these smoke rings.

'Unless there were other photos I didn't know about?'

'As if I'd do that. Those were our private moments.'

'Everyone thought you must have.'

'Conjecture. Pure conjecture, Damian. I found out that he'd been sleeping with at least three other girls besides me. Any one of them could have somehow seen, or got hold of, those photos. The simple fact is he couldn't keep it in his pants. He got what he deserved.'

'His wife sliced his testicles!'

I shrugged my shoulders. 'He survived. Who knew she was nuts?' I laughed. 'You were talking about testicles and I said nuts ...'.

'Yeah, but poor guy.' Dame stopped on seeing my not-smiling-now face. 'I honestly thought you had lost the plot Josie – you seemed more cut up about him than anyone else.'

'It's all in the past, Dame.'

I smiled, not wanting to relive how hurt and vulnerable I had felt. How that had been the moment when I'd struggled to get out of bed, to make it to lectures. To find motivation for anything. I'd almost quit my course on several occasions and would have done so, had it not been for Dame and his support, his friendship.

'Can we please change the subject and order that dish I love from the local takeout? I'm starving.'

He got up from the sofa, wobbling slightly as he picked up the telephone and pressed 3 on the speed dial.

'The usual please. Half an hour. Thanks. Bye.' Dame put the phone down noisily, staggered around the room and plonked himself back on the sofa. We sighed heavily in unison.

'I just want you to be happy, Josie. To find someone who treats you right. First off, you have to let go of the past. I know! Let's construct a DUMPED MANIFESTO.'

Dame looked excited.

I groaned loudly. 'A *what*?'

'A manifesto for the dumped,' he said, as if it made perfect sense. Twenty minutes later, the manifesto read something like this:

THE DUMPSVILLE MANIFESTO

- Playing of soppy sad love songs is absolutely forbidden.
- Wallowing in endless self-blame and pity is strictly prohibited.
- I will nurture and love my inner child (*that was my idea*).
- Consumption of chocolate and all chocolate produce is good for the soul … but will stop if blow up like a whale.
- Belief in self as sultry sex kitten is paramount as will encourage wild flirting with sexy strangers.
- I will pamper myself with new fragrances, essen-

tial oils and long hot bubble baths every night if I so please (*that was my idea, too*).

- Indulge in new activities such as salsa classes, belly dancing or just go out and have lots of FUN!!
- Buy new wardrobe (as in clothes, not actual wardrobe – *also my idea*).
- Release negative feelings by partaking in vigorous exercise such as running, kickboxing, etc. rather than destroying any part of ex-beloved's body or possessions.
- Do not under any circumstances phone ex-beloved, text him or Facebook him, especially when drunk (i.e. when had more than one glass of wine).
- Lastly, do not act over-eager or desperate when meeting a new man (no matter how shag-worthy he may be!).

I had to admit, rather reluctantly, that I had entertained several fantasies of body dismembering. Not that I would have known where to find Niles. But Dame insisted that this Manifesto showed a commitment to letting go and becoming really mature. Mature was not a word I usually associated with Dame, unless he was going through a phase of dating older men.

Dame leaped off the sofa at the shrill sound of the doorbell. 'At last! I'm bloody starving.' He ran to the door and flung it open, exclaiming loudly, 'What took you so long?'

He suddenly froze.

'Easy, Tiger!' came a smooth voice from the other side of the door. Dame said nothing, rooted to the spot.

'Well, are you just going to leave me standing here all night?' came the silky voice again.

'I … I …' Dame floundered, 'I left a message on your mobile phone.'

'I've come straight from work and the network reception's really poor,' replied George, coming into the flat when Dame finally stepped out of the way.

'I'm sorry I'm late but work has been a fucking pig and traffic was murder coming over. What did your message say?' he said, running his fingers through his thick shiny black hair.

'Huh?' said Dame, dumbly.

'Your voicemail message?'

'Oh, it's not important!' said Dame absently, waving his hands in the air and smiling like a maniac.

'I've been thinking about you all day …' purred George, teasingly. 'And I'm very hungry.'

'Well there's an Indian on its way.' Dame was drooling on the carpet, weakening at the sight of the taut, lean, muscular body in front of him.

'It's not an Indian I fancy tonight,' said George pointedly.

Suddenly they were all over each other, sucking each other's faces off and tearing at each other's clothes like wild animals. This was a very depressing sight for someone who had just been dumped.

'So much for *not* acting over-eager and desperate,' I muttered under my breath.

They disappeared into the bedroom, slamming the door hard. I stood up feeling really queasy and wobbled over to the bathroom where I chucked my guts up. I went to bed feeling lousier than I had felt for a long time, my last thoughts being on the Indian takeaway that hadn't shown up. Just as well, as no one would be needing it now.

Chapter Two
Blue Monday

I HAD A NIGHTMARE-FILLED SLEEP WHERE vicious hounds chased me across a deserted moor, the lashing rain making me slip and slide. A real-life storm woke me with a start, gusting winds rattling the windowpanes. That was nothing compared to the banging and commotion emanating from the next room. It was 6.35am and I was being subjected to high-pitched sexual shrieks and moans that could be heard clearly through the paper-thin walls. I buried my head under my pillow.

'Doctor, Doctor, I've got a rather uncomfortable stiffness and swelling that I think you should take a look at.' After a few seconds, 'OOOOOOOHHH Doctor!' Dame screamed. Oh, what a carry on!

It wouldn't have been so bad if there hadn't been a power drill going off in my head, with a cement mixer churning up my stomach. I opened one bleary eye.

'Will you give it a rest?' I hollered.

Dame was certainly making up for his three-month sex drought and boy, did he want the whole street to know it.

It was my first day back at work after the new year break and I felt like the worst kind of crap imaginable. I pulled open the curtains and was faced with a blanket of mist. Perhaps it would brighten later. I dragged myself from my bed and into the hallway, hearing giggling from Dame's room. Then Dame's bedroom door opened as he glided out, with gleaming eyes and a florid face.

'Sorry for waking you sweetie. It was George's EEME.'

'Emy?,' I asked.

'Enormous Early Morning Erection.'

I sighed heavily. Did he have to look so bloody gleeful?

'Sooorry.' He at least had the good grace to look contrite.

'It's fine,' I mumbled, making a dash for the shower. I didn't want to be late. Punctuality certainly wasn't my strong point and it had already cost me a written warning. I'd show Bitchy Bernice that I could be reliable and on time for a change. Twenty minutes later I was showered and dressed, feeling somewhat perkier. I ambled into the small but immaculate kitchen. George was propped up on a breakfast stool in Dame's dressing gown, his black hair sticking up at varying angles. He was slurping milk eagerly from his cereal bowl.

'Morning darling!' he said, looking up at me, smiling with a milk moustache.

'Had a good night then?' I raised my eyebrows at him.

'Pretty great actually.'

At least he had the decency to look at least a little bit embarrassed. My stomach rumbled at the smell of bacon and eggs, but I sensibly put two slices of whole-wheat bread in the toaster and poured myself a cup of coffee. He dished out four slices of bacon and three fried eggs for himself, wolfing them down in a matter of minutes, burping loudly and proudly.

Dame was in the shower singing at the top of his voice, sounding ecstatic but like an X-Factor reject. I watched George curiously over my coffee cup; he was sprawled out across the counter, brown sauce on the sleeve of Dame's fluffy dressing gown. Dame would not have been impressed, clean freak that he was. Mind you, he may have forgiven George's grubbiness given his current sex suffused state. Dame even made being violently sick - in the toilet bowl with no spillage - look dignified, after a large curry and six beers.

'Got to go,' I said, pointing at my watch as if I were Ms. Conscientious. I grabbed my toast and legged it out of the door. George lazily waved goodbye at me.

'Bye Dame!' I called out, but I don't think he heard me, what with the racket he was making.

I smiled; maybe some of his positive energy was rubbing off on me. I prayed that George would turn out to be a good thing, especially after some of the losers Dame had been out with. I stepped out into the cold damp morning and was just contemplating whether to leg it across the common when I was stopped in my tracks by a most peculiar sight on the corner of the street.

I strained my eyes to see through the mist. An elderly lady wearing a long brown suede coat appeared to be dancing solo, but she was making gestures, her arms held up as if she were stepping in time with a partner. I got closer and was stunned to see my neighbour, Pru Morel, laughing and chattering to herself, continuing to swish and twirl around. She had a fixed intensity about her, not seeming to notice anything or anyone. A small group of schoolboys stopped at the corner, pointing and laughing at her.

'What a freak!' I heard one of them call out. Pru continued

to dance, humming under her breath, oblivious to the world. A tall burly boy picked up a stone and got ready to aim it at her.

'Don't even *think* about it,' I growled threateningly at him.

'Looks like your granny's got a screw loose, shouldn't be let out on the streets,' squeaked a little ginger-haired boy. The taller boy clobbered him over the head.

'Just piss off, all of you.' I must have been sufficiently scary as they sloped off, tittering amongst themselves.

'Mrs Morel …?' I began, hesitantly. Nothing. I felt sure that she'd recognise me. I had picked up her post a couple of times before now and we'd had a few conversations in the corridor, mostly about baking, even though my scones turned out more like stones. She'd always been keen to linger and chat. I think she was rather lonely.

'Mrs Morel, can you hear me?' I said, a little louder in case she was going deaf. Still nothing.

I tapped her gently on the shoulder. She jerked, looking up at me with startled blue eyes. I noticed she was wearing an elegant black evening dress underneath her coat, and her silver hair was fastened with diamond clips.

'Is that you, Josie?' she said, sounding more shocked than I was.

'What are you doing out here?' I asked.

'Isn't it obvious? I'm doing the foxtrot, Bert's favourite.' Her eyes were dancing merrily and her ruby red lips curled into a smile.

'Bert?'

'He was my late husband, died five years ago today. I was just off to the cemetery to visit him,' she said, pointing to a bunch of flowers on the pavement beside her.

'Which cemetery is that, Mrs Morel?'

'St. Mary's in Battersea. And please, call me Pru.'

'OK, Pru.' I smiled.

'This is where Bert and I danced for the last time, but it was under the glistening moonlight. We often did crazy things together,' she confided. 'We made love sometimes,' she whispered, 'just over there.' She pointed to a patch of dense bushes.

I flushed, hoping she was joking and feeling grateful she hadn't taken it upon herself to re-enact their love-making scene, solo. I felt a deep wave of sadness and concern for her. Pru had told Dame that she had no living relatives close by, except for her grandson Melvin who rarely took the trouble to visit her, although he only lived the other side of London.

'Bert made me promise to dance with life, to live with sunshine and lightness, and to do the daftest, craziest things possible if it should take my fancy,' she continued wistfully. 'He would be tickled pink right now to see me, because that's what life was to him – a big long celebration. He was my hero.'

'How did he die?' I asked, cautiously.

'He had a massive heart attack, shouldn't have been such a shock. He was into his rich food, rich wine, and a big belly full of laughter.' Her eyes were misting over. I squeezed her hand tightly.

'This was the dress I wore when he took me to my very first ball.' She opened her coat and spun around, the black sequins catching the sunbeams that managed to break through the mist. 'And it still fits perfectly,' she said proudly. I looked down at the beautiful black dress hanging limply from her slight frame. My guess was that she had filled it more generously at the time.

'How long were you married, Pru?'

'Fifty-five happy years,' she glowed.

I smiled. 'I'm hoping to get married.'

'Who's the lucky fella?' she asked, nudging me gently with her elbow.

'I'm still working on that part.'

Suddenly out of the corner of my eye I saw a bus whizz past. I could have made it had I been Usain Bolt, or even Penelope Pitstop, but as I was neither I decided to watch the bus speed off into the distance. I probably could have made it at a push but I wanted to make sure Pru was going to be ok.

She picked up the flowers and smoothed down her dress. 'Oh dear, it seems like I've missed my bus.'

***

I decided to accompany Pru on the bus, heading to the tube station. I was bound to be late anyway, so I tried not to worry about the bollocking that would be waiting for me at work.

We waited a few minutes for the next bus. A crowd of mums with whining, snivelling children joined the queue, as did a group of rowdy teenagers. It got my hackles up but Pru didn't seem phased by anything. She continued chattering away nineteen-to-the-dozen. The doors swung open and people crowded onto the bus, pushing in front of each other. Pru glided on gracefully, in true Greta Garbo style, stepping in front of a leather-clad man with multiple tattoos and piercings. She looked at him, speaking in a loud but polite voice, 'I think you will find we were here before you, young man.' He scrunched up his face in a way that looked really painful, but said nothing.

We found two empty seats on the lower deck. Pru had

totally exhausted herself with all her dancing, and was thankful to be off her feet. The bus moved slowly through heavy commuter traffic. At the next stop a rather portly man got on, panting heavily with beads of perspiration trickling off his forehead. He dabbed himself with a white handkerchief. Although there were no free seats available on the lower deck, he seemed to decide swiftly against the idea of heading up the stairs as soon as he heard what sounded like a gang of hooligans making a sacrifice on the upstairs deck.

'Wanna sit your lardy arse over here?' called out one of the rowdy teenagers on the back seat. The other three boys were laughing, egging him on. The man began to wipe his clammy hands on the handkerchief, flushing crimson while keeping his eyes down, looking down at the floor.

'Hey, why don't you look at me when I'm speaking to you?' the teenager shouted out aggressively. I felt a bubble of rage that was floating inside of me getting bigger and bigger. And then that bubble exploded.

'What gives you the right to harass someone because of their size, or any other reason, you pig-ignorant bunch of bullies?' My whole body was shaking, not least because I would probably get a good beating. But I couldn't - and wouldn't - tolerate injustice of any kind.

'She's right, you morons; I simply won't hear of you terrifying that poor man any longer.' Pru got up, shaking her fist at them. Oh my god, what the hell was she thinking? I knew she was batty but now she had propelled herself into the Premier League of Battiness. She walked straight towards the teenage bully; a collective gasp could be heard rippling through the lower deck of the bus.

'Oh yeah? What are you gonna do about it, you daft old cow?,' he sneered at her.

'I'm going to … I'm going to …' and she paused dramatically, not looking like she had a clue. I jumped out of my seat ready to rescue her.

'I'm going to kiss you.' And with that, she leaned over and planted a noisy kiss on his forehead. 'It's obvious you didn't get enough love as a child, such a shame to have so much hatred in one so young.' The teenage boys stared at her, mouths hanging open, completely flummoxed. Eventually they just shrugged, scratching their heads in bewilderment.

Pru walked back to her seat, to the sounds of clapping and cheering. 'Go Grannie Go,' called out the pierced, tattooed man. The portly man nodded gratefully to her. The boys on the back seat remained subdued for the rest of the bus journey.

'So, did I tell you about the cross-stitch pattern I'm working on?' Pru said.

***

I decided from that moment on: Pru was a true legend and we were kindred spirits. We parted company on the bus, and I felt comfortable in the knowledge that she would be more than a match for any gang of thugs. The rest of my journey was uneventful in comparison, just the usual delays caused by a signal failure on the line.

I closed my eyes, reflecting on the morning so far. Something that Pru had said kept playing on my mind. *'Bert was my soul-mate and when he died I was heartbroken, naturally. But I've moved on and still seem to find joy in everything I do. Some nights I just lie awake smiling to myself, looking forward to what the next day will bring.'* She had also described some of her dreams to me: of waterfalls, boat rides on sparkling river fronts, but most commonly, walking through fields of purple flowers holding hands with Bert. She said that dreams were about the subconscious trying to tell us something, or guide us through life.

I wondered if I would ever find my Bert, my soul-mate to dance through life with. My mind flitted to memories of Niles and of all the other wrong-ones, and I was consumed with a pain and emptiness that seemed to grip my very soul. What had I done wrong?

I always scrubbed up well on dates, turning up with polished nails and glossy hair. Was it that one time when Niles saw me bent over the toilet bowl, cleaning the inside rim with an old electric toothbrush? I had been wearing paint-stained jogging bottoms. I shuddered at the memory of his less-than-impressed face. I was jolted back to reality by the loudspeaker announcing Pimlico was the next stop.

I looked at my watch. SHIT, SHIT, SHIT. It was twenty-past nine. Bernie was going to have a field day with me. I stepped out of Pimlico tube station to be greeted by fat raindrops plopping from the sky like an angry assault of tears. Minutes later I walked through the Gallery doors, damp hair hanging from my face, trying not to look too flustered.

'Well if it isn't Ms. Green?' boomed a voice from behind me. 'Strolling in late as if you owned the place. I was rather hoping punctuality was going to be on your list of New Year's resolutions. What's your excuse this time, Green? Been attacked by a ferocious dog, an evil armed robber or have you just returned from the planet Zoltac following an alien abduction?'

Bernice - or Bernie as she was more commonly known

(because she was stout and solid like a bloke) - was glaring at me, her foot tapping impatiently. I had come up with a whole range of excuses in the past but none of them had been quite as ridiculous as what I was about to tell her.

'Missed the bus,' I said feebly, not thinking she would be interested in my neighbourly concern for Pru Morel, let alone accept it as a plausible excuse.

'Well you know what the missed bus means, don't you?' she said, smirking nastily. Great. Happy New Year. My second written warning.

I felt low for the rest of the day but managed to perform the duties expected of me, with all the enthusiasm of a brick. I did manage to snap out of my mood for a while, when a group of camera-happy Japanese tourists bundled in off the street. I showed them around the gallery, pointing out the latest exhibits. They seemed fascinated, intrigued, clicking away madly.

The Japanese tourists were most impressed by the Street Art Collection which consisted of unknown artists depicting images of sleeping rough. Things like empty beer cans, whisky bottles, tatty old blankets, torn boxes, etc. The tourists bowed at me repeatedly, suggesting I should visit Japan someday. I nodded politely but there was no way I'd be jetting off to the other side of the world, thank you very much. Not in a million years. Even the mini break in Brighton last autumn had been an ordeal for me. I fretted about silly things like the weather, breaking down on the motorway, running out of money … it just didn't seem worth the bother. I liked knowing what to expect. Fiorentina pizza Fridays, wine-on Wednesdays, or shoe shopping Saturdays. Nothing wrong with that. For all his order in the home, Dame was the more adventurous one and was always trying to get me to deviate from my regular plans.

I wandered into the room where the Impressionist collection was hung and sighed dreamily, a feeling of peace enveloping me. But that didn't last long.

'Phone-call, Green!' Alex shouted. 'You know we are not supposed to accept personal calls,' he tutted loudly. I swear he was giving Bernie one. They always seemed so chummy, whispering together conspiratorially in corners – and how else had he been promoted to Senior Information Assistant in the space of a month? I shuddered at the thought. I would have to be extra careful now she had appointed beady eyes to watch my every move.

'Hello, Pimlico Gallery. Where art comes to life,' I answered the phone, with all the cheeriness I could muster.

'Hey Jose, I heard about Niles. What a fucking shit. Fancy getting legless?' It was Babs, my best friend, a modern dance teacher with bouncing red curls and an incessantly cheerful manner. She had the energy and vitality of those multivitamin women appearing in the glossy ads.

'Can't. I'm totally shattered B. All I want is an early night. Sorry.'

Babe suggested a comedy movie night with a Thai curry takeaway, but I insisted that I just needed some time to myself. 'Look, I can't talk now, Beadle's About. Got to go. Bye.'

'OK, talk later, love you honey.' Babs knew exactly who I was talking about. Alex was watching me steadily from across the room, pretending to dust a sculpture. I glared back at him, at which point he strutted off with his head held high like a peacock. In search of Bernie, no doubt.

***

Later that evening I sank into a warm bath topped with lavender oil, letting the sweet calming aroma wash over me. I began to drift off, feeling truly relaxed for the first time all day. Dame was out with George, so I'd switched my phone off and

I wasn't answering the door to anyone. Niles had only crossed my mind about twenty times. Pretty good going.

After my bath, I made a steaming hot mug of cocoa, stirring in two heaped spoonfuls of sugar and headed straight for bed. I paused, contemplating the 'Endless Love for Always' compilation CD accompanied with a good cry, but I was too exhausted. I did, however, get around to removing 'In a relationship' from my Facebook status. Yet again. I had changed my relationship status more often than my bedsheets. Well not quite. I wasn't a complete slob.

My fingers hovered over Nile's picture. I was desperate to find out what he was doing and if he had also declared himself single. I clicked on to his page and found no new updates. Hardly surprising, considering that he rarely used Facebook. I 'deactivated' myself, deciding it best to avoid social media with all the smug smiling faces of loved-up couples for the time being.

That night I dreamed of Pru and Bert dancing in the moonlight, laughing and dancing until a brilliant orange sun filled the sky. A love like theirs seemed aspirational and out of reach but Pru had made it sound so simple - and therefore entirely possible, surely?

Chapter Three
Leaf In A Pond

THE NEXT FEW WEEKS SEEMED to pass by in a daze. My days consisted of getting up, dragging myself to work and avoiding Bernie and Alex as much as humanly possible. I'd come home and crash on the sofa, hot chocolate in one hand and a good book in the other. Dame complained that I had turned into an old biddy 'just like the one downstairs'.

I had, in fact, drawn comfort from spending time with Pru in her flat. Eating her homemade banana loaf, drinking endless cups of tea out of real bone china teacups, and watching nature programmes like the one about Elli, an orphan elephant. The programme was both heartbreaking and heartwarming. Pru and I sobbed throughout the entire episode when Elli was rescued and taken to a sanctuary where good people (and other elephants) looked after her.

We also talked about the war, rationing and, most importantly, men. Bert, (short for Bertrand) had, in his time, been something of a studmuffin. Pru had the pictures to prove it, some of them a little too compromising for comfortable viewing. I shared with her my own dream wedding visions, describing everything in meticulous detail. From the ivory lace dress, to the iced flowers on my wedding sponge cake, and the outdoor Mozart-playing orchestra at my reception. I had only been fantasising about my wedding day since I was five years old, after all.

Despite spending lot of time with Pru, I still had moments where I felt completely discombobulated. How could it be that birds still chirped, daffodils were beginning to bloom and the sun had shone for a whole week, yet I was moving around in some strange, dark alternate world where my dreams all amounted to nothing?

I eventually confessed all to Mum, after she remarked (for about the hundredth time) how gloomy I seemed. She fed me with her homemade triple chocolate cheesecake and then panicked me when she suggested moving into the flat. No doubt to keep an eye on me in the manner of prisoner on suicide watch, I thought to myself. I quickly plastered a smile on my dial, insisting I was fine. Just fine.

Dame and George were protective over me too, complaining that I had 'let myself go.' I kept insisting there was nothing wrong with my bird's nest hair, or wearing the same t-shirt three days in a row, or not ironing anything. In fact, it was quite liberating to slob about and not care how I looked, especially after months of sucking in my stomach.

What seemed to be more concerning to them was my new-found inclination to spend time alone. Usually I hated being alone, even for an hour, but I was getting used to it. Kind of. They managed not to grope each other in my presence, apart from the odd furtive fumble when they thought I wasn't looking. Besides that, they seemed to have settled into a routine. George worked long and erratic hours at the hospital and Dame was forever working and socialising in the City. But every spare moment they had, they spent together.

Even Babs tended to me as you would a sick bird with a broken wing, too fragile to lift a feather or finger. Frankly, it was a bit weird with her fluffing up my pillows and talking to me like I was a five year old. Thankfully this uber-sensitive side didn't last too long and she was soon back to her slightly-scary-Babs self.

She marched me into the kitchen one day and tapped the side of the fridge with a long ruler.

'When was the last time you studied the Dumpsville Manifesto, Green?'

Oh hell. Sure, I had given the list a cursory glance every now and then, but I hadn't really thought seriously about putting it into action. I mean how could I see myself as a sultry sex kitten or imagine myself flirting with strangers when the thought of going out filled me with dread? Although I had indulged in new fragrances, if you counted stale sweat and congealed-on-t-shirt-ketchup.

'I have been trying,' I said, looking at the floor in the manner of a naughty schoolgirl standing in front of her strict headmistress.

'Look here … *Wallowing in endless self-blame and pity is strictly prohibited … I will nurture and love my inner child …* See these?' she said, tapping at points 2 and 3. 'Too much wallowing and not enough nurturing, Green. Let's start with some feel good movies!' 'Silver Linings Playbook' (our go-to inspirational Bradley Cooper movie), Amelie (cute and French) and 'Kill Bill' (bad-ass girl power) were chosen.

'Then we will go to a kick-boxing class this evening. Give us a chance to work off the excess food and alcohol we will be having. It's *on* the list,' she pointed out when I stared at her, aghast. Despite my desire to crawl back into bed, I knew better than to argue with her and I had to admit to feeling better for it afterwards, especially when I imagined Niles' head as target practice.

In keeping with the Dumpsville Manifesto, Babs managed to persuade me out beyond my four walls one sunny Saturday afternoon for a spot of indulgent shopping. We walked along Kew Bridge clutching strawberry ice-cream cones and eventually came to a halt on the balcony of Café Rouge, settling down at an outdoor table. I felt life stirring within me, almost unconsciously aware of the pungent smells, soft breeze and pretty boats bobbing along the river in front of us.

Babs was truly the best friend a girl could have. We met aged six at St. Anne's Primary School. We were two innocent looking girls with bushy bunches of hair, green striped shirts, flared purple skirts, matching brown buckled shoes and off-white knee-high socks with our initials sewn into the sides. Inseparable in every way, we sat together in assembly, shared our packed lunches, and quickly earned the nickname of 'the Terrible Two' because bubbling beneath the butter-wouldn't-melt-exterior were two mischievous little girls. We flushed some girl's bobble hat down the toilet for a laugh and reduced little boys into quivering wrecks during games of 'kiss chase.' I smiled at the memories, looking over at Babs. We had lost touch for a while when she went to Durham University and I remained in London, studying, but she hadn't changed one bit.

She still had the same enthusiastic nature with a cheeky little grin and bouncy red curls. She was forever dashing around, from one dance class to the next. Babs also had a part-time job at a bookstore yet still found time to volunteer with children who had learning difficulties. She also cycled, rollerbladed, painted, sculpted and had a steady, if somewhat tempestuous, relationship with Jake. She had been with Jake for nearly four years; he was a mostly-out-of-work actor, prone to long brooding silences with the occasional burst of temper. He was also adventurous, exciting, and dynamite between the sheets, according to Babs.

'Do you think you two will ever get married?' I ventured.

Babs screwed up her freckled face. 'Doubt it,' she shrugged. 'Every time I try to introduce the topic, he suddenly remembers he has to fix a shelf or rush down the pub for ten pints with his mates. Or he distracts me by nuzzling my neck in a way that he knows gets me horny.'

'But what if he never agrees to the idea of you two marrying?'

'No biggie,' she said, stretching out her petite frame to turn and face the sun. 'I like what we have and besides, there are more important things in life.'

'Such as?'

'Such as world peace. The latest sales and … ooh! Not forgetting dancing the night away occasionally.'

I slumped deeper into my seat, staring at my frothy café latte.

'It's just that I feel so lost and empty at the moment. Nothing seems to make sense. I had it all worked out, you know? The one thing I felt sure of in life was that I wanted to fall in love, get married and have a family.' Plus the whole internet dating thing really didn't appeal to me, I thought. I'd heard enough no-hoper and semi-stalker type horror stories from my single friends, to put me off for life.

I know life's not all about being with someone,' I began 'but it is important to me. I also really want to figure out what the hell I'm meant to be doing with my life.' I smiled ruefully.

I don't think I'd ever known what that was, but I was desperate to find something. 'I feel like a leaf in a pond, making small movements round and round, but getting nowhere.' I looked to Babs for some reassurance and support, in the hope that she wouldn't think I was just 'wallowing,' but she seemed preoccupied with something behind me.

'Don't look now,' Babs said, as she leaned in and whispered out of the corner of her mouth, 'but that tall, fit waiter seems to be checking you out.'

I glanced casually over my shoulder, just in time to see a waiter ducking furtively behind a large green spider plant.

'How strange ...' I said.

'Not strange, just shy. He must be new. I've never seen him here before,' said Babs.

I glanced back over to where he was serving a middle-aged couple a few tables away. He suddenly looked up, staring directly at me with the most intense, turquoise blue eyes I had ever seen. Like the warmest, tropical part of an ocean. He quickly returned his attention to the couple in front of him. He had a kind of clumsy, boyish quality to him; he tried brushing his hair out of his face which had flopped lazily over his left eye.

'Oh my god!' Babs shrieked, 'you have to go over and talk to him.'

'I don't think so. No way!' I spluttered.

'Yes you can, and you *will*,' declared Babs. 'You haven't had whole milk for a long time. I'm going to call him over.'

The thing with Babs and me was that we had created this

milk system for rating men's looks. 'Creamy' was the cream of the crop, 'whole' was hot, 'semi-skimmed' was quite cute in the right light, and 'skimmed' was ok-if-you-are-desperate. 'Gone off' was even-his-mother-would-find-him-ugly.

'Babs, No!' I bellowed, but she was already motioning him over.

The waiter glanced over and seemed to hesitate, a conflict of emotions crossing his face. He seemed nervous, as if he didn't quite know what to do with himself but he settled for smiling at me, a shy but warm smile which I quickly returned.

Our eyes locked for a few seconds. Mmm, Babs was right. He was teetering on the 'whole' scale.

He then hurried inside the restaurant. I watched his retreating buttocks sashay away. Definitely 'wholesome,' I agreed.

A portly waiter with a thick black moustache came over to our table a couple of minutes later.

'What can I get you ladies?' he said pleasantly.

'Just the bill please,' Babs replied, huffily.

'Maybe he had something urgent to do?' I said to Babs when the bill arrived. 'I'm still kind of cut up about Niles, in case you hadn't noticed.'

'I saw you checking him out,' she said, wiggling her eyebrows at me, laughing.

On our way out Babs insisted we walk through the restaurant, to try and find our enigmatic waiter. We drifted by the kitchen and heard loud clanging sounds, followed by a huge crash and a stream of raised voices, but no-one appeared.

'Do you know him?' Babs asked me.

I shook my head but there *was* something slightly familiar and, dare I say it, a little bit intriguing about him.

'It's just that he got quite agitated when he saw you, like he was blinded by your beauty,' she teased.

'I think he's just a bit clumsy or something,' I replied modestly, but inside I was secretly cheerleading. Who didn't like to be noticed?

'Have you ever really studied a leaf in a pond?' Babs asked me suddenly. 'They are really quite beautiful and serene – just like you. And FYI, no one really knows what they're doing in life. I just make it up as I go along.' She winked at me.

So she had been listening to me earlier. I smiled, feeling very grateful for the love and support of my best friend.

***

I woke on Sunday morning feeling refreshed, rather than in my usual state of grogginess. I followed the aroma of coffee and croissants, grateful that Dame was home alone for a change. It wasn't that I didn't like George but he had taken over the flat and our lives; his magazines, briefcase and discarded items of clothing could be found in the oddest of places. But Dame had made huge allowances for him and happily tidied his things away. If George was responsible for the warm glow, soft-eyed twinkle and altogether more compassionate nature in Dame, then it really couldn't be a bad thing. Even Dame's whinging and moaning had ceased. There could only be one explanation. Dame was in love.

'Jos, I am so deliriously happy!' he shared, confirming my suspicions. 'I think George could be The One. He's asked me to move in with him.'

Shit.

'Isn't it a bit soon?' I said, trying not to sound too alarmed. 'You already see enough of each other, so why change things?'

'It just feels right,' Dame shrugged, 'for both of us.'

'What about me, what will I do?' I widened my eyes, as a way of trying to convey the enormity of what I was feeling to Dame.

'Come here,' he said, stretching his arms out to me. I hugged his chest and we stood in the middle of the room for a few minutes in complete silence. 'I'm not throwing you out, and it's not like I'm moving to Guatemala. Just Hampstead Heath. You can visit anytime.'

I smiled up at him sheepishly, wondering where Guatemala was.

I tried not to blub. True, I was getting used to my own company but that didn't translate into wanting to *live* alone. I thought about Niles and how perfect this arrangement would have been if we had still been together. He could have moved out of his rented, run-down terrace in Tooting and moved in with me. He was always saying how much he loved Clapham. Anyhow, he was probably halfway around the world by now. Maybe even in Guatemala, wherever that was.

'It's fine. Just means I can operate my secret drugs den from here, invite my gambling mates over, have orgies that kind of thing,' I said, with a long sulky face.

He burst out laughing. 'Or I could get someone in to keep you company?'

'Do you have someone in mind?'

'No. I was thinking more like getting a lodger. If I advertise now, I'm sure the place would be snapped up in no time, being in such a sought-after area.' The words were rolling off his tongue, like he'd already placed the advert.

I hesitated. 'I'm not sure if I could live with a complete

stranger. What if they act nice but they are actually a bit psycho and end up stabbing me in the shower?'

'You could get a girl lodger?' Dame smiled.

'Don't tell me you've never seen the film Single White Female?' I responded dramatically.

'Oh come on Jos, that's just a movie!'

'It could be my reality if you leave. Be it on your conscience if they find my body parts stuffed underneath the floorboards.' Now I was starting to freak myself out.

He raised a half-weary, half-persuasive eyebrow at me. I could see he was desperate for me to give him permission to move into his boyfriend's shag pad. Not that he needed my permission.

'OK. I agree to meet prospective lodgers and if there aren't any, you should still go,' I said.

'You'll see. It will all work out perfectly,' Dame nodded wisely.

***

I headed to Hyde Park later that afternoon, hoping that the fresh air would help clear my mind. A group of rollerbladers whizzed past me, nearly knocking me off my feet. A young couple cycled by, side-by-side, and a lady with a boisterous yapping puppy briskly walked by. I sat down on a bench near the Serpentine; the sun was sinking lower in the sky, fanning out a blanket of orange, purple and pink hues. The blue sky darkened making me feel sluggish, but peaceful. I closed my eyes.

Some time later, I suddenly bolted upright. What was that, jabbing at my arm? Night had fallen and there was a distinct nip in the air. A haggard-looking man was poking me in the arm with something and I flinched, almost jumping out of my skin.

'Can ya spare us some change. I jus' need a quid,' he garbled. His hand was wrinkled, although he couldn't have been more than in his mid-fifties.

'I don't have any change, sorry.'

'Pull the other one,' he chortled. His breath smelt rancid, an unpleasant combination of booze, cigarettes and, I suspected, no toothpaste for quite a while.

'OK, here you go.' I shoved a pound coin into his hand, just wanting to be rid of him and quickly got up to walk away.

'It's alright for some,' he sniffed angrily, 'some of us don't have a place we can call home.'

I turned to face the scraggy man. His long tousled hair was falling into his eyes.

'What happened to you?'

He was silent for a moment. 'What do you care? Just piss off. Go on!'

Ungrateful sod. I would have brought him a burger and coffee had he been a bit nicer to me. Maybe it was best that I didn't engage in conversation as he seemed a bit unhinged, I thought to myself.

I started walking away and heard him shuffling behind me. Oh shit. I quickened my pace. Suddenly I heard a yelp behind me. I turned to find he had tripped over a fallen branch.

I couldn't leave him alone now, could I? Bloody hell.

'I've hurt me ankle,' he said, struggling to get the words out. His face looked even paler in the moonlight.

'Do you think you've broken it?'

'Probably just a sprain. Damn fuckin' branch.' He pulled his hair back and tied it with a rubber band.

'Can you move it at all?' He tried wriggling his foot around, but grimaced and yelped sharply.

'I'm going to call an ambulance,' I said, reaching into my pocket for my mobile.

'No,' he said quickly, 'please just go. I'll be fine.'

'I can't leave you here all night.' I looked around to see if there was anyone who could help us, but there wasn't another soul in sight. I tried Dame's mobile, but no response.

'What you helping a dirty old beggar for?' he asked me suspiciously.

'Because you're hurt!' I said, matter-of-factly. I squatted to the ground next to him, dialled 999 and asked for the Ambulance Service, briefly explaining the situation and our location. I was now feeling a lot calmer myself, knowing that I wasn't going to get mugged or battered to death. Actually, there was no guarantee of that, as he still had use of other limbs to attack me with, but the fall seemed to knock the stuffing right out of him.

He remained quiet for several minutes. I looked at him with curiosity; there was something about him. His face looked familiar. Maybe I had brought him a coffee in the past?

So how did you end up homeless?' I hoped he would answer this time.

'I wasn't always like this, you know. I had a wife, couple of kids, nice home and a good job.' He paused for a while; it didn't look as if he was going to continue to share his story with me.

'What happened?' I gently urged him on.

'I lost me job, fell to pieces, took up the bottle, and one day I jus' lost it. Started shouting nasty things and smashed up the place. I shall never forget the look of disappointment on me wife's face. I felt so disgusted and ashamed of myself. She asked me to pack me bags and leave. So I did.'

'Did you go back and try to explain things to her?' I asked.

'How could I? I had fallen in with bad people, started drinking more heavy, and much worse …' He paused again; pain etched deeply into his face. 'No, I haven't seen me family for gone twenty years, and the only friend I had were Arthur and even he's gone now, up in doggie heaven.' He looked up to the sky, lapsing into silent despair once more.

'There are places that can help you get back on your feet. I can help you if you let me,' I said earnestly. I don't know what made me say that to him, to be honest. My mum was always berating me for wanting to help others. Said I was too trusting, but kindness and humanity were important to me. I had done a shift at Crisis last Christmas and it was true, homelessness could happen to anyone, at any time.

He looked at me like I was very silly and more than a bit naive.

'There ain't no one that can help me, it's all up to Him up there, and whatever He decides.' He looked up towards the dark sky again.

'It's not too late!' I said angrily. 'You can't just give up on life. *He's* not going to help you, if you don't even try and help yourself,' I said, looking up at the sky too. 'You know what I think? I think you're a coward. Your wife and children are probably heartbroken, they don't know where you are, if you are even ok. All those years of pain you have inflicted on them.

'My dad left when I was five and not a day goes by when I don't think about him. All we get is the odd post card, whoopee-do. He needs help too, but he won't let us. He's left this big aching hole in my heart, and no matter what I do, I can't seem to fill it.' I was shaking violently, and not just because there was a chill in the air.

'For all I know *you* could be my dad.' I laughed at the crazy notion. I really had lost the plot. What with Niles having left me, Dame about to move in with George and the distant but painful memory of my dad leaving, I seemed to be desperate for someone to be there for me, even if it was a homeless stranger in the park.

He stared at me, shaking his head sadly. 'Trust me, you wouldn't want a dad like me.'

The ambulance turned up minutes later and took him away. I wanted to go with him to make sure he would be alright. An insane notion to try and fix things and makes things right for this man took hold of me, but he didn't want that.

'I'm not your father, you crazy gal,' were his parting words to me. 'I have, or should I say had, two sons. So just leave me be.'

I stood there and sobbed my heart out, those words ringing in my ears. Surely it couldn't be right that someone could be so utterly alone; it just wasn't fair. I pulled my coat tightly around me and began walking home, grateful that I had a place I could call home.

***

I got back to the flat, shivering as I entered the communal landing. I banged the time-sensitive light switch and ran up the stairs, hoping I could make it to the top before it went out. I didn't, but thankfully there was a light shining on the stairs. Someone's door was wide open and as I approached, I heard hushed voices speaking together. Suddenly a man stepped out into the landing outside Pru's flat on the floor below mine.

'Hello. You must be Josie. I'm Melvin, Pru's Grandson.' He spoke in a dull even tone, but was eyeing me quizzically.

'Yes, that's right. Umm, is everything ok?'

'She's in hospital, had a bit of a fall.'

'In hospital? Pru's in hospital?' I parroted, a sudden bout of nausea gripping my stomach.

'Daft thing climbed onto a chair, trying to reach some old photographs in the cupboard above the bed. Just a few bruises, she'll probably be home in a couple of days.' He spoke as though he found it faintly amusing, while maintaining the same nondescript expression as before.

I disliked him immediately and wasn't at all surprised that he rarely bothered to visit Pru.

'I'd like to visit her,' I said, with a trembling voice and a wobbly lip as I tried to hold back the tears. My head was throbbing and weary exhaustion spilled into my veins. Suddenly my legs buckled and I fell to the ground.

Chapter Four
Into The Groove

I WAS ONLY OUT OF IT for a minute at most. Once I had regained my senses, I set about phoning the hospital. It turned out that Pru was fine. She was to remain in hospital under observation for a couple of nights. I visited her the next morning with a big bunch of English daffodils, her favourite flowers since reading Wordsworth's poem, 'I wandered lonely as a cloud'. She was sitting up in bed, munching her way through a box of Maltesers, watching a crackling TV.

'Jerry Springer is a hoot! That man on the show is dating his son's girlfriend and daughter's boyfriend simultaneously. It could only happen in America, right?' Pru shook her head, laughing.

'You had me worried, Mrs. M.' I said, perching on the edge of her bed.

'Apart from having a very bruised behind, I'm fine,' she said cheerily. 'But you wouldn't believe some of the old fogeys in here. That's Nelson,' she pointed to a grey-complexioned, frail-looking man who was snoring lightly. 'He's only 63 but you wouldn't think it to look at him. He's been moaning and complaining about this and that. Don't think there's much wrong with him apart from a very bad wind problem, to be honest,' she wrinkled up her nose. 'No wonder he doesn't get many visitors.' I looked over at Nelson who seemed fairly placid and non-stinky for the time being.

'I met your grandson, Melvin.'

'An old head on young shoulders,' she said, gazing back at the television.

'He certainly seemed very – formal,' I replied, not knowing how to express my unease about him. 'Is he married?'

'Afraid so,' she trilled, winking at me. 'They're expecting a baby in a few months and I'm going to be a great granny!'

'I wasn't asking about Melvin for me!' My stomach turned at the very thought of it. 'I just wondered why he doesn't visit you more often, that's all.'

'That boy is in a world of his own, and a very busy and materialistic one at that. He's a bank manager, you see, and he's always going on about having a better car, bigger house, the latest gadgets … getting more, more, more. Takes life far too seriously if you ask me,' she said, sighing. 'Still, I suppose he just wants the best for his family.'

'Oh, I see.' That information did nothing to endear him to me. I don't know what it was but the way he stood silhouetted on the landing last night and his odd manner, he seemed almost sinister. I tried to shake the doubts out of my head. He was Pru's grandson after all, and she was obviously concerned about him.

'What about the rest of your family? I'm guessing you have children if you have a grandson?'

'I had a daughter but she passed away suddenly quite a few years ago.'

'Oh Pru, I'm so sorry,' I said, feeling shocked.

'It's alright, dear,' she replied, patting my hand as if to comfort me. 'She was very beautiful and very sweet. I will tell you about her one day but for now, can we talk about other things?'

'Of course.' Poor Pru had lost her daughter and her husband yet I don't think she had a self-pitying bone in her body. I looked at her jolly face and squeezed her hand tight. We watched another episode of Jerry Springer, tittering to ourselves. After a while I grew thoughtful, remembering what happened yesterday in Hyde Park.

'Are you alright, dear?' she asked, her blue eyes growing wide. 'You look agitated.'

'I met a strange man last night. In the park,' and I proceeded to tell her about the homeless man.

'I think I saw a man of that description being wheeled past me last night. I remember him because he was kicking up such a fuss, said he was perfectly healthy and had no need for hospitals.'

'He could still be here, then,' I said, anxious to find out. 'I'd really like to check if he's ok.'

'Did you catch his name?'

'Err … John, I think. At least that's what he said to the ambulance crew.'

'Go try find him,' Pru said, her eyelids drooping. 'I'm feeling rather tired now.'

I found a doctor on the ward and began to explain the situation. He nodded as I began to describe him, but he didn't remember the name.

'Yes, we had a somewhat dirty-looking man of that description come in last night. Fractured his foot in two places, looks like he will need crutches for the next six months.' The doctor had a haughty air about him.

'Can I see him?'

'Well, strictly speaking no, as you're not family, but as he won't give us details of family or next of kin, then I guess you can. Although I can't imagine why you'd want to. Straight through there,' he said, pointing to a single bed. He turned away and walked briskly down the corridor, leaving behind a sterile smell of antiseptic.

I entered the bed area slowly, feeling the nerves prickle at my stomach. I didn't have a clue what to say but I just knew that I wanted to see him.

I edged towards the bed, my view obscured by the raised leg.

'Umm, excuse me. I just wanted to see how you're doing. I'm here visiting a friend of mine… Oh, I'm sorry. I must have the wrong room. Really sorry.'

I backed out of the room at the sight of a bearded man with a blank face. It wasn't him. I went to find the doctor again. That that was the only vagrant they'd had in last night. I went back to check on Pru, feeling strangely disappointed.

***

After what had been a disconcerting few weeks, I began to settle into a routine of comfort and security once again. Pru made a sterling recovery, celebrating her return home with tea, crumpets and more than a tinkle of whisky with her friends from bingo. I hadn't encountered the strange man in the park since, and probably wasn't likely to. It had been silly to think he would be in the same hospital as Pru. More likely he had been taken to a hospital nearer to Hyde Park or, stubborn fool that he was, maybe he had demanded the ambulance stop and let him out. In which case he would still be hobbling around somewhere. I tried to push him out of my mind. The truth was that our conversation had stirred something deep inside of me.

Perhaps I just felt a kinship for those who go through life unnoticed, isolated from others.

I took to spending blissful unexpected moments in solitude, browsing through bookstores or eating lunch in the park. I still felt lost, but strangely not alone. I even felt more at ease with Dame moving out but as no one suitable had answered the advert for a lodger, Dame said he would hold off leaving. Babs and Dame were convinced that I was on the verge of clinical depression, so rare was it that I preferred my own company.

'What you need is a big night out,' announced Babs one evening.

'Yeah, you seriously need to get your fanny pumped, clear out some of those cobwebs,' Dame interjected.

'Don't be so gross!' I said, chucking a pillow at Dame.

'All I'm saying is that if you're not careful you'll turn into an old prune, Pru … I mean Jos.'

'Pru is a vibrant, funny and kind woman,' I said, defending Pru hotly. 'And I would be proud to be half the woman she is.'

'Well, you're not even half her age so there's no need to take up the knitting needles just yet,' said Dame, opening up another bottle of wine and a packet of Doritos.

'Knitting requires a great deal of skill and concentration and isn't just for old people.' Oh god, I did sound a bit senior saying that, didn't I?

'We are going to help you get your sparkle and shine back - starting with tonight!' said an enthusiastic Babs.

'Tonight?' I stretched my legs out lazily, pointing my tattered slippers to the floor. 'What's going down tonight?'

'Hopefully you are. Going down on someone cute, that is.' Trust Dame to go below the belt. I choked on a Dorito.

'Salsa,' Babs replied, 'and it's on the list.'

'What, a salsa to go with the Doritos?'

'No. Salsa as in the Cuban dance!' she said, leaping up to give me a demo.

'So it is,' I said, trying to sound enthusiastic before she turned into the Manifesto Nazi. 'But I haven't got anything to wear.'

'I've fixed that,' said Babs, 'and first off, we have to get rid of these …' she said, carefully picking up my slippers and holding them away from her as if they were flea-ridden or full of poo. She discarded the offending footwear.

'Now this is more like it,' she said, appearing from the hallway with elegant strappy silver sandals and a dozen carrier bags.

'Oh my god, they're the Karen Millen sandals, the ones I've wanted for ages!' I breathed, suddenly snapping out of my drink-infused bleariness.

'They're yours!'

I blinked. Right now she was the Manifesto Angel. Sorting out my wardrobe was definitely on the list. 'How did you manage to …?'

'You remember Anna, don't you?' I stared at her blankly. 'You must remember Anna. Blonde, pert, chain smoking chic. Works for Red or Dead Public Relations?'

'Oh yes.' I hopped about, getting excited at the prospect of peeking into the bags.

'Well she owed me a biggie. Last year I caught her boy-friend up some blonde girl's skirt in the ladies loos, so I decided to fix her up with one of Jake's friends. Now they are blissfully happy and engaged to be married. I should be re-named Emma.'

'Emma?'

'Emma. Jane Austen's Emma. You know, the story of the prolific matchmaker?'

"Isn't that the one who sorted out everyone else's love life, apart from her own?'

'Well yes, but my love life is going swimmingly and maybe now Jake's friend is getting hitched, marriage won't seem like such as scary thing to him.'

'I don't want to hear about happy couples or weddings right now,' I said, burying my face in my hands.

'OK, let's do the wardrobe thing,' Babs said, pointing to the bags. 'The clothes, however, are only on loan for tonight so we'll have to be really careful not to spill anything on them.' Babs hiccuped loudly, tipping the red wine bottle dangerously close to the bags.

'These are gorgeous!' I gasped, pulling out gold and silver shimmering sequinned dresses, some of which were designer and very expensive.

'Hey, what about me?' squeaked Dame from the corner of room, lolling his head around.

'Sorry darling, we only have dresses,' Babs said, emptying out the contents of the bags.

'George is taking me out on a mystery date, he won't say

where, but he's been acting really peculiar all day, so I don't have a clue what to wear,' he moaned.

'Tight black trousers, new blue shirt …' Babs and I chimed together.

'Do you think?' he said, hesitating.

'Definitely!' said Babs.

'For the maximising-lunchbox effect,' I added.

He puffed his chest out and strutted off like a proud peacock.

Babs and I stripped off in the front room, trying on numerous posh frocks from the likes of Donna Karen, Jasper Conran, and Prada, but it was a deep red chiffon number that caught my eye. Not designer but classy, from Warehouse.

'Wow, if it isn't Julia Roberts in 'Pretty Woman' … ' Babs sang the lyrics into the empty wine bottle, accompanying it with a little jig around the room.

But she was right, I did feel like a Pretty Woman. The dress brought out the olive tones in my skin and accentuated every curve to maximum effect. I studied the mirror, just for a moment concerned about the plunging neckline and the huge split riding up to the top of my thigh.

'You are going to drive the men wild tonight, you look gorgeous!' Babs complimented me.

'And you, my dear, are simply stunning. As always!'

I slipped on the strappy sandals and felt a million dollars. Babs picked out a sparkling silver dress from Jigsaw. An hour later we were hair-sprayed and lip-glossed to perfection, ready to paint the town red.

At 9pm on the dot a white limo pulled into our narrow quiet street to pick us up and take us anywhere we wanted to go. Yet another surprise.

'In case I forget to tell you later, tonight has been amazing and I've already had the best time ever. You are a brilliant friend.' I hugged her tightly and we opened a bottle of champagne in the back of the limo.

***

What I hadn't realised at the time was that Babs had set me up on a blind date with Jeremy, an actor friend of Jake's, who looked like he'd just been auditioning for the part of Frank Spencer's character in 'Some Mothers Do 'Ave 'Em'.

The evening began well. We got to Bar Med just in time for the start of the salsa lesson. The place was heaving, full of tall, tanned and toned men with a Latin look about them. I took a deep swig of sangria.

'I think we'll be needing 'nother pitcher,' I slurred, the combination of wine, champagne and sangria having gone completely to my head and back down to my Karen Millen-clad feet, which were quickly flowing into the basic step, the side and cross step and even the cucaracha, which I'd always ballsed up before.

'I'm completely tanked up to the eyeballs, feeling really woozy. Think I might be sick ...' Babs said faintly, wobbling around the dance floor.

'I'll get you some water,' I shouted.

'No, no. I just need a bit of air,' she shouted back, disappearing before I could argue with her.

'Right, now change partners!' boomed the salsa teacher.'

I eagerly moved on, not missing an opportunity to flaunt my gorgeous dress and shoes, turning this way and that, gyrating my hips rhythmically to the Latin groove. The bootilicious babe was back with a vengeance.

My head was spinning with all the twists and turns, but it added to the frenzied excitement … especially when I noticed him. He was tall and broad, with dark hair and sparkling dark eyes. Sexy and self-assured, he also moved like a dream. He stared at me from the other side of the room, licking his lips slowly, the mischievous glint in eyes deepening, taking on a raw, hungry look. I stared back at him brazenly, pouting my lips and cheekily poking out my tongue at him. He grinned back, winking.

I slowly advanced towards him, shifting from one partner to the next; soon I would be dancing with him.

'OK, now let's put all those moves together – I want you to watch carefully,' said the salsa teacher.

We all stopped to watch the demonstration. He was standing to the other side of me. Only one more man to get through.

'I'm having trouble getting the hang of this,' squeaked the thin, wiry man I was currently with. I looked at him bemusedly. He was wearing a little black beret, with tufts of ginger hair poking through. He was squeezing my hands a little too tightly with his own clammy ones.

'Oh I'm such a moose,' he said stepping on my beautifully-clad foot, laughing nervously and somewhat insanely.

'It's fine,' I said, irritated but desperate to dance with the stallion by my side. I looked over at him. He pretended to be concentrating on the moves but I saw the corners of his mouth twitch, like he was trying to suppress a laugh.

The odd-looking man in front of me, dressed in tight beige trousers and a belted jacket, moved in a completely uncoordinated fashion. He managed to trip me up and send me flying. I just about managed to stop my boobs falling out of my dress but could do nothing to prevent the split in my dress riding higher to reveal my lacy red knickers. Luckily, I had also managed to re-engage the interest of the sexy man on my right, judging by his wolfish grin. Thank god I had had the sense to change out of my greying granny pants.

'Hi, you must be Josie.'

The thin ginger man was speaking to me. *OH MY GOD. HOW THE HELL DID HE KNOW MY NAME?* I opened and closed my mouth, unable to utter a sound, suddenly reminded of being unnerved by Pru's grandson Melvin knowing who I was when we had met.

'I didn't want to introduce myself to you earlier, in case I … you know, umm, put you off.' He was stumbling on his words. 'Thought we'd better get to know each other a little first.' Hee Heeeee, Haa, Hee. There it was again, that high-pitched squeaky laugh that made me want to sock him in the gob.

'I thought Babs was going to do the honours. She was supposed to meet me, but I couldn't find her.'

'Are you a friend of Babs?' I asked in amazement.

From the corner of my eye I saw Babs had re-joined the group on the dance floor. She was looking a lot healthier and put her thumb up to me, to indicate that she was fine. She was also shrugging her shoulders and mouthing something at me: Sherry? No. From the look on her face it was more like 'Sorry.' She was with Jake, who was beaming at me.

'No, I'm Jeremy, a friend of Jake's. He said you were a stunner and he wasn't wrong.'

I looked over at Babs and Jake. Suddenly the confusion lifted, and everything was crystal clear. I had been set up on a blind date. Worse still, I hadn't been told. Even worse, my blind date was a bumbling idiot, strangely reminiscent of someone I couldn't quite put my finger on (and wouldn't want to).

I didn't think things could get any worse but as I glanced to my right, I was horrified to find that my man had gone. Disappeared. I ran off the dance floor, wanting to cry, but unfortunately Jeremy chased after me.

'Josie, Josie what's wrong? We were getting on so well …'.

I stopped in my tracks, then wished I hadn't as he crashed into me.

'There that's better, isn't it? Standing still is better. I find that jogging is best reserved for mornings in the park when you're not trying to do too many things at once. Anyway, what can I get you?' he blabbered on.

'Look Jeremy,' I said, trying to be kind, 'I wasn't told about this blind date. If I had been, I would never have agreed to it because I'm nowhere near ready for a relationship. I've just split up with someone, you see.'

'I know,' he said brightly, 'but I'm totally reliable, committed and ready to settle down, start a family - just say the word.' I stared at him. 'We even sound good together. Jeremy and Josie Jones.' He finished off with his hyena laugh. It sounded like he needed to be committed. To a mental asylum, and fast.

'Umm … I'm desperate for the loo.'

I dashed off once again, tearing across the bar and straight into the arms of the tall, brooding stranger. A slow smile spread across his face.

'Where are you off to in such a hurry?' he said, stroking my face.

I swallowed hard. 'Umm, I was just looking for the loos,' I said shakily. 'Haven't seen them by any chance, have you?'

'Follow me,' the stranger said, grabbing my arm urgently and pulling me through the crowd to the other side of the room. We followed the sign to the toilets but bypassed them, where instead he opened a door just a bit further along and pulled me in roughly. I was breathing hard, feeling scared, but exhilarated.

'We were about to dance together,' he whispered, sliding his hand around my waist and pressing me in towards him, then moving his hips expertly forward and back. My heart was hammering against my chest. I felt reckless, it wasn't like me to get frisky with a stranger in what was probably a mop cupboard but I couldn't help myself. We pounced on each other desperately, his hands slid up my dress and easily found my red lacy knickers. He groaned.

'You are a sexy minx ...' he said hoarsely, now cupping my breasts. He kissed me slowly at first, then with greater passion. I started ripping at his shirt, burying my face in his chest. Just at that moment the door swung open, the sudden bright light invading our shared intimacy. I blinked my eyes, not quite believing that Jeremy was standing in the doorway, his eyes wide open in horror.

'I thought you got lost finding the loos, but I guess you found exactly what you were looking for, you ... *hussy.*' He hissed out the last word, turned on his heels and slammed the door shut behind him.

Chapter Five
The Morning After

I WOKE UP FEELING DISORIENTATED, NOT quite knowing where I was but reassured by the sight of the glittery sandals and chiffon dress hanging on the back of my bedroom door. Memories from the night before flashed through my head like disco lights. I cringed with embarrassment on remembering what happened with that bumbling buffoon Jeremy, and also with that rather gorgeous sex beast. I doubt I would see either again. Thankfully not the former, and most regrettably not the latter.

I had fled the scene in shame, just stopping briefly to put my tits back in my dress and readjust my red lace panties. I heard someone call after me but I didn't stop to look back. Thankfully I was able to jump straight into a waiting taxi.

I couldn't remember anything after that, but at least I had made it home safe and sound. A peek under the bed sheets confirmed I was in one piece, wearing my sensible pyjamas. I was just thinking how lucky I was when the telephone shrilled loudly in the hallway. I groaned, pulling my head under the duvet. I couldn't face anyone right now, especially if that someone was my mother. Which was very likely, considering that she didn't own a mobile phone, far too modern for her liking. I think Dame got the landline just so that our mothers could keep in touch. The phone rang again.

'I said I don't want to talk to anyone right now,' I yelled. The ringing continued. 'For god's sake ....' I got out of bed, a little unsteady on my feet. Whoever it was wasn't giving up. Abruptly the ringing stopped and the answering machine clicked on.

'Umm hello, if you're there Josie, please pick up the phone,' came the rapid tones of the urgent, deep familiar voice I had wanted to hear for so long. 'I know you are probably standing there in shock, wearing your pink pyjamas and wondering why the hell it's taken me so long to realise that I'm lost without you and want more than anything in the world for you to be my wife.' There was a pause. 'Well, it's because I'm a total moron but I guess you knew that already. Umm, hope you are well, Josie. Please call me back. Please. I love you. Bye.'

I stood in the doorway, shaking.

I couldn't believe it ... Niles? Niles! Finally, he had come to his senses. I ran to the phone, almost tripping over the duvet I had wrapped tightly around me. Jubilant and triumphant, I started laughing and whooping. My heart was thudding, my head was spinning. I tried to gather myself together but my hands were trembling something fierce. I stopped for a moment. What should I say to him? Why had it taken him so long to contact me?

'It doesn't matter!' came back my chirpy reply. He made a mistake but has realised he loves you, wants to marry you. I located my mobile phone. Yup, he'd already tried to call twelve times. I took a deep breath and went to press the callback button but was interrupted by the doorbell, followed quickly by a loud knock on the door.

'What now?' Exasperated, I threw the phone on my bed. 'You're always forgetting your bloody keys!' I yelled, stomping to the door.

I flung open the front door, expecting to see Dame but was astonished to find myself face-to-face with the rugged man I'd almost romped in the mop cupboard last night.

'It's you. You from last night. How did you find me?"

'Good morning, Josie' he said, leaning in to give me a hug and waving a bag in front of my face. 'Breakfast time. I hope you like coffee and blueberry muffins, it's the only kind they had. Did you sleep well?'

'What are you doing here?' I asked slowly.

'Don't you remember, Josie? I followed you in the taxi last night to make sure you got home safely. Things went a bit pear shaped when your boyfriend found us at it in the storeroom.'

'Yes, I remember that bit … and that wasn't my boyfriend,' I said crossly.

'Whatever. Anyway you seemed a bit upset so I wanted to make sure you were ok.'

'Do you mean to say you slept here last night? With me?'

'Well, yes and no.'

'What do you mean by 'yes and no'?' I asked, feeling a bit sick.

'Well I definitely remember putting you to bed,' he said with a lascivious smile.

'Oh god!' I said, burying my head in my hands. 'So, did we … you know?'

'What?' he asked innocently, his dark smouldering eyes turning puppy-dog on me.

'Shag!' I shouted at him.

'Yes please!' he grinned widely.

'Did. We. Shag?' I demanded to know.

'Well …' he drawled, 'you have to understand it was very hard to fight you off. You were wild, look what you did to my neck.' He showed me a purple bruise on his neck that could well have been a love-bite. 'And that's just for starters … after that, you seemed to lose all coordination, stumbled around for a while, tripped up on the coffee table and threw up in that bin …' he said, pointing at the small bin near the sofa.

'Great.' I said, thinking things couldn't really have got much worse.

'At least your aim was good. You didn't get any sick on the carpet and only a bit on yourself.'

'So, where did you end up sleeping?' I asked, still suspicious.

'After I cleaned you up, emptied the sick in the bin and put you in your spotty pink pyjamas, I found some spare bedding and slept on the couch. I even checked up on you a couple of times in the night to make sure you hadn't choked on your own vomit.'

'Thanks,' I mumbled, feeling very grateful but totally ashamed. Yet again.

'All in all, I was the perfect gentleman so I think it's only fair that you shag me now.'

He looked at me with those dark penetrating eyes, leaning in closer to brush away a loose strand of hair from my face. His full red lips parted and moved closer to mine. I pushed him away gently.

'I can't. I'm sorry,' I whispered.

'Why not? You didn't seem so shy at the club?'

'I can't ... because I'm engaged.'

'That didn't seem to bother you last night ... oh, I get it,' he said in realisation, 'that man who caught us was your fiancé?'

'No, that most definitely wasn't my fiancé. That was Jeremy, some silly man that my even sillier friends set me up on a blind date with.'

I then told him the whole sorry story about Niles, and how last night had been about trying to forget him and get on with my life, and how this morning he had called to say that he wanted me back.

'If you ask me, I think this Niles sounds like a right plonker. I mean how could he dump someone as gorgeous as you? Last night you wanted me, you were acting on raw, basic instinct ... and that, Josie,' he whispered, leaning in towards me, 'was so powerful, sexy and irresistible. You were enjoying yourself and totally getting on with your life. I thought we had a connection.'

I flushed crimson despite myself. We chatted some more while devouring the coffee and muffins but I knew the time had come to sort things out.

'I'm really sorry ... Umm, what was your name again?'

'Chris.'

'Chris, you've been really sweet and everything and indeed, a true gentleman if what you say is true. But I'm going to have to ask you to leave now as I've got to go and see Niles. I really want to work things out with him.'

'OK,' he shrugged. 'He clicks his fingers and you go running, it's a shame ...a real shame.' He looked at me regretfully and walked towards the door. He paused as he turned the door handle, and turned to me once more. 'If he disappoints or lets you down in anyway, call me.' With that, he offered me his business card, giving me one last lingering look as he walked out of the door.

***

'Josie, it's so good to hear your voice … you sound great!' Niles sounded relieved when I called him.

'We should talk in person, Niles. Shall I pop over in, say, an hour?'

'An hour is good for me … I can't wait to see you.'

'Me too.' I felt oddly calm now but maybe I was just in shock.

I took one last approving look in the mirror. My cheeks were flushed, eyes bright and hair glossy. Maybe this had something to do with the booze and excitement from the night before. The black belted dress accentuated my best bits. I grabbed my bag, coat and keys and headed straight for Niles' place.

I couldn't quite believe that I was about to see him. I honestly thought I would never see him again. I got off the tube and headed towards his house. I paused outside his front door and took a deep breath, suddenly feeling really apprehensive. The door was flung open before I even had a chance to buzz.

'Josie, what took you so long? You didn't get lost, did you?' He laughed nervously but gave me a warm embrace. 'God, I've missed you.'

'You know what the weekend tube service is like,' I laughed awkwardly, my stomach churning.

'Anyway, don't just stand there on the doorstep like a lemon. Come in. Here, let me take your coat.'

I stepped into his hallway gingerly, as if I were treading in something unpleasant.

'Can I get you a tea or coffee?' he asked hurriedly, ushering me into the front room.

Nothing, thanks.' I smoothed out my dress and sat down. 'I like the new coffee table, the colour goes nicely with the flooring.'

'Thanks Jos. Anyway, enough of the small talk, let's talk about us.' He sat next to me on the sofa and took my hands in his. I looked up into his soft grey eyes, framed by the steel spectacles which made him look a combination of bookish intellectual and super sensitive. Since hearing his voice on my answering machine, I had experienced a whole array of emotions from excitement, fear, nerves, shock and mild disbelief. But now, as I sat next to him looking into his face which appeared so calm and collected, I felt a shot of pure anger run through me.

'Niles, you dumped me with zero explanation, and then disappeared from my life for over three months. And now you expect me to throw my arms open and welcome you back into my life. I left hundreds of messages on your mobile which was permanently switched off and you didn't return one single call.' (That is something I hadn't confessed to Babs or Dame as it contravened the Dumped Manifesto but come on, I'm only human.)

'Jos, I was a mess. I wanted time and space to think without any distractions, so I left my mobile at home. I didn't contact anyone except my mum and that was only once to stop her sending a police search party out looking for me. I didn't think you would try and call me so often, considering that I said it was over.'

'Don't remind me. So, did you have fun deep-sea diving in Guatemala?'

'Where's Guatemala?'

'Never mind that! Did you find what you were looking for?'

'No, not really, because what I was looking for was back at home all along.'

'So, where have you been all this time?'

'I know this is going to sound lame but mostly I was with my mate Dan in Ireland, getting drunk and generally feeling like shit.'

'You dumped me for a three-month booze-fest with your mate?' I asked incredulously. 'What happened to deep sea diving and travelling the world?'

'I did sign up for a two-week diving course in Greece, but it turns out I wasn't very good under water.'

That would have sounded funny if it hadn't sounded so pathetic.

'I can't believe that all this time you have been on an extended boy's night out, getting drunk and partying in Ireland while I've been crying myself to sleep wondering what I did wrong.' I tried to fight back the tears. I didn't want Niles to see how much he had hurt me, but I had already admitted to crying myself to sleep.

'I know I've hurt you, Jos, but I was scared and confused. I got cold feet, but this time away from you has been hell. While everyone around me was laughing, I was miserable. I thought that I could do without you, but I can't. I want to be with you for the rest of my life. Please forgive me, Josie.' He buried his head in his hands.

'So why didn't you pick up the phone and call me then when you realised that you were so miserable without me?'

He shrugged his shoulders lamely. 'I wanted to, but Dan convinced me I should think it through before I jumped back in.'

'Some friend he turned out to be,' I fumed. 'So how do I know you won't up and leave again?'

'It won't happen. I'm never letting you go again.'

'How can I be sure?'

'I guess you have to trust me, trust that I've grown up. I know what I want now, Josie.' He looked up at me earnestly. 'I was foolish enough to think I didn't need you, that there was something else out there for me, but I was wrong.' His thoughtful grey eyes looked deeply into mine as he leaned forward to gently caress my face, my hair.

I jerked my head away. 'What were you searching for?'

'Myself, I guess. I felt inadequate, disillusioned. I've worked hard all my life, not taken a single sick day. Stuck to the book but I began to wonder if it's all been worth it. My first wife certainly didn't think so.' (Niles married his first proper girlfriend when he was 20. She later accused him of being a workaholic and ran off with his charming, out-of-work younger brother some 15 years later). Niles continued, 'I wanted to rediscover my purpose in life. but then I realised that as long as you're by my side, I can do anything'.

I was silent for a few moments. 'So basically you were having a mid-life crisis?'

'Of sorts. Although I don't quite see myself as middle aged,' he said, smoothing down his fine hair.

I smiled for the first time. 'The difference between us, Niles, is that when I met you I felt like we were a team, that we would face all challenges or adventures together. Niles, you have to learn to leave the past in the past. This could have been a new start for the both of us.'

'That can still be the case, Josie. I don't expect you to forgive me straight away but I do love you and I'll spend the rest of my life making this up to you.' He looked so sincere, so heartfelt, that it was all I could do to stop myself from covering him in kisses and telling him that of course I could forgive him. I took a deep breath to steady myself.

He pulled me towards him and kissed me so softly, so tenderly that the pain of the last few months began to melt away. We continued talking, holding each other for what felt like hours.

He eyed me appreciatively. 'I love that dress on you … but I think the dress would look even better on my bedroom floor.' That was the first line he had used on me -with the desired result - and I think he was trying to be funny by using it now, but it jolted me back to reality.

'I've got to go, Niles. I need some time …'.

'But I thought you came here to …?' he stammered.

I glared at him. 'To do what?'

'To give us another go, because you love me too?' he asked, hopeful.

'I do, Niles. But you left me heartbroken and now you are trying to rush me.' I stood up. 'And maybe, just maybe, I've changed.'

'You've found someone else?'

'No!' I replied indignantly, as a quick flash of Chris from

last night entered my mind.' 'But it would serve you right if I had.' He looked hurt.

'And when did you get that coffee table?'

He looked down shiftily. 'A couple of weeks ago,' he mumbled.

'You've been back a few weeks and you only just thought to call me?' Niles said nothing.

'Unbelievable!'

With that I grabbed my coat and left.

***

I opened the door to the flat, half expecting to see Dame and George cavorting on the living room floor, but was pleasantly surprised to find myself home alone and with the space to think things through. The fact was that last night I had thrown myself at a very handsome, rugged stranger, only to later decline the advances of a man who I had once had every intention of marrying. I poured myself a large brandy for the shock. What was happening to me and what was I going to do?

Ten minutes later I was on the phone with Babs, who had left several apologetic messages on my mobile.

'I had no idea how ghastly and gone-off Jeremy was.' ('Gone-off' referring to our male milk rating system.) It was all Jake's idea. He told me he was funny and decent-looking so I agreed to let him set you up.'

'More like funny-looking or belonging on a funny farm,' I laughed.

'So *tell me*,' she said breathlessly, 'did you catch up with that other bloke?'

'What bloke?' I asked innocently.

'Josie, this is no time to act all coy. I want *details*, girl.'

I spilled the beans to her about my drunken shenanigans with 'creamy' Chris in the mop cupboard.

'I thought you two would get it on - even on the dance floor! The sexual tension between you was palpable. Josie, I'm really proud of the way you're getting through the Dumpsville list. Wild flirting with sexy strangers - big tick!' she said gleefully.

Oh god. 'You haven't heard the half of it yet,' I said.

I then retold the whole tale to Babs, interspersed with many 'Oh my god's' from her.

'Well, at least you managed to get some love action *and* you've finally found out what a louse Niles is.'

I stayed silent for a few moments. 'So, you don't think I should give Niles another go?'

'No way, Jos! You said yourself that he's been swanning around pub-crawling in Ireland, not giving you a second thought. Now he expects you to drop your drawers and get on with it.' Babs had such an eloquent way of putting things but I loved her for being so straightforward and caring, if at times a little bit too brutal.

'I know, but I hate the way I left things with him. Now I know he's back, we've got to at least communicate.'

Babs remained quiet.

'Anyway, I really need to lie down. It looks like Dame is still with George so I might just get a couple of hours of peace.'

'Yeah, once you've had some rest I am sure you'll be thinking more clearly.'

With that, we said our goodbyes and I lay my weary, befuddled mind and body down to sleep.

***

I got up around 6pm and the good news was that I could smell food. It was coming from the kitchen and it smelled delicious; my stomach rumbled in agreement. I put on my slippers, padding into the kitchen. Dame was stirring a thick tomato sauce on the stove, sporting his chef hat.

'Bonsoir my lovely, spaghetti a la meatballs will be served in deux minutes,' he said, in a crap French accent.

'Spaghetti meatballs is meant to be Italian, you idiot.'

'Yeah, but I don't know how to say 'a la meatballs' in Italian. Anyway, will Madam please refrain from arguing with the chef and be seated.' He pushed me towards the table and pulled out a chair. He had gone to a lot of effort. The table was adorned with scented candles and fancy napkins. Dame was top-grade husband material. George was a lucky man.

'Are we expecting George, or George's parents for that matter? I mean you've gone to a lot of trouble.'

'No, but it's funny you should mention George's parents, because George drove us out to this lovely spot near Oxfordshire last night and we had a moonlight picnic. It was so romantic, I couldn't believe it. The most romantic thing a man has ever done for me before that was hold my hand while I was being sick in his toilet …'.

'What's that got to do with George's parents? Did they turn up or something?' I interrupted.

'I'm getting to that part,' he said, rolling his eyes at me. 'Anyway, while he was feeding me strawberries and getting me drunk on champagne, he mentioned that his parents would like to meet me and he was quite insistent on wanting to meet *my* parents.' He looked at me expectantly.

'And?'

'*And,*' he stressed like I was a two-year-old, 'you know what my parents are like. They've got it into their tiny minds that I'm only gay because I haven't found the right woman, then hinted that Lydia was looking for a husband.'

'Who's Lydia?'

'The daughter of my dad's business partner. Boring, stuck-up, but of very good breeding according to my mum. Or failing that, they said even you would do.'

'Charming,' I replied, shoving forkfuls of spaghetti meatballs in my mouth. 'Look Dame, the way I see it is that maybe your parents need to be shocked into realisation. Take George to meet them, introduce him as your boyfriend. They will have to accept it then.'

Dame didn't look convinced.

'They're not as bad as you think, just a bit old-fashioned, but if they know you're serious, they will come around - eventually,' I promised him.

Dame got up suddenly and dashed to get a notebook, furiously scribbling something down.

'I'm glad you are taking note of my advice,' I said, feeling pleased with myself.

'I'm jotting down a few ideas of what to cook for George's parents. Apparently they're take-out people and probably haven't had a decent home-cooked meal in decades. George reckons they'll be practically eating out of my hand by the end of the night.'

'No need for plates then,' I joked.

Dame sighed. 'George is so lucky to have parents who accept him for who he is, and they even seem cool with us moving in together.'

'Well on that note,' I said brightly, 'I may have found the perfect flatmate, leaving you free to move in with George.'

'Well don't keep me in suspense ...' said Dame excitedly.

'Niles.' I hadn't actually decided, but thought I'd sound Dame out.

'Niles?' Dame almost spat out a meatball in my face.

'It's a long story ....'

'I know you almost shagged him earlier ... Babs told me everything,' he explained, when he saw my expression. 'But I hoped you might have come to your senses by now. Getting back with your loser ex was definitely not on the list.'

What was it with this bloody list? It was just some stupid thing we had created in a few minutes, months ago. The truth is what I had secretly wanted all along was for Niles to come back to me. Which he had.

Dame was looking at me in the manner of a stern father. 'That man is no good for you, Jos.'

'I didn't mean that he should move in tomorrow or next week, but who knows? In time, maybe?'

'Niles can move in here ... Over. My. Dead. Body. Unfortunately I can't stop you from seeing him though.' Dame rarely spoke in such serious tones. 'You should have got it on with that Chris bloke. According to Babs he was hotter than a Chicken Madras.'

Dame looked at me sadly. 'You know what, Jos? You were actually getting along just fine without Niles. You were even beginning to have some fun, and now he's going to smash your heart into tiny pieces again.'

With that, Dame stabbed a fork into his last meatball, cleared up the plates in silence and retreated to his bedroom.

Chapter Six
A New Flatmate

DAME CONTINUED TO BE FROSTY with me over the next couple of weeks, especially when I told him that Niles and I were having discussions. He wasn't much into giving people second chances. I reminded him of just how ludicrously loved up he was with George and that he could *try* being happy for me too. Dame conceded to '*give it a go*' but warned me that he would '*kung fu*' Niles into the middle of next week should he so much as harm a hair on my head.

Naturally I had my reservations about Niles, too. It wasn't a case of just falling back into his arms, like some sap. We'd spent hours going through everything. He'd explained how he wanted a passionate, honest relationship, not a calm but dull one like his parents had. Yes, they were pleasant to each other and hardly ever exchanged a cross word, but beneath it all, there was this forced politeness, which while growing up had been horribly oppressive. No one dared speak about real issues or emotions and Niles had felt this silent scream building up inside him, which he had finally released twenty-five years later while sitting in an Irish pub.

Pru was always talking about having faith and trust in a higher force. Perhaps in some mystical way the Universe had conspired to bring me back the thing my heart most desired.

Monday morning rolled around all too quickly again but I woke up with a genius idea. Call in sick and invite Niles over. I messaged him my plan and he approved wholeheartedly. I read somewhere that taking the occasional duvet day was good for mental health and general wellbeing, and could increase motivation and productivity in the workplace: a concept which my bitchy boss Bernice wouldn't have bought in a month of Sundays.

'Calling in sick again are we, Green? Interesting to note how this will be your fourth sick absence on a Monday,' she drawled in a snide tone. 'Report to my office so we can have a talk on your return to work, *only* when you're feeling completely better,' she added, with a large dollop of sarcasm.

I didn't let her unfeeling attitude dampen my spirits. As soon as I was showered, moisturised and perfumed in Coco Chanel, I revelled in the fact that I would be spending a whole delicious day with Niles all to myself.

Niles must have broken the speed limit as he was at my door within twenty minutes, presenting me with a beautiful bouquet of red roses and a dashing smile. He wore fitted jeans and a tight white t-shirt which emphasised his slim frame to perfection. Dame often commented on how Niles looked slightly malnourished whilst patting his own slightly porky belly, which was not helped by his beer-swigging, client-entertaining lifestyle. Far from looking underfed, Niles appeared relaxed, tanned and toned, like he had just returned from an exotic spa holiday in the Maldives.

Nile's face nestled into my neck. 'I'm about to show you

just how much I've missed you Ms Green,' he whispered seductively. His breath felt hot and sweet and his lips traced their way down my neck to my shoulder blade. He stopped briefly to gaze lovingly into my eyes. Then he kissed me fiercely, passionately, like never before. I hardly had time to catch my breath when he ripped open my creamy silk blouse, the buttons pinging to the floor. He pushed me roughly up against the wall pinning my arms to the side, his finger nails digging into my wrists.

'Niles, why are you being like this?' I asked with a mixture of fear and excitement.

He didn't reply but grabbed my breasts and squeezed them hard like he was trying to milk them.

'Easy tiger,' I said feeling a bit scared and trying to push him away a little.

He released me suddenly and told me to face the wall in a more soothing tone. I obliged.

His hands slid up under my black skirt, caressing my thighs, squeezing and worshipping my buttocks. My nipples were rock hard pressed against the wall. Suddenly he yanked down my knickers and delivered a hard slap across my bare behind.

'Niles!' I protested, the sound of the thwack shocking me more than anything.

Just then there was a loud sharp knock at the door. I gasped and attempted to cover myself up. Maybe Pru had heard a commotion and thought I was being attacked by burglars or maybe my suspicious boss had worked out the real reason for my absence… the possibilities raced through my mind.

'Leave it!' growled Niles.

I held my breath, hoping that the visitor had gone.

A few seconds later the knocking resumed.

"I thought you said we wouldn't be disturbed today?' Niles' voice was thick with irritation.

I shrugged my shoulders in response. Finally, footsteps could be heard walking away. It was probably one of those pushy utilities sales people.

Niles motioned me into the bedroom, his ardour seemingly having returned.

Afterwards I lay there shivering, despite our heated lovemaking session. Niles was snoring loudly, his arm flopped over the side of the bed. At least some things hadn't changed. I drifted in and out of sleep and woke an hour later to find that Niles was still in a deep slumber.

I got up and realised I was famished. The sex had certainly restored my appetite and burned off a few calories in the process, no doubt. I raided Dame's cupboard for his secret supply of Marks & Spencer shortbread biscuits and found the last two. Hopefully I would remember to replace the packet tomorrow. After making a sandwich and a cup of tea, I settled down in front of a repeat episode of Diagnosis Murder. I was just getting into the plot when there was a knock at the door. It made me jump. Why didn't whoever it was just use the doorbell? Knocking seemed more sinister somehow, especially when I had just witnessed the murder of a woman alone in her flat on TV.

I felt the hairs prickle on the back of my neck. I was tempted to ignore it but the knocking sounded again, louder and more insistent. I figured that if someone did want to murder me then they would hardly draw attention to themselves by banging the hell out of the door. Niles was also on hand, should I need any protection, even though he wouldn't be much good in the semi-comatose state he was currently in.

I flung open the door annoyed as hell, ready to hurl abuse at the overly-keen gas man.

Except that he looked rather strange for a man wanting me to switch energy suppliers. For a start, he was wearing a waistcoat and tight trousers and looked like he belonged on the cover of Horse and Hound. He was red and puffed out, like he could well have just been riding his horse.

'Umm. Hi. Hello there. I'm Ed. Ed Chancellor,' he said, shaking my hand. It even sounded like a horsey name. 'I'm so sorry to have disturbed you, I wasn't sure if there would be anyone at home, but then I thought I heard people talking.' He spoke in clear-cut, public schoolboy tones. He also had a distinctly boyish, clumsy quality about him, with his ginger blonde hair tumbling into his face which he tried desperately to control.

'What can I do for you, Mr. Chancellor?'

'I heard that you were looking for a flat mate,' he said, looking at me briefly before staring intently at the floor like it had suddenly become fascinating. Maybe he wasn't a horsing enthusiast after all, but a flooring specialist?

He'd seen Dame's advert and just turned up to the flat instead of making an appointment. How presumptuous of him.

'I just thought I'd try popping in on the off-chance, as I happened to be visiting someone in the block.'

'Best if you come back later and meet Dame, the owner of the flat,' I said. I was ready to shut the door on him.

'Gran said you wouldn't mind.' *Gran?*

He looked up at me with twinkling blue eyes.

My stomach did a flip. 'Whoa. Have we met?'

He looked puzzled for a moment, before turning away. Yes, those intense turquoise-blue eyes were most definitely familiar. Café-Rouge-man was standing in my doorway.

'Oh yes. Of course!' he said, slapping his hand on his forehand. 'You were at the restaurant, what … a few weeks ago now? With your friend. I wanted to talk to you, you looked familiar. Unbelievable!' He ran his hands through his unruly hair.

I stared at him, wide-eyed. Unbelievable was one word. Highly peculiar were two better words, maybe.

'So, you said your gran told you about this place?'

'Yes, I believe you are quite well acquainted with her?'

'No, I don't think so?' The only other elderly lady in the block was Mrs Olsen; Pru was quite friendly with her.

'Yeah, she said you sometimes pop over for a cake and cuppa. She lives directly downstairs.'

'Oh, you mean Pru!' I said, startled. 'Pru has only ever mentioned having one grandson," I said, thinking of Malevolent Melvin. 'And he's certainly a lot different to you.'

'That he is,' he said, chuckling. 'Me and Melvin don't exactly see eye-to-eye, he's rather mercenary and a bit mean, I find. But I haven't seen him for a while as I've been in Australia.'

'Oh yes, that's right. She did say something about having a grandson living abroad.'

'That would be me,' he said, holding up his hands.

Well, you definitely have her eyes, I thought to myself, looking into their turquoise depths.

I relaxed now I had determined he wasn't a psycho stalker but Pru's travelling grandson.

I invited him in, hastily retrieving my black mini skirt from the lampshade and throwing it behind the sofa where he sat.

'Can I get you a drink, Ed?'

'Cup of tea, two sugars if you are making one. I've got it,' he announced suddenly. 'Where I've seen you. It was right here, just before I went to Australia.'

'But I only moved in a few months ago?' I said.

'Your mate Damian was having a party. A very loud one if I remember correctly. I was visiting Gran. Anyway, I bumped into you and your mate in the corridor.'

'I don't seem to remember that,' I said, frowning. I wouldn't have forgotten someone as distinctive as Ed.

'I looked very different at the time. Thin long greasy hair, chain smoking crackhead.'

I burst out laughing.

'No. I'm being serious. Long story. The short version is that my mum died suddenly and I kind of went off the rails for a few years. Most people avoided me in those days, except other crackheads. My dad carted me off to an Australian boot-camp to sort me out; it only took six years and counting.'

'Oh. Wow. Sorry to hear that,' I said, touched by his honesty while trying (and failing) to conjure up an image of him as a thin greasy-haired junkie.

'So why don't you just move in with your gran? I'm sure she'd be glad of the company and you might even get away with living rent-free,' I said, winking at him. Oh god, did I just wink? Thankfully he hadn't seemed to have noticed my twitchy eye.

'I haven't seen much of Gran since I got clean. I want to prove to her that I've changed. Live independently, be there for her when she needs me. Besides, it was Gran's idea that I should enquire about moving in. She reckoned that we'd get on like a house on fire,' he said, winking back at me.

There was a bit of an awkward silence. Maybe he felt a bit silly about the whole winking thing too. I fussed with one of the cushions and he looked intently at the floor again.

'So this is, of course, the living room,' I said, somewhat unnecessarily. 'Which I think you'd agree has some nice touches,' I pointed at the arty vase and Picasso painting behind the black leather sofa.

I led him through to the kitchen. 'Dame had this kitchen installed last year. Don't you just love the worktops and the cupboard space?'

Ed looked impressed and was making appreciative noises. I was clearly in the wrong career.

'As for the bedrooms, Dame's bedroom is definitely the more spacious of the two, as well as being very light and airy. But I'm not sure if it's safe to go in. I think it's best if I check first. Just a moment …'.

I hurried over to Dame's room and took a quick peek inside. It was as immaculate as usual, very minimalist apart from what looked like a very long riding crop, a pair of pink furry handcuffs and a black leather thong laid out neatly on his silk white sheets.

It wasn't as bad as I'd been expecting. I shoved the items in a drawer.

'Safe to enter!' I called out into the hallway.

'Are you sure?' said Ed, as he poked his head around the door nervously.

'This is fantastic,' he said, visibly relieved. 'A lot bigger than I was expecting.'

'That's what I hear they all say in Dame's bedroom,' I chuckled.

I told him to take another look around, almost forgetting Niles was napping.

'Except in there,' I said, pointing to the closed bedroom door. 'My boyfriend Niles is in there, sleeping.' I found that I was whispering, even though a lumberjack probably wouldn't have woken him up.

'Oh, I didn't realise there were three of you living here?'

'He doesn't live here. He's just visiting,' I said, smiling.

As we sat on the sofa drinking tea and chatting away, I realised that I had a good feeling about Ed, probably on account of him being Pru's grandson and a much nicer one than Malevolent Melvin. Thankfully it seemed that we had also got past the initial awkwardness, which no doubt was down to our mutual surprise at seeing each other again in my doorway, of all places. It was like I was nattering away with an old school friend. And I'm sure as flatmates go, he'd be pleasant and handy with the hoover. In addition to that, he worked at Café Rouge and therefore knew how to make real coffee *and* he would probably bring home a supply of leftover pastries at the end of the day ...!

Ed seemed to think we were getting along well too, and asked if he could move in on a trial basis. I told him that while it was fine with me, Dame would have to make the final call as it was his flat. Having said that, I didn't think Dame would have an issue, what with him being desperate to move out.

There was only one thing left to do. I presented Ed with the flatmate questionnaire, which read like so:

Q1. How would you deal with a large spider in the kitchen sink?

a) I would leave it in the sink
b) I would drown it
c) I would run off screaming
d) I would remove it from the sink.
(please specify how: ______________)
e) Other: ____________________________
(please specify)

Ed lifted one eyebrow. 'Mmm …' he said thoughtfully. 'I would opt for d) I would pick up the spider from the sink, pull off its legs slowly, one at a time, before finally putting it out of its misery and battering it to death.' He said all of this deadpan.

I scribbled down 'Evil sadistic bastard with insects, clearly displays psychopathic tendencies,' although I think he was joking.

Q2. What chores do you most dislike?
a) Washing-up
b) Cooking
c) Cleaning floors/hoovering
d) Cleaning toilets/bathtubs
e) Other: ____________________________
(please specify)

'Actually, I'm fairly well domesticated and happy to do my fair share of any chores. And I don't want to blow my trumpet or anything, but I make a fairly decent lamb shank,' replied Ed.

I scribbled down 'Helpful with housework. Excellent cook, and not forgetting the leftovers he will bring home from Café Rouge.'

Q3. What is your favourite dish?

'That's easy. Lamb Shank. I also love mushroom pizzas and Belgian Chocolate Haagen Daas.'

I scribbled down 'Seems almost too good to be true, could he be gay too?'

Hence the next question was:

Q4. Do you have a partner? Y___ N ___

If Yes, how often on average would they come over/sleep over at the flat?

a) At weekends

b) Once a week

c) Two or three times a week

d) More often

The logic behind this question was that if he had a partner who popped over occasionally he would be less likely to object if Niles stayed over every now and then.

'No time for all that.' He saw me frown and read my mind. 'But I'm totally ok with you having your boyfriend over. What you do in your spare time is your business, as long as he doesn't spend three hours in the shower.'

'Hardly.' I said. 'He's not gay. Obviously.'

He grinned. 'In fact, we probably won't cross paths all that much as I work different shifts and hang out with my work-mates quite a lot.'

I scribbled: 'Sympathetic about having partners stay over. Out a lot, so won't interrupt my life. Very Good.'

Q5. What's your worst, or most annoying, habit?

a) Poor hygiene

b) Untidy

c) Listen to heavy metal (or any very loud music)

d) Watch a lot of sport

e) Trainspotting

f) Other: ______________________

(please be honest)

Niles chose that precise moment to stumble out of the bedroom in his underpants looking bleary-eyed, with his hair sticking up at varying angles.

'Josie, make us a cuppa will ya?' He was taking a while to focus, then he noticed Ed sitting all cosy on the sofa next to me.

'Who the hell is that?' he spluttered. 'I knew you had another fella!' He glared at Ed, looking like he was ready to box his head in.

Ed looked at me guiltily, declaring 'I do watch a lot of sport but the good news is that I am a recovered trainspotter. I used to hang around Clapham Junction a lot until they escorted me off the platform one day, they thought I was a jumper.' He said this with mock seriousness but again, I think he was joking. I did wonder if his 'trainspotting' was a reference to his former drug use, like the film 'Trainspotting.' No one was perfect, I guess.

Niles stood looking completely bewildered. 'Sit down,' I told him calmly, 'and have a cuppa and a Hobnob; I'll fill you in."

Chapter Seven
Ed Cooks Up A Treat

THINGS COULDN'T HAVE WORKED OUT better. Dame was thrilled about Ed moving in, and he, in turn, moved in with George at lightning speed. Most of his stuff was there already. The couple seemed blissfully and puke-inducingly happy.

The dinner with George's parents had gone exceptionally well. They had taken to him like a son-in-law, gushing how he was the nicest, most decent man that George had ever been out with. Fortunately, they didn't know what a trollop Dame really was. Feeling buoyed by their reaction, Dame summoned up the courage to introduce George to his parents and even that hadn't been a total disaster. Dame's mum Irene had spent the entire evening fluttering her eyelashes at him, cooing that he looked like a young George Clooney. She remained in full flirt mode until she remembered that he was Dame's *gay* partner. Dame's dad, Gary, had been a bit gruff and distant with George to begin with, but after a couple of beers and a couple of hours talking football and the economy all seemed to be going well. George could pretty much charm anyone.

Ed was almost as good a flatmate as Dame, just not quite

as hilarious or cleanliness obsessed (thank god). In fact, he had a habit of forgetting to empty out the dryer, leaving me to find his forgotten Bart Simpson boxers or Mr. Happy socks, but he was a dream in the kitchen. After a day of hell at work which, for me, was most days, he'd knock out his signature hot chocolate with whipped cream, crumbled flake and marshmallows. I'd come home ranting and raving and he would gently bring the steaming mug under my nose. Pure heaven. I'd probably end up the size of a house but it would be well worth it.

He also had a hidden talent for proofing job applications. I'd spent a few sleep-deprived days applying for numerous marketing posts in a vain bid to escape the monotony of my current job. I was fast losing motivation and had fallen asleep in front of my computer. Ed helped me beef up my person spec, encouraging me to keep going with the help of strong coffee and the occasional can of Red Bull (or three). Fingers crossed that I might just score myself an interview after all this hard work.

He also seemed to have made amends with Pru, considering the amount of time he was spending there. Maybe she loved his hot chocolate delight as much as I did, but judging from his happy glow it seemed they were getting on in more ways than just a mutual love of hot chocolate.

Yes, things couldn't have been better, except that Niles didn't seem too keen on Ed. I couldn't understand why. Well maybe I did, but it had all been perfectly innocent.

Niles had walked in on Ed crouching down and holding my leg up, supporting it onto a chair and gently placing a bag of ice on the affected area. I had twisted my ankle quite painfully while jumping up and down a little too enthusiastically in an attempt to keep up with the latest keep-fit DVD.

I'd fallen awkwardly and screamed. Ed had rushed out of his room to help me. Niles had been in the toilet for an inordinately long time (reading his car magazines no doubt), but had finally come out to see what all the commotion was about. He'd apparently stood there for a full minute before any of us had noticed him. It didn't take him long to surmise what was going on, i.e that I was injured and in total agony, but he still huffed and puffed about what it looked like. No danger of him having any concern for me then. I thought the whole thing had been forgotten but it seemed like a cloud of suspicion had formed in his mind.

'It's not that I'm jealous,' he protested, 'it's just that he gives me the creeps. It's like he's watching me when he thinks I'm not looking. But it's a bit bloody hard to ignore those huge blue eyes peering at me from over the top of his newspaper.'

'Perhaps he's gay and you're the man of his dreams? Maybe the newspaper is covering the bulge in his pants?' I said in a playful tone, but Niles' face was like a clap of thunder.

'Gay, my arse,' was his unfortunately-phrased reply. 'Maybe he's got the hots for you and is trying to cover it up by staring at me.'

I burst out laughing, patting his knee affectionately. 'Look, Ed told me that he had a difficult break-up in Australia; he won't go into details, but I think he's finding it tough. He's just a bit awkward and probably a bit lonely, so just give him a chance.'

Niles looked furious. 'Why can't he just go on bloody Tinder if he's lonely, instead of crying to you about it? I know how blokes think, Josie, you'll only encourage him by being so nice.'

'It's not like that at all. We live together, so of course we're going to talk. I thought you of all people would have encouraged that, being a counsellor and all …'.

Niles sat there sulking, made worse by me trying to explain how nice and decent Ed was.

'Even Babs likes him, and you know how harsh Babs is on blokes.'

Niles gave me the sort of look to suggest that he didn't care much for Babs' opinion.

'Have you shagged him?' he asked me abruptly.

'Are you being serious?' I was shocked at his outburst and wondered if this was all down the fact Ed had the sheer audacity to tend to my twisted ankle.

Niles' phone started buzzing, and he pointedly ignored it.

'He's tried it on with you, hasn't he?'

The buzzing continued.

'No. Of course not!" I bellowed back at him.

Niles answered the phone and after listening for a couple of minutes, he hastily ended the call mumbling something about not being interested in what they were trying to sell him.

He didn't bother with any more accusations after that but raised an eyebrow at me, turned on the TV and sat down to watch the cricket like everything was normal.

But it wasn't normal. Niles was becoming increasingly controlling and clingy. He had stayed over for the last five nights in a row and hadn't once trusted me to be alone with Ed, making things very awkward indeed. The strange thing was that it wasn't like him. Usually he was mild-mannered and easy-going. Not the type to get jealous at all. However, I expect I wouldn't have been too thrilled if the tables were turned and he had an attractive woman living with him. Although

I'm hoping that I would have been more trusting. I sat looking at Niles, feeling frustrated that he couldn't just tell me how he was feeling.

His phone started buzzing again. 'What is it with some people?' he said, angrily switching off his phone and staring into space.

'I thought you didn't want us to end up like your parents?' I muttered.

Niles said nothing.

Thankfully there was the welcome intrusion of someone knocking at the door. I couldn't bear another minute of sitting in silence with Niles.

'Don't bother yourself,' I said to Niles, who was sitting closer to the door. Maybe Dame or Babs had received my telepathic signal to get me the hell out of here.

I was just as pleased to see Pru standing in the hallway, wearing a bright red dress with matching lips and accessories.

'Wow, Pru! You look amazing, have you got a hot date?' I teased her.

'I'm off to Bingo with Flora and Rose. This was one of Bert's favourite dresses, I wore it a lot while we were courting. 'Do you like?' she said, twirling around.

'I *love* it!'

'I trust you also love coconut and raspberry cake?'

'Goes without saying,' I nodded.

'Good!' she said triumphantly. 'I don't think Ed's had a chance to tell you yet but he's invited me over for dinner tomorrow night. He'll be serving up his famous Lamb Shank and I'm bringing dessert. I hope that you will be joining us.'

'There's no need to be kind, Pru,' I said, feeling a little

awkward. 'Don't you want to spend some time alone with Ed? You've probably still got a lot to catch up on?'

'Ohh, I'm not one to say things just to be kind. You're the granddaughter I wish I had, so make an old lady happy and say yes.'

I don't know what it was, maybe my row with Niles or the fact that I was stressed at work, but at that moment, I felt really emotional. Pru seemed to sense my vulnerability and put her arms around me and stroked my hair in the way my own grandmother had done many years ago.

'Don't worry, dear. Everything will be just fine - I know it, I can feel it in my bones.'

It was funny how elderly people could always feel things in their bones. Maybe it was their arthritis or something. My Nan had been the same.

***

Pru always had a way of making things seem brighter. I bounced back into the room and Niles looked over at me curiously. He held out his arms and beckoned me over.

'I'm so sorry, Josie. I've been a total moron,' he said, looking ashamed.

'Yup,' I agreed. 'But for some reason I still love you anyway.'

'Come here, Pumpkin.' Pumpkin was his affectionate pet name for me (because I apparently had a wide, pumpkin shaped face) but I kind of liked it.

I trotted over to where he was on the sofa. His arms were still outstretched and I hugged him, feeling thankful that his bad mood had passed.

'It's just that I get insecure sometimes and say things I

don't mean. All I want is to make you happy,' he mumbled into my hair.

'There's nothing to be insecure about. As long as we trust and respect each other and keep on talking, everything will be fine.'

'You are so wise, Pumpkin,' he whispered. 'I'm so looking forward to spending the rest of my life with you.'

Later, while we were wrapped in each other's arms, I felt relieved that the Niles I knew and loved was still there. I couldn't bear it if things were to fall apart now, not after losing him once. I was discovering a side to him that I'd never seen before. Fortunately, he was also still sweet, kind, generous and affectionate, all the things that made me fall in love with him in the first place. I hoped that our union would be as long and as happy as Pru's and Bert's had been.

***

The following evening, I tried to help Ed prepare the meal but he was worse than Gordon Ramsey, swearing at me, barking orders and getting red and sweaty, even though he clearly had things under control. Anyone would think that he was cooking for royalty. I left the kitchen, offering to do the washing up instead as soon as I realised all I was doing was getting in the way.

Pru came over promptly at 7pm, armed with a bottle of Merlot and the promised raspberry and coconut cake. By this time Ed was looking calm and unflappable, opening the wine and pouring both Pru and I a very generous glassful. I was grateful that Niles was spending the night at his own place, it showed that he did trust me after all. He had even suggested we all share a meal together soon.

The lamb shank was tender, cooked to perfection, and the conversation was flowing nicely along with the wine. I sometimes forgot that Pru was well into her eighties; she had the energy and vitality of a woman less than half her age. I imagined Babs being the same at her age and made a mental note to introduce the two of them. Plus Babs was itching to see Ed again; she'd already rushed over to meet him after I explained my new flatmate was the mysterious waiter from Café Rouge.

'It's all fate,' she said mystically, when I told her about the other coincidence: that he was Pru's long-lost (well, if long-lost meant having lived in Australia for the last six years) grandson.

'If you ask me, I think he's in love with you. He fancied you when he was a drugged-up hippy all those years ago, then he got all flustered when he saw you at Café Rouge. Now he's cooking you a slap-up meal …'.

'He's cooking for Pru. She was just kind enough to invite me.'

'Ha!' she exclaimed. 'All I'm saying is that you'd better lock your bedroom door at night, or maybe you could leave it slightly ajar …' she said, winking at me.

'Don't let Niles hear you say that,' I said, in all seriousness.

'*Sooo,* what is happening with you and Niles?'

'I'm taking things slowly. I still love him and want to get married but there's no need to rush.'

'You don't know the meaning of *slooow.*' Babs was being deliberately annoying. 'You are more the meet-move-in-get-married type of girl.'

'So, how's the lamb?' Ed's anxious words cut into my thoughts. He must have noticed my faraway look.

'It's not very nice,' I said, shaking my head and putting my hands across my stomach and groaning. 'In fact, I feel quite sick.'

'Oh god. I knew I should have defrosted the lamb for longer.' Ed was going all red again. I was fast realising that Ed's cooking was not a subject I could joke about.

'Relax, I was just kidding. It's delicious - as if you didn't know it.'

Pru had witnessed this exchange with an amused expression. 'If I didn't know any better, I'd say that you too are quite fond of each other.'

Ed and I exchanged looks. Pru and Babs were definitely alike. The truth is that it was impossible *not* to like Ed - unless you were Niles, of course. He had the goofiness of Kris Marshall in *My Family*, the heat of Gordon Ramsey and the stumbling, bumbling manner of Hugh Grant. The best thing was that hours could fly by and we'd still be chatting away. It was quite rare that I felt so comfortable with someone so soon after meeting them, Pru being the exception. You could definitely tell he was Pru's grandson.

Admittedly Ed was attractive, but romantically ... purrlease. Besides the dubious dress sense and orangutan hairiness, the only ginger-nuts I liked were of the biscuit variety. Not that I had thought about going down there. Eeew. Babs, my flame-haired friend, would have branded me a 'gingerphobe' if I had admitted to such thoughts, but it wasn't that I was anti-ginger, I just happened to prefer tall, dark and handsome, that was all.

'If you two lovebirds can take your eyes off each other I'd like to tell you about my friends, Flora and Fred.'

As it turned out, Flora had met Fred at the Bingo Hall. She had lost her first husband quite tragically, but had become enamoured with the call-master. She was a regular punter at bingo, and was Pru's best friend.

'Anyway, it was love at first sight when he called out 'legs eleven' and got Flora her first full house in twenty-five years. Today is their twenty-fifth wedding anniversary and he's only gone and taken her to bingo!' she said, throwing her head back with laughter. 'Bert took me ballroom dancing on our twenty-fifth wedding anniversary, it was even hotter than that film Dirty Dancing. Not in an obvious way, mind you, but Bert had more sex appeal in his knuckles than Patrick Swayze had in his entire body.'

I almost choked on my wine. Ed went all red again, trying not to laugh. Dame would have slapped Pru for saying that, as he practically licked the TV screen whenever Patrick Swayze was 'Dirty Dancing'. He had seen that damn film at least seven times - and probably a few more times in the theatre with George.

'You may laugh, young Josie, but Bert knew how to woo me in style. He was loving and attentive. Even after twenty-five years of marriage, even after fifty years. We were together for fifty-five happy years.' Pru's eyes were misty.

I thought about Niles and wondered if we would last fifty-five years.

'It won't be long now before we're together again.'

'Don't go getting all morbid, Gran. You'll be stuck with us until you are at least a hundred.'

'I think it will be a lot sooner than that,' she said, matter-of-factly.

'Are you ill, Gran?' Ed looked scared.

'No, of course not. I'm as fit as a fiddle, but I'd rather go with all my mental and physical faculties intact. I don't want to live so long that I forget my name or where I live or so that I can't get to the toilet on time. I'd hate to be a burden to anyone.'

'You'd never be a burden, Gran,' Ed said, hugging her fiercely. 'And I'd never abandon you the way I did when Mum died.'

Pru looked at him for a moment, squeezing his hand. 'I never blamed you for going off the rails. You were distraught. We were all a mess when she died. Besides, we all make mistakes.' She paused, and for a minute I thought she was going to say more but she didn't.

'Anyway, I don't know why I'm being so silly. Like you said I'll probably live past a hundred, I always wanted to get a card from the Queen,' she hooted. Yes, silly indeed. Like I said, she had more energy and vitality than a woman half her age, she wasn't like one of those elderly, sick people you see hunched over a Zimmer frame. The notion was ridiculous unless Pru was keeping something from us. More than likely Pru was just feeling nostalgic and missing Bert. Maybe she was just lonely. I gave her a big hug.

Joviality was restored, but I felt like I had intruded on a private moment and that there was more she had wanted to say. A lot more. Her smile wobbled but it stayed in place. I wanted to make my excuses and go to bed but Pru kept patting my arm, asking me inane questions like 'was I happy working at the gallery?' Short answer: hell no. What did I really want from life? Short answer: not sure, but I told her that I had started testing the waters, applying for jobs.

'You know that I'm really proud of you both? Ed, you are a fine young man with a bright future ahead of you as a top chef. You already are, if tonight's meal is anything to go by.

And Josie, you are a real treasure, I'm sure you have many wonderful adventures ahead of you. I'm blessed to have you both in my life.' Pru's eyes were glistening with tears.

'Life is so short, my dears. Please make the most of it, that is all I ask.' She looked at us intently. There she went again, talking about life and death. It sent a shiver down my spine. 'Go on, love. Cut me a slice of that coconut and raspberry cake,' she said, deftly changing the subject again.

After that we sat munching the delicious cake with a cup of tea, watching a repeat of 'Some Mothers Do 'Ave 'Em' and laughing when I told them about my blind date with Jeremy, the Frank Spencer lookalike.

***

All the while Pru was thinking about what she had kept from them. Since her fall a couple of months ago, she hadn't felt quite right. She was getting more dizzy spells and had even blacked out on one occasion. That terrified her. But she didn't want to worry anyone. It was important that she enjoyed what time she had left with them, not waste time worrying. Maybe she was being selfish in not telling them. Maybe she was selfish for not telling them the biggest secret of all. Perhaps she should have got checked out again, but she felt it was time to move on. Bert was calling her home.

Pru had carefully laid out her plans of what was going to happen after her death with a calm assurance. Josie reminded her so much of herself; she knew they had a special connection from the moment they met. Ed coming back into her life had brought her more joy than he could ever possibly know. She only hoped they would forgive her when they found out the truth. But for now, both Josie and Ed remained completely oblivious to the changes about to hit them, and that conversation about Pru dying had been dismissed, forgotten like the wind blowing away the rain.

Chapter Eight
Meet The Greens

HAVE YOU EVER WATCHED THAT film 'Meet the Fockers'? I can't imagine the Fockers being any worse than my family. In the absence of my dad, my twenty-five-year-old brother Ant had played to perfection the role of over-protective, nosy and slightly irritating man-of-the-house. At 6ft 4 with broad chest, beefy arms and scowling furrowed face, he had a tendency to frighten prospective partners away. If they happened to be the slightly shy or sensitive type, then god help them. I was naïve to think that introducing them to my actual fiancés would be any different.

My first fiancé, Geoff, had been in the doghouse from the first instant they met, all because he'd forgotten to wipe his feet at the door. Admittedly, bringing muddy feet into the house hadn't created the best first impression but Ant could hardly bring himself to raise a smile or word of greeting forever after. And if that hadn't been bad enough, Ant had interrupted us whilst we were kissing and canoodling in the kitchen. He'd handed Geoff his coat, announced in a loud voice that it was getting rather late and it wouldn't be right to overstay his welcome. I had been nineteen at the time, not twelve.

I was sure that everyone would get on with my next fiancé, Dan, because although he had a domineering character, he seemed to charm most people. Mum, however, seemed to think he looked and smelled like he was on strong medication. Ant liked him but I think that was on account of them sharing a passion for - you guessed it – football. Dan was an Arsenal season ticket holder with the occasional spare ticket going, which meant he was in Ant's good books right from the beginning.

Why I thought they would get on with my third fiancé, Stewart, was anyone's guess. I thought Stewart (out of all of my fiancés) seemed the most normal and homely. He had a steady job as an accountant and had lived on his own since he was eighteen; he also owned his own house. He'd told me he wanted to get married, but actually I think he was far too used to his own space to let me in. Compromise turned out to be too much of a challenge for him, so he cut things off with me very cleanly. There were certainly no theatrics involved where Stewart was concerned.

So I decided, all things being considered, not to introduce them to Niles too soon. You can imagine my nervousness when Niles rushed to pick up the telephone that day, engaging in a lengthy conversation with my mum. The outcome of which was an invitation to Sunday lunch, just three days away.

'Your mum is a delight,' Niles said, passing the phone over to me.

'Hi Mum,' I said, forcing a smile.

'Josie!' she shrieked into my ear, 'Niles sounds absolutely divine. Thank god you two worked things out. I think he could very well be *The One*. I can just hear it now,' she said, growing audibly more excited. 'Da Da Da Da, Josie's going be a bride, Da, Da, Da, Da, Da, finally getting hitched! Don't let this one slip through your fingers darling, you are not getting any younger. Got to knock out a few before it's too late …'.

I held the phone away from my ear, cringing, and feeling annoyed with Niles for a) picking up the phone, and b) blabbing away to Mum.

I had planned to tell Mum about my reconciliation with Niles eventually. I was just hoping to have him to myself for a few weeks. Was that too much to ask? I glared at the back of his mousy wavy locks, cursing him silently while he happily flicked through the paper, totally oblivious of the awkward predicament he had put me in. Well, just let him wait until Sunday … then he would see what they were really like.

'Yes Mum. So am I.' I ended the call, trying to sound calm. 'Really looking forward to lunch on Sunday. Byeee.'

Sunday morning arrived. I looked over at Niles, sound asleep and snoring lightly. My heart swelled with love. He was a bit daft and jealous at times but only because he loved me so much. I dreamed about my wedding last night, the same dream I had been having for the last two weeks, and everything had been just how I imagined. My mum, brother, aunties, uncles and cousins were all smiling with pride. Babs and Dame looked like they were fit to burst with happiness as I walked down the aisle. This was the most perfect moment of my life. I was buzzing with a mixture of excitement and a deep feeling of contentment. As I approached the altar I turned and looked up expectantly at Niles … and at this point I woke up suddenly. Every dream ended like this, including last night's dream.

Some nights I even dreamed about my wedding reception. I was laughing and dancing, drinking champagne and not making a tit of myself for a change. In fact I looked freer, more confident, than I had ever felt in real life.

I would always wake up from my dreams thinking of Pru, remembering her dreams of Bert. I felt her guiding me into the decision I was about to make. The wedding was back on. It felt absolutely like the right thing to do, and I knew Niles wanted it too.

Niles began wriggling around next to me, opening one eye. 'Morning Pumpkin,' he yawned, as his arm flopped across my belly.

Come Sunday afternoon, Mum would be delirious with joy as Niles and I were once again officially engaged. We decided that Mum should be the first to know, although she had already predicted it. I felt a bit apprehensive at the prospect of telling Babs and Dame but pushed that to the back of my mind.

Niles pulled me on top of him, kissing me passionately and getting very frisky indeed, but I was too nervous about this afternoon to join in.

'Later Niles, when we get back. I'm taking a shower.' I unpeeled myself from his embrace.

'Spoilsport!' he complained.

While the shower hadn't really helped quieten my nerves, Niles was clearly in good spirits as I heard him laughing when I entered the bedroom.

'No, of course not. We just have to be careful.' He was talking into his phone, smiling broadly.

He continued smiling when he saw me, but something in

his eyes looked a bit shifty. 'Look, I've got to go mate, talk to you soon.'

'Another woman?' I joked.

'Dan.' Ah. Dan. No wonder he looked uncomfortable. The infamous Dan who had kept him so drunk in an Irish pub for three months that he forgot to call me.

'Dan.' I repeated grimly.

'Yeah, I was just saying that we have to be careful about our drinking. He really is a bad influence, but he's my best mate.'

'I know,' I said, not wanting to think about him. 'So, what do you think I should wear?'

***

We arrived at my Mum's in good time. Niles wanted to impress his future mother-in-law with his punctuality - and the brightly coloured gerberas which I had carefully selected. Mum opened the door, dressed in a multi-coloured stripy dress which matched the flowers perfectly. She grinned widely at us.

'You must be my soon-to-be son-in-law … and a clever, thoughtful one at that,' she said, giving him a little wink. 'Gerberas are my favourite flowers. How did you know?' she sniffed them dramatically while running a carefully manicured hand through her curls. Could there be anything more embarrassing than my mum fawning and fluttering her eyelashes at my future husband? And so much for announcing our engagement. Mum already had the wedding in the bag. She had probably booked the local church for a week on Sunday. I fervently hoped that Mum's zealous enthusiasm wouldn't have Niles running for the hills.

I glanced at Niles. Thankfully they seemed mutually charmed with each other, exchanging compliments and big smiles. Just to balance things out, Ant strode into the kitchen and placed a protective hand on my arm.

'Josie told us how you done a runner. I trust that you are planning on sticking around this time?' For a moment Ant and Niles stared each other square in the eye. I almost thought they were going to get their pistols out.

'Most definitely, and I'll do all that I can to make Josie happy. I'm a very lucky man,' Niles said unwaveringly.

'Yes. Yes, you are.' Ant was glaring at him. 'Let's hope it's fourth time lucky for you,' he said, raising his eyebrows in my direction.

Mum shot Ant a furious look. 'Can you help me take the food through to the dining room, Niles?' she said, picking up the chicken casserole.

'Of course.' Niles rushed to help, picking up the plates and cutlery.

'I don't like him,' Ant said, when Niles was out of earshot.

'You've not even given him a chance,' I said, feeling hurt. 'Why can't you try? Just for once, for me?'

'I'm sorry, sis,' he said, wrapping his arms around me. 'There's just something about him. I get the feeling he's hiding something.'

'Ant!' I said, warningly. 'Niles has proved himself to me. He loves me and I love him, so please try to be happy for me.'

'If he makes you happy, who am I to grumble? I just don't want to see you getting hurt again. Just be sure.'

'I am sure,' I said, smiling up at him, knowing that the only thing Niles was hiding was a boxed-shaped package containing a diamond ring somewhere.

What was worrying me was the sight of Mum pouring her third glass of prosecco on an empty stomach.

'Steady on, Mum.'

'I'm steady as a cliff-face, sweetie' she said, going all Ab Fab on me, waving her glass merrily and somewhat dangerously in the air. 'Well, darling!' she added, hissing behind her serviette, 'what do you expect? I was nervous about meeting your future husband and needed a little something to take the edge off. I've already smoked a 20-pack of Silk Cut.'

'Top up, Mrs. G.?' asked Niles.

My laser-like glare in his direction had zero effect on him.

'Don't mind if I do,' Mum tinkled, wobbling her glass in his direction.

Mum was getting merrier by the minute, just as Ant was getting frostier.

'So, what did you say you do for a living?' he enquired.

'I'm a couple's counsellor.'

'Really? People pay *you* for relationship advice?'

I turned my laser-beam glare towards Ant.

'Well I think that's a marvellous job, just marvellous.' Mum chimed, rocking excitedly in her seat. 'So, when are you two getting married?'

'We haven't set a date yet. I wanted to run it past you first. Make sure you approved of me marrying your lovely daughter.' Niles bestowed a ravishing smile on me, while Ant made gagging noises. 'And might I add that this is the best chicken casserole I have ever had the pleasure of tasting.'

Mum glowed with pride. 'Why, thank you Niles. Glad you like it. And of course you have my approval. It's about time she tied the knot. I couldn't be happier that it's with someone as mature and responsible as you.' No mention of the fact he had dumped me without a word for three months. Mum had chosen to conveniently forget that minor detail, but I could see it was at the forefront of Ant's mind.

Mum placed a hand over Niles,' looking as if she was about to cry with pride, while Ant was ferociously pointing a fork in the direction of Niles. Ready, no doubt, to launch into a protective brotherly speech.

The shrill sound of the doorbell interrupted the proceedings.

'You're not expecting anyone are you, Mum?' I asked, glancing anxiously at the door.

'I don't think so,' she said, looking confused.

Ant sprang to the door.

'Aunty Pam!' he announced. 'Great to see you!'

Oh. Dear. God.

Aunty Pam didn't just make an entrance. She filled every corner of the room with her presence.

'Hello darlings!' she boomed, as if she was standing on one side of a football pitch with us far away on the other side.

'You are gorgeous, you are!' she said, making her way over to a startled-looking Niles.

'Really nice to meet you,' Aunty Pam said, gripping his hand firmly and pumping it up and down rhythmically, her 6ft 2 frame towering over the table.

'Umm, good to meet you too,' he squeaked.

'Where are my manners?' she said, slapping her forehead. 'I should welcome you properly. You are practically family now, after all!' she said, winking at him while simultaneously lifting him off his chair, embracing him enthusiastically. Mum had no doubt filled Aunty Pam in on the details of my reconciliation with Niles.

He looked like he was about to protest and I spotted a hint of terror in his eyes, which wasn't visible for long as Aunty Pam pressed him into the folds of her abundant bosom, much to my horror and Ant's amusement.

Niles emerged some time later with a red face and crooked glasses.

'May I be excused, I need the bathroom?' he croaked.

'Where's the wine I gave you? Ant, my boy, come on. Get pouring,' Aunty Pam demanded.

'Is that rosé?' Mum seemed to be disorientated, in an inebriated world of her own.

'Aunty Pam's brought us a bottle of sparkling rosé, Mum, but you've had more than enough already,' I said firmly.

'Well I never,' Aunty Pam said, only just noticing Mum. 'You are completely hammered. Oh, how funny!' She clapped her hands over her mouth, laughing uncontrollably. Ant joined in laughing.

Great. This was going just great.

By Mum's second glass of rosé, she started fondly recalling Magnum PI's strong and shapely thighs, the contours being of perfect proportion she insisted. (Magnum PI was one of Mum's golden oldie programmes; I swear she still lived in the 80s).

'I bet you look good in a pair of shorts,' Aunty Pam nodded towards Niles, who had drunk rather a large quantity of alcohol himself.

'You have to ask Josie,' he slurred.

At that moment Salt N Pepper's 'Let's talk about Sex' blared out from somewhere. I looked around, startled. Aunty Pam started singing and dancing, waving her arms about enthusiastically, rotating her hips for good measure. 'Oh, that would be me,' she said, fishing her phone from out of her bag. She was another relic from the 80s.

'Gets me going every single time. I'll just see who it is,' she whispered conspiratorially, heading out of the room.

A few moments of silence filled the room, then a vibrating noise which rapidly grew more insistent.

'Niles, isn't that your phone?' I asked him. He pulled his phone out his pocket, a look of alarm crossing his face when he saw the screen display.

'Aren't you going to answer it?' Ant asked.

Niles hesitated briefly before pressing the answer button.

'Hey,' he said brightly, mouthing to me 'I'll just take this outside'.

Ant raised an eyebrow at me. 'He seemed a bit rattled with whoever that was?'

'He always gets a bit flustered when he's had a few.'

'Mmm.'

Still, I couldn't help feeling slightly suspicious. I was probably just being silly, but just in case …

I went out into the corridor and heard his muffled voice in the front room. I leaned in towards the closed door to see if I could hear what was being said.

'Don't be like that, of course I'm happy to hear from you.' Niles laughed, 'No, don't be silly, of course I do. Just give me some time … don't worry. Bye.'

I stumbled away from the door, back into dining room where Ant, bless him, had cleared away the dishes while Mum and Aunty Pam were doing something resembling the conga around the table, wearing party hats of all things. I had no idea where they had found those.

'Who was that, darling?' I asked casually as Niles came back into the room.

'Oh, just John.'

'Just John?'

'From Ireland. Dan's mate. We were just reminiscing about the good times.'

'Good times? When you were supposedly cut up about me?' I said furiously.

'That's why I didn't want to answer the phone,' he said, sulkily. I glared at him.

'Don't be like that, Jos,' he said, widening his eyes innocently. 'It was just good to catch up, that's all.' He hugged me tightly. First Dan and now John. Were they planning a reunion or something?

Niles slapped my bum looking rather pleased with himself. 'I think I'm slightly sloshed.'

'You think?' I said, sarcastically.

Ant came back into the room and raised his eyebrows again. I chucked a serviette at him, wanting to block out those accusing eyebrows.

'I think I'm going to vomit,' Mum announced mid conga, which made Aunty Pam laugh hysterically.

I ran into the kitchen and grabbed a saucepan for Mum to be sick in. Which she was, and quite violently so.

I stroked her hair and then helped her upstairs, feeling ashamed of her but then immediately flushed with guilt for feeling ashamed as I remembered my own 'sick in the bin' encounter with Chris as my saviour. Ahh Chris, now that was something to smile about … not that I should be thinking or smiling about him now that I was an almost-married woman.

Still, Niles had really pissed me off today. Oh well, at least

Mum and Aunty Pam liked him. I helped Mum into bed. She had sobered up a little since being sick, and she was groaning. 'Darling, I'm so sorry I ruined lunch by getting drunk. I hope Niles understands.'

'You're not the only one who's had one too many, Mum. Niles and Aunty Pam were pretty far gone too, and actually it's been nice to see you smile and have fun.'

She started to cry, although I didn't realise at first as she tried her best to hold it in.

'Niles is a good man, Josie. I am so happy for you and very proud. I just wish I had someone too.'

'You do?' I was taken back. Mum always insisted she was better off without a man in her life. She'd been on a few dates since Dad left, but nothing serious.

'Maybe I'll give this internet dating a go. It won't be long before Ant leaves home too, then It will just be me. Pam said she would help me set up my profile.' God help Mum, I thought.

She grasped my hands, suddenly looking very serious. 'You know I love you, Josie. Maybe I was overly-protective of you when your dad left, but I thought that somehow you were going to slip through my fingers too. But I'm ready to let you go now, Josie,' she said bravely. 'Go fly, make your dreams come true, do whatever it takes to make you happy, and I will always be here for you.'

'Ditto,' I said, overwhelmed with feeling.

'And Josie?'

'Yes?'

Mum bit her lower lip. 'Never mind.' She pushed away whatever was on her mind. I stayed with her until she fell asleep and noticed, for the first time in a long time, how vulnerable she looked. I guess we all needed to feel loved.

I came back down to find Niles and Aunty Pam playing a game of Twister. Really, that was so unnecessary. Thankfully it wasn't naked Twister, just the regular variety. Ant was enjoying the show, taking photos on his iPhone.

'These are SO going on Facebook!' he chortled with glee.

Great, just another Sunday afternoon in the Green household.

***

After Josie had gone downstairs, Josie's mum sat up in bed and opened the top drawer of her bedside table. She studied the postcard she had received yesterday morning. A hummingbird with a purple shimmery breast and a long thin beak nestled into a bright yellow flower. She turned the postcard over. 'Graceful and floating free, this bird captivates with its beauty and elegance.' Small neat handwriting in a black ink pen.

That summer's day in the back garden, laid out on a picnic blanket with a cold, crisp white wine and not a care in the world. That was when she had first spotted a hummingbird, flitting from flower to flower. That was when he'd proposed. It was a long time ago. She exhaled slowly, her fingers trembling. It was far better for Josie to think that she was moving on, rather than revealing that she had a small glimmer of hope in her heart that he might be ready to return. Only time would tell if that hope would bear fruit.

Chapter Nine
Message From The Grave

THE NEXT COUPLE OF WEEKS were pretty uneventful. Mum vowed never to drink again. Aunty Pam changed her ringtone after her phone started belting out crude lyrics in the lingerie department of Marks and Spencers. 'Oh, the shame of it!' exclaimed Mum, 'I didn't know where to look!'

Still, at least they were getting out and about. I asked Mum how the internet dating was going, and she had been rather evasive in her response. If Auntie Pam was taking her underwear shopping perhaps there was hope on the horizon, and perhaps it was best that I didn't know any of the details.

I heard back from two of the jobs that I had applied for. One of them said they really liked my application, but I didn't have the 'right kind' of experience. They offered to keep my record on file, should a more junior position become available. At least that was something. The other company wrote to let me know they were going into liquidation! Typical. I guess I was lucky to have a job at all. Bitchy Bernice was in Las Vegas with her brother for a fortnight, so at least I had a two-week reprieve from her breathing down my neck and monitoring my loo breaks.

Jake had landed a year of paid acting work, so him and Babs were excitedly making plans to move out of their tiny bedsit and into a one-bedroom flat. Dame had recently invested in a steam cleaner which apparently gave him an endless amount of satisfaction. How he managed to live in harmony with grubby George I had no idea.

Niles was being the perfect fiancé for a change, surprising me with little gifts and cards. He finally admitted that the boys in Ireland were trying to persuade him to join them on a lads holiday.

'Are you seriously thinking of going?"

'I've already told them No,' he said, with a determined look, 'but you know what the lads are like.'

'They'll probably brainwash you into leaving me again.' My stomach knotted up tightly.

'That's not going to happen. Besides, we've got wedding plans to make. I think we should set a date and get things moving.' He smiled at me reassuringly. 5th July was raised as a possible date, and I smiled as the flicker of worry and doubt eased itself from my mind.

Almost three months had passed since that dinner with Pru, where she'd hinted that her days were numbered. As it turned out, her words had been prophetic.

On a sticky July evening, she telephoned Ed and asked him to pop over for breakfast the next day. When she didn't answer the door, he used his key to let himself in and was devastated to find her lying motionless in bed. The creeping hand of dread had pulled his stomach tight when he tried, and failed, to rouse her.

A medical examination confirmed that she had experienced a severe stroke, a massive bleed in the brain, and most likely would have died instantly. The grief and shock hit me like an express train. Ed kept himself busy, contacting family members, making funeral arrangements and doing whatever it took to stop himself falling apart.

I finally managed to get some time alone with him.

'Ed, do you think she knew this might happen? I know a lot of people survive strokes, or at least get them tested for when they have symptoms. Did you see any of the signs?'

He sighed heavily, his shoulders dropping and his face crumpling like a paper bag.

'I've been going over and over it in my head. She seemed a bit off balance at times, but I just put that down to age. Whenever I tried to raise a concern, she reassured me that she was just tired.'

I had noticed Pru looking more weary than usual but hadn't thought anything of it. If only I had insisted that she see a doctor. I'm sure Ed was thinking exactly the same thing.

'Do you remember that conversation we had a few weeks ago?' he said, shivering. 'Part of me thinks she wanted to die. How could she, when everything was going so well? I had only just got to know her again, and now she's gone …'. The anguish on his face was heartbreaking.

'Ed,' I said, touching his arm, 'she had a terrible stroke which she had no control over. It's not like she was depressed and lost the will to live. In fact, I never saw her look so content as in her last few months – and that had *everything* to do with you.' I paused, then continued, 'In a strange way, I think she was at total peace with death because she lived her life so well, with such love and kindness. She had done everything she needed to do.'

'Perhaps I was the last piece of the puzzle for her, and when it was complete she was ready to go?' He looked unbearably sad.

'What matters, Ed, is that you made her happy. She absolutely doted on you.'

'I know,' he said in a strangled voice, a single tear making its way down his cheek.

I held him tightly, letting my own tears spill. She had become a huge part of my life in the little time that I had known her. I still couldn't believe she was gone; it just didn't feel real.

A few days later Ed handed me two crisp white envelopes with my name printed in small black writing in the middle of each envelope. They were labelled *Josie 1* and *Josie 2*.

'I found these on her bedside cabinet.'

Surprised, I took both envelopes from him.

'The funeral has been arranged for next Friday, 10.30am at St. Mary's Cemetery.' He shared this information in a flat voice, then stood up abruptly, ready to leave.

'Ed, I'm a good listener, if you need to …'.

'I'm fine, Josie, really.' He smiled at me thinly, trying to make it stretch across his face. 'I just need some time. Please just let me have that.' With those words, he left.

I felt so damn helpless. I wanted more than anything to comfort Ed. I thought back to a couple of weeks ago when he found me drinking a bottle of malbec alone, reminiscing about Dad. I don't know why I still got like that sometimes. You would have thought after almost twenty-five years of not seeing him, I would be used to it by now.

Ed had sat with me and listened, encouraging me to shout, scream, cry, do whatever I needed to do.

He then spoke about his mum, how kind and sweet she had been, how losing her had shattered his world. He had been nineteen at the time and fallen prey to an addiction that had stopped him from feeling anything other than self-disgust. That phase lasted for more than three years, and then he had moved to Australia. Fending in the bush had been a wake-up call. Getting to know his gran again when he returned home had made him feel close to both his gran and his mum.

The ironic thing was that that night we ended up watching 'Four Weddings and a Funeral,' saying 'fuck' a lot, and laughing like hyenas when we watched the scene where Hugh Grant breathes the word 'divine,' in response to Andie McDowell's character trying on dresses. And we both said, 'That's not the last time he'll be saying that,' referring to his incident years later with a prostitute called Divine Brown. I smiled at the memory.

Ed needed some privacy, time to be alone with his thoughts. Part of me wanted to run after him, but I sensed that he wasn't ready for that just yet. I also couldn't shake the feeling that there was something he wasn't telling me, something that had made him leave the flat so abruptly. It puzzled me but I just had to make sure I was there for him when he was ready to talk.

I sat down and held the envelope labelled *Josie 1* for a long time. It was with trembling fingers that I finally opened it, somehow knowing that the contents would prove life-changing.

17 April 2013
Dear Josie

If you are reading this letter then I have departed this wonderful world, but don't be too sad, you can be sure that I am laughing and dancing in a field full of daffodils with Bert somewhere. You may think that I was keeping something from you. Well, yes. I've been feeling a bit dizzy since my fall, but I didn't want to worry anyone. Please forgive me, but I just kept feeling a sense of Bert around me and knew that the time was close.

My eyes flicked to the date at the top of the page, 17 April. Almost three months ago, probably around the time of our dinner together. She'd been saying peculiar things about life and death. I should have paid more attention. I struggled to read on, but I had to.

Life is a continuous journey. I am pleased to say that I take many wonderful memories and a peaceful heart on the next phase of my journey. I am one of the lucky ones, I lived out my dreams, I had a wealth of friends and loved ones (you included) and now I have Bert to keep me company forevermore. Now Josie, pet, please don't cry onto this page as I have something very important to tell you …

I grabbed a tissue as a big fat tear threatened to plop on to the page.

I would like you to carry out a special request for me, please see it as an experiment in living your life to the full. I do worry that your life is passing you by, so forgive me for intervening!

All I ask is that you help retrieve something important to me. I will be watching over you, Josie.

I stopped reading, suddenly feeling apprehensive as a

shudder went down my spine. I looked over my shoulder and screamed at the sight of myself in the mirror, it was like I had seen a ghost. 'Pru, I know you are there!' I whispered loudly. 'Pru?'

Of course there was no reply but I felt Pru's presence as strongly as if she was sitting next to me. I couldn't go on reading as my hands were trembling so much. It wasn't like I even believed in ghosts, but I could have sworn that Pru had just breathed down my neck and I could smell daffodils. Dame would have testified that ghosts do exist, having watched the film 'Ghost' a dozen times, mainly due to Patrick Swayze's seductive ways with pottery. He made a very convincing ghost, Dame informed me, but I guess that was his job, to make us believe. I tried to shake off the spooked feeling spiking my veins and continued reading ...

> *Anyway, I don't want to frighten you child.* ('yeah, not half!' I thought to myself) *It's no big deal, really. Before I sign off I just want to wish you lots of luck. I'm sure that happiness won't elude you for much longer, remember have no fear, I'll be with you every step of the way.*
>
> *All my love and more.*
> *Pru xxxx*
>
> *P.S. Josie, before you open the second envelope please remember that one of the keys to successful living is to create something, to feel empowered, be it a painting, a poem a piece of music. To get you started, I'd like you to write a poem, on any subject, right now. Here's my favourite one to give you some inspiration!*

Enclosed with Pru's letter was a copy of Wordsworth's famous 'I wandered lonely as a cloud' poem. I smiled to myself. What was it with Pru and her daffodils? I could see their appeal, but she was crazy for them.

I wandered lonely as a cloud
That floats on high o'er vales and hills,
When all at once I saw a crowd,
A host of golden daffodils;
Beside the lake, beneath the trees,
Fluttering and dancing in the breeze.

Continuous as the stars that shine
And twinkle on the milky way,
They stretched in never-ending line
Along the margin of the bay:
Ten thousand saw I at a glance,
Tossing their heads in sprightly dance.

The waves beside them danced; but they
Out-did the sparkly waves in glee:
A poet could not be more gay
In such a jocund company:
I gazed and gazed but little thought
What wealth to me the show had brought.

For oft, when on my couch I lie
In vacant or in pensive mood,
They flash upon that inward eye,
Which is the bliss of solitude
And then my heart with pleasure fills
And dances with the daffodils.

Wow, that was the first time I had read the poem right through. An image of Pru filled my mind, of her swaying with the breeze and joyfully dancing with the daffodils. I smiled but inside my heart I felt a lump, like a heavy stone, weighing me down.

I looked at my reflection in the mirror again. My eyes were red, my skin pale, my hair tousled and wild. But who was I? Pru had faced her death with peace and contentment. Even though she wasn't here in body, I was convinced that her spirit was eternal, more whole and real than I was sitting here. I wondered if I would ever feel that way.

I picked up my notebook and pen, and started to write.

Mirror mirror, who am I?
This vacant, desperate, craving I.
Kind I know, sweet I can be,
But content and whole are far from me.
A glance, a kiss, a whispered charm;
All have me dancing in a trance.
Of a hope, a promise to be adored
And to be cherished forevermore.
But sometimes I think there could more.
There's more to me then I can see.

Startled, I blinked back at myself. Tears were rolling down my cheeks. Where had those words come from? Images of my former lovers and fiancés swirled and twirled before me. All my life I had longed for affection, searching for The One, a promise of Forever to make me feel on solid ground. And I had tried to mould myself to become someone I thought would be worthy of their love. But who was I beneath that need? The mirror didn't answer me.

As I sat alone, it became clear that there was more to

me than I had known before. I had grown to like my own company. Indulging in long baths, going for walks, browsing through bookstores. It's like I had recovered a lost part of me. I smiled thinking how Ed had brought me a copy of his favourite book, 'To Kill a Mockingbird'. I delighted in the characters of Atticus, principled and kind; Scout, his impulsive tomboy of a daughter.

I thought about Niles. Jealous and daft at times, but sweet and loving too. He had encouraged me to broaden my horizons, hinting that we were going somewhere exotic for our honeymoon. I twisted a tissue around my finger, trying to conjure up a picture of what our life would be like together. Getting married, having children. I saw an image of Niles sleeping through the sound of a crying baby, but he'd definitely pull his weight in other ways, wouldn't he? Then I thought about the milestones we'd be facing. Like the kids leaving home, us growing old together. My head felt fuzzy and my stomach gurgled. I needed to talk to him, to be sure.

I focused back on the task at hand. I was sure glad that Pru had asked me to write a poem and not have to paint a picture or create a piece of music. Despite working in an art gallery, I had no artistic inclination at all, and I hadn't played a musical instrument since the recorder when I was ten - and not very well, either.

I paused before opening the larger envelope, *Josie 2*. Should I call Dame and Babs for support? Niles? No, he'd been working long hours in preparation for being away at a work retreat next week. I needed to be brave even though my heart was pounding. Pru said something about a special request to collect something, that didn't sound too difficult. A diamond tiara maybe? I wouldn't put it past her to own one. I wondered if she'd made me a list, like with the Dumpsville Manifesto. What was it about people wanting me to do things? I smiled to myself. Ok, so the Manifesto had got me out of my comfort zone, having fun and feeling better about myself, so maybe there was something in it after all.

And now Pru was giving me instructions from the grave.

In big bold letters on the centre of the page were the words:

YOUR MISSION

Dear Josie,

Now that you are warmed up, here are your specific instructions:

1. On Monday 2 August at 2.20pm, you and a friend will take a flight to Nice, France. You will then take a train to Juan les Pins, where you will be staying in a private apartment for the week, which is next to the most wonderful yoga studio.

Holy fuck. Flying in a plane, of all things. My most dreaded fear, my biggest nightmare. I'm sure I told her. I tried to muster my inner Scout, my inner Warrior, but all I saw was a plane crash, then me drowning in the sea. 'Breathe … breathe …' I told myself. It's not like I had never flown before; I had flown once, when I was little. Disneyland Paris had been fun, but the flight there had been an ordeal. The size and noise of the aircraft had scared me and I'd screamed loudly when the plane took a nose-dive. Thankfully Mum had managed to settle me to sleep on the way back.

Maybe I could get hypnotised into believing that I loved to fly, that flying was my greatest passion, that I was daring and adventurous. Eat your heart out, Amelia Earhart! Ok, now I was being ridiculous but at least I was trying to get into the spirit of things. What I really needed was some quality time with Niles, and what better way than to fly away together? While I wasn't exactly thrilled by the prospect of a week abroad, Niles' mate Dan was forever boasting about the number of countries he had visited and the number of stamps in his passport like it was a badge of honour. No doubt that's what put the crazy notion into Niles' head in the first place. This would be the perfect opportunity to prove to Niles that I could be adventurous, even though it made me feel sick thinking about it.

I could hardly complain though. If Pru thought that I needed to get on a plane, broaden my horizons and get bendy doing yoga then by god, I was going to give it my best shot. It would also be good preparation for my exotic honeymoon which was bound to be thousands of miles away. Good job I had a passport, thanks to Niles filling in and posting my forms off in readiness for our first trip abroad. And now I was off to Nice, France. Fancy that! Actually, I was staying in Juan-les-Pins. Never heard of it, but it sounded posh.

I continued to read on:

> *2. On Tuesday 3 August at 2pm, you will go to the Musée Picasso in Antibes and meet with Tebor (Bert's brother who lives out there, photo enclosed). He will give you a parcel. I can't tell you what it is as that would spoil everything :)*

I stared at the photo. This was strange. Intriguing, but strange. Why was Pru being so mysterious? Why couldn't she just tell me what I was collecting? And when had she started using smiley faces? I started dialling Bab's number, bursting to tell her all, when I happened to glance at item number 3.

3. To prepare you for being up high, I have asked a Trusted Other to book a hot air balloon experience for you.

Oh my god! What was she thinking? And who was this 'Trusted Other?' Ed was my guess. It was bad enough being encased in a metal aircraft, but floating across the sky in a flimsy basket was taking it a step too far. I wondered what next. A bungee jump off the Eiffel Tower, perhaps? I could almost hear Pru's wicked tinkling laughter ringing in my ears.

'This is not funny! It's alright for you, you're already dead!' I was shocked at how angry and ungrateful I sounded at that moment.

I thought this whole experience was supposed to empower me, not give me a heart attack. I thought maybe I would get a choice, like a) Go bungee jumping, or b) a £1,000 gift voucher for Selfridges, but no such luck. At least it wasn't bungee jumping and I was allowed to take someone with me.

OK, I could do this, no biggie. This year I had been heartbroken then given a chance to love again; almost shagged a stranger in a mop cupboard; danced in some fabulous heels, lived with someone new and strange (ok, so he wasn't so strange after finding out he was Pru's grandson) and I had spent time willingly on my own. I kicked arse. I looked in the mirror again. 'You can do this!' I nodded to myself, bravely affirming my intention.

That's all for now, Josie. I know you're probably feeling totally bewildered and scared but just trust me, you'll see, and believe me that hot air ballooning is a totally calm and serene experience. You will feel like you're floating in the sky, Bert and I did it once.

Am getting a little tired, so will sign off now … Bon voyage, dear Josie, I am excited for you.

Pru xxxx

Chapter Ten
The Funeral

LATER THAT EVENING I DISCUSSED my imminent trip with Dame and George, while contemplating the bright pink walls in their living room.

'So, it looks like I'm going to France, picking up a parcel and flying in a hot air balloon,' I concluded, toasting myself with a large glass of red rioja.

'Bloody bananas, Josie. And you're ok with all this?' Dame gaped at me.

'Well … not exactly,' I admitted, letting out a deep breath. It was like I was on a pendulum, swinging from being brave to fearing the worst, including getting mugged and shot abroad, having my kidneys sold on the black market and a hundred other atrocities that could befall me.

'I need a fag and another large glass of this …' I said, waving my glass in the air.

'Yeah, you might need more than that, because I've just booked the hot air balloon flight for next Sunday,' Dame said slowly.

'You are kidding. So you're the 'Trusted Other?' I asked, amazed.

'Don't sound so surprised. I am the epitome of trustworthy,' said Dame, puffing out his chest. 'It seems Pru is rather fond of her letters and instructions. She wanted me to book the hot air balloon flight preferably before your trip to France, and I managed it for the day before. How's that for timing?' he said, beaming at me.

I gulped down the rest of my wine.

'YOLO,' George declared, assessing the situation.

'YOLO?' I raised an eyebrow.

'You Only Live Once,' Dame nodded sagely.

'Hopefully I will still be living after next Sunday,' I replied, slugging down the rest of my rioja.

'I don't know anyone who has died from flying in a hot air balloon, so unless you wilfully jump out of the basket, I think you'll be fine.'

'Strictly speaking, there have been rare incidents …' George began, until Dame shot him a warning look.

'What if I vomit out of the basket? Will it fly back in my face?'

Dame and George shook their heads in unison.

Perfectly reasonable question, I thought to myself.

'You'll be fine,' they chorused.

'You won't even feel like you are up in the air.' George added, 'it's so serene.'

There wasn't much that George hadn't tried, from swimming with sharks to nearly getting trampled on by an elephant. Maybe I could convince him to be on standby to make sure I didn't faint and fall out of the balloon. He *was* a doctor, after all.

All I had to do was get through was a funeral, a hot air balloon ride and a trip to France. 'One step at a time, Josie, one step at a time' I told myself. My stomach gurgled. Oh god. Too much rioja.

The funeral was booked for Friday. I wish Niles could have been there, the need to talk to him was growing urgent but it conflicted with his therapeutic Welsh retreat. It was a work thing, booked weeks ago so he couldn't get out of it. His phone kept going to voicemail, they must be working him really hard. I thought back to how wonderful he had been, the day I found out Pru had died. I was inconsolable and he knew exactly what to do, comforting me throughout the night, stroking my hair and holding me close. I eventually slept in the early hours of the morning and when I eventually woke up, Niles had brought up a breakfast tray for me with coffee, croissants and a red rose. I couldn't ask for more, and he couldn't exactly tell work to stick it just because I was going through a personal crisis. I hadn't even had the opportunity to discuss the letter with him, or our imminent (fingers crossed) French trip, but I had to concede that getting him to cancel his clients at short notice was slim. They needed him I guess, but then so did I. Thankfully he was back on Friday night and I couldn't wait to see him.

Fortunately, Dame managed to pull a few strings and get the day off work. The benefits of being in a senior position, he told me, but I could tell that he judged Niles for not being there for me.

'You are marrying the man, surely he should be by your side, Josie. And another thing, please tell me that you are keeping your own name when you tie the knot?'

I shook my head, feeling the heat rising in my face.

'I would cordially like to invite you to the wedding of Mr and Mrs Niles The Plank … I mean, Mr & Mrs Dunplank,' he said, creasing over with laughter.

I was getting tired of defending Niles and I was furious with Dame for ridiculing him and, in turn, my decision to be with Niles.

'If you've got nothing nice to say, then don't bother talking to me.' I could barely get the words out, I was that upset. I turned to leave, but Dame called out to me.

'Sorry, Jos, I'm being a dick. You've been through a shitty time and I'm not helping matters.' He held both my hands. 'All I want is for you to be happy and I'm going to be here for you, no matter what.'

I felt my anger fall away. Dame was just looking out for me, but it still hurt that nobody seemed to support my decisions as far as my love life was concerned. Maybe with good reason, if my previous dating history was anything to go by.

I was grateful that Dame was going to be at the funeral, to make sure I didn't crumble and blubber too loudly throughout the service.

The funny thing with death is that you just don't know how it's going to hit you. On the day of the funeral I felt numb, but apprehensive. I still couldn't quite believe that she was gone. I had the sick feeling that she might suddenly open her eyes and grab my arm while I was peering into the coffin to pay my last respects and say, 'Don't even think about chickening out of going to France. I'm keeping an eye on you.' Then her eye would pop out of its socket and hit me on the forehead, along with a profuse amount of blood and fluid. At least that's what happened in my dream last night.

I knocked back a neat brandy even though it was only

9am. Ed was doing the eulogy; I couldn't bring myself to speak, it was hard enough to just turn up, let alone talk in front of the forty or so guests that Ed estimated would attend. She was much loved and not just by the ladies at Bingo. Ed's dad and some other relatives were coming over from Brisbane. Malevolent Melvin would be there with his family, as well as some of Bert's family. I'm guessing that Tebor wouldn't be turning up, otherwise there would be no need for me to go and collect this package from him in Antibes which I had discovered was in the South of France, relatively close to Cannes. I hadn't had a chance to speak to Ed about the letter, but now was hardly a good time.

I told Dame that I wanted to take the bus to the cemetery even though Ed had offered for me to ride in the car behind the funeral hearse, but that was too morbid. Dame went with Ed and I travelled alone by bus, remembering the day Pru had gone to visit her beloved Bert at the cemetery, how I had shared that bus journey with her. Oh, happy times. And now she was gone. It really didn't make any sense. At least now she would be buried alongside Bert and I knew they would be dancing together, forevermore.

I took a seat beside Dame on one of the pews at the front. Ed was standing by the minister, looking understandably quite solemn but composed, or maybe a bit numb like me. He seemed to look through people when they spoke to him, except for one man. This had to be his dad. He had the same gingery hair, just a little less of it and the same broad shoulders, which proved very useful as Ed collapsed into his father's arms for the briefest of moments before he composed himself again. I felt a pang when I saw this tender exchange, thinking of my own absent father.

The minister addressed us with words of welcome and comfort. There was a prayer and some passages from the Bible. His voice was hypnotic but I couldn't concentrate on his words. This might have been on account of the fairly substantial measure of brandy that was swilling around my brain.

I spotted Melvin in the second pew on the right. He looked less miserable than usual. In fact, he looked quite cheerful. He was with his wife and their very small baby, who couldn't be more than a few weeks old. Pru had been totally stoked when she found out that she was going to be a great granny, but I'm not sure she even got to meet her great grandchild. I sighed heavily. The walls of the church seemed to be closing in on us.

Something the minister was saying caught my attention: that the body is just a costume we wear, that our soul is eternal and that we can't take anything with us so not to be too attached to anything. That was exactly how Pru wore life, like a loose blanket, unhindered. I thought about her letter, about the mirror, and about how today was acknowledging her continued journey … and mine.

Dame took my hand and squeezed it gently, handing me a tissue. I wiped away a few tears but felt peace nestle deep in my heart.

The service continued with the hymn, 'All things bright and beautiful,' one that I remembered singing heartily in school assembly. Babs and I had voices of angels in those days. I could see why Pru had chosen this hymn, it was filled with a gratitude and wonder that resonated strongly in her own life and character. Then Ed stood up and moved towards the pulpit, his steps slow and deliberate like he was trying his best to stay composed. His red face and trembling hands gave him away. He unfolded a piece of paper and set it down in front of him. He cleared his throat.

'My gran Pru was a larger-than-life character, as I'm sure many of you will know. Her love for life was unbounded. I will miss those twinkling blue eyes and the way she was always plotting some mischief. I will be forever grateful and touched by the way she welcomed me back into her life after so many years apart, and forever saddened that our time together was so brief. I yearn for just one more slice of her famous fruit cake, for one more hearty hug, for one more line of wisdom …' He stopped to cough.

'She used to tell me that I worry too much. That I should just hang up my tatty old worry-coat and have some fun. Being quite stubborn, she was rather insistent that we all get up and have some fun today, so without further ado … hit it.'

Chic's 'Everybody Dance' boomed out from a stereo somewhere, filling the entire church. Ed starting dancing and clapping.

Melvin's face was a picture of horror and his wife looked embarrassed, but their baby was gleefully bouncing its head in time to the music. Ed motioned for people to get up. One by one, people stood up. Dancing, clapping, and even laughing.

The lyrics put a smile on my face, especially the line about spinning all around the floor like Rogers and Astaire. Just like that day when I caught Pru at it on the corner of the road, merrily dancing the foxtrot with her memory of Bert. Pru certainly knew how to get people in the celebratory mood. Well. Most people anyhow, I observed, noting Melvin's thunderous expression. Someone popped a champagne cork and we were toasting Pru's dancing feet.

This would have been exactly what she wanted. As people

were swinging and swaying - and even Melvin had given in to the music, shuffling awkwardly from foot to foot - I looked around, hoping that Ed would introduce me to Bert's family. I wanted to know more about Bert's brother, Tebor, and wondered if anyone could shed any light on this mysterious package.

But Ed had joined his father and other relatives, so I took the opportunity to scan the guests for anyone who looked like they might have flown in from the south of France. The minister indicated that it was time to leave the church for the burial service. I followed the guests out, still holding on to Dame's supportive arm.

'I reckon they look a bit continental,' Dame said, gesturing towards a middle-aged couple in front of us. 'Bonjour!' he called out to them. They turned around, looking confused.

'Umm, hello,' the woman replied, sounding very definitely British.

'I'm Damian and this is Josie. Pru lived in our block of flats. Are you from Bert's side of the family?' he enquired pleasantly.

'I'm Alan,' replied the man, extending his hand to us, 'and this is my wife, Gill.' She smiled at us politely. 'Bert was friends with my parents. We got to know Pru quite well too, what an angel, such joie de vivre and famous for her cakes. She was always baking and said that being pregnant gave her the most extraordinary cake cravings. Happily she always made enough for us.'

His eyes were twinkling with the memory. 'Sorry, I'm wittering on.'

'Not at all,' I said, 'and you know what? Pru still made the most fabulous cakes.' I smiled, remembering our dinner together and thinking about the daughter that she never got to tell me about. Ed had told me how she got killed suddenly in a car crash. So tragic.

'I seem to remember that Bert stayed with us a couple of times without Pru.' Alan's foreheard wrinkled in confusion. 'That can't be right though, as he was with always with Pru. I was just a kid at the time, so I probably don't remember right.'

That did sound a bit odd. From the way Pru described it, they were practically joined at the hip but in a good way.

'Did Bert happen to mention his brother, Tebor, in the south of France?'

'Can't say that I remember. He was friends with my parents, so they might have known him.'

'And your parents, are they here today?' I waited with baited breath, maybe they could at least tell me a bit more about Tebor.

'No. Sadly Mum passed away a couple of years ago and Dad died shortly afterwards.'

'Oh, I'm sorry,' I mumbled, feeling awkward all of a sudden. He must have wondered why I was asking so many questions.

Alan was indeed regarding me curiously.

'Anyway, nice meeting you,' I said, giving them a little wave as I walked away with Dame. My flight was in ten days so I guess I would have to wait until then before getting my questions answered. Dame reminded me that all I had to do was collect a parcel, not shag a tribe of Tibetan monks. What was it about Dame and shagging? Didn't he know that monks were likely to be celibate spiritual beings?

The minister led us to the graveyard where Pru's coffin was

lowered down into the ground. A feeling of peace washed over me as he spoke:

'We now commit her body to the ground, earth to earth, ashes to ashes, dust to dust, in the sure and certain hope of resurrection to eternal life.'

Pru was everywhere. She was in the gentle blowing breeze, in the distant birdsong, in the rhythmic swaying of the trees. Yes, I definitely felt like Pru was accompanying me on my onward journey, and a whisper in the air seemed to tell me that I need not worry at all.

Chapter Eleven
Not Again?!

My feeling of calm at the graveside had turned to panic. I couldn't stop thinking about Pru's last wishes for me. I'd had more ups and downs than a rollercoaster: one minute I felt emboldened by the adventure that lay ahead of me, the next minute I was petrified. There was only one person I wanted to discuss this with. Niles. I tried calling but got his voicemail yet again. I sent him a cheery WhatsApp message, instead making some wise crack about sheep shagging on his Welsh retreat. I retrieved his spare keys from the drawer. If I couldn't get hold of Niles, then I'd just have to wait at his place until he showed up.

I made my way over to his flat with Pru's letter clenched in my hand, my knuckles white with tension. The contents of the letter were emblazoned into my brain. Although Pru's request wasn't that peculiar, I felt like there was something she wasn't telling me, something significant that I had missed and I was rubbish at reading between the lines. Nerves were prickling my stomach. Whether it was to do with the letter or something else, I couldn't be sure. The thought made me feel rather unsettled. Niles, being a typical two-and-two-is-four type of bloke was bound to see things clearly. I realised I was shaking and struggling to breathe. I rang the doorbell twice, just in case he had got back early. No answer. I let myself in, surely he'd be okay with that, what with us being engaged. Engaged. The thought still made me smile. He had given me a temporary ring saying that he was having a special one made. 'Special' sounded expensive.

I sat in Niles' armchair, a well-worn faded chocolate brown chair, and looked around the sparsely decorated room. It felt suddenly peculiar sitting here waiting for him. I flicked through a magazine. I sat for a while longer, but it was eerily quiet, oppressively so. Well, of course it's quiet, Josie, I told myself. Niles always has Radio 4 on, or a history programme on in the background. I thought about turning the TV on but decided against it, thinking it might be best that I come back later. Not before using the loo though.

As I approached the top of the stairs I thought I heard someone speak. I stopped and listened, holding my breath. Nothing. Oh god, Pru's death had really rattled me to the extent I was hearing voices again. I continued to the top landing. There it was again, a soft voice with a lyrical note to it. It was coming from Niles' room. Typical. Niles had fallen asleep in front of the TV again. I creeped over to his room, the door was ajar. I slowly pushed the door open, not wanting to wake him suddenly. But then remembering that not even a rocket could wake him at the best of times, I flung the door open, shouting out 'Surprise!'

The first thing I saw was the look of horror and utter disbelief on two faces. One was the ashen face and staring grey eyes I knew so well. The other face belonged to a blonde-haired, fair skinned lady with green eyes and smudged red lips. She looked from me to Niles.

'What's she doing here?'

He shrugged his shoulders stupidly, but then spotted the keys in my hand.

The next thing I saw was my pale face and shaking body in the mirror behind the bed they were in.

'It's not what it looks like.' Niles was getting up, pushing his hand through his ruffled hair. 'We met in Ireland, she just popped round to say hi ...' he tailed off weakly, looking at the indignant half-dressed woman opening her mouth to say something, but seeming to change her mind.

And still I couldn't speak. Shock had seized up my airways and frozen me to the spot. All his promises were nothing more than lies. My heart thudded painfully. I knew it. I bloody well knew it. I just hadn't wanted to admit it to myself.

'I just came to tell you that I'm going to Antibes,' I managed at last, my voice barely a whisper. And to think I had wanted him to come with me.

'Where? Josie, look we can talk about this, maybe when you've calmed down. I really wanted to be there for you at the funeral. I know how devastating it must have been for you, how much Pru meant to you. This ...' he said, waving his arm dismissively towards the blonde, 'was never meant to happen.'

I heard him speak with that same earnest expression he used when he'd forgotten to buy the milk or put the dishes away, but this was just completely incomprehensible. His words barely registered.

'Oh right, so you just accidentally fell into bed together?'

He looked at me helplessly.

'I'm leaving,' I said, far more calmly than I felt.

'Josie, I'll call you ...' he said, then he froze as I walked towards them. Terror swept over both their faces. Snatching his phone off the bedside table, I went over to his fish tank and momentarily paused to watch the array of exotic fish swimming in circles. I felt like I was one of the fish inside the tank, going round and round in circles and not getting anywhere. Except I wasn't quite so colourful.

I dropped his phone into the tank.

Next, I took off my ring and dropped that into the tank too, followed by his door keys.

'No, you won't. I don't ever want to see you again.' With that, I somehow found the strength and use of my legs to run down the stairs and out of the house.

'Pumpkin,' he called after me, 'Pumpkin! I've bought you a diamond ring and everything, I promise.'

'You know where you can shove your ring!' I shouted, before slamming the front door shut.

I ran down the street howling like a tortured, anguished creature. Even though I knew deep down that things hadn't been right, how could he have done this to me? How could he have been so cruel? Why had we just talked about getting married with my family, for god's sake? My cheeks flamed in humiliation and I could just see my mum's pitying but slightly accusing expression, reminding me that I had screwed up yet another relationship. I felt like a prize fool. Everyone had warned me but I refused to listen, especially to Ant who would have no hesitation in beating him to a pulp.

Love stinks, I thought miserably. Love stinks so bad. Worse than a pile of rotting corpses, worse than the foulest smelling rubbish, and even worse than my brother's socks after football practice. My only hope was that god could grant me total oblivion.

Total oblivion from the pain, total oblivion from the charms of men. And god could also grant me the good sense not to be sucked in *ever* again.

I looked up into the sky mouthing a silent prayer. But then again, god was probably a bloke, laughing his head off at me from up there on his cushioned cloud. A stream of angry tears poured down my face. I had been faithful, loving, forgiving. I had let him back into my life, he must have seen MUG in flashing fluorescent letters written across my forehead. Who the hell was she anyway?

Nile's words came back to haunt me. '*We met in Ireland …*'. The realisation of what those words meant made my heart crash to the floor. He had met her during his three-month booze fest in Ireland, where he had supposedly reached the decision that he couldn't live without me.

I'm sure his best mate Dan had encouraged him to 'get back out there' with anyone willing, and that happened to be with a peroxide blonde. What was I thinking? He probably hadn't needed much persuasion at all. The thought of him consoling himself against her frankly rather-flat chest made me want to scream. It all made perfect sense now, the mysterious whispered conversations, his suspicious behaviour.

Niles and his platitudes of remorse for leaving me together with his renewed undying love mocked me while I walked. I wiped my eyes furiously, pounding all the way to Babs' home. She would know what to do.

As expected, she was outraged and I had to physically restrain her from going over there to 'sort him out.' Two bottles of pinot and a family-size bar of Cadbury's Whole Nut chocolate later, I was still bawling my eyes out. Anger had given way to overwhelming sadness.

'I did everything I could to keep him interested. I even brought new lingerie from Figleaves,' I sighed deeply. 'I waxed and preened myself to perfection, and endured all number of sit ups and squats. I didn't want him to think I was letting myself go.'

Babs shook her head sadly. 'All you've been doing is living in fear of him leaving you again since he came back. That's not the way it should be. He was supposed to be the one proving himself to you, but all he's proved is just how much of a cheating knob he really is.'

I stared at her silently. 'I'm sorry, Josie, but it's true. You are far too good for him.'

'I know,' I croaked.

And suddenly I felt something unexpected. Relief. Finally, the spell had been broken, the trance of seeing things as I wanted them to be. That day in front of the mirror I had realised something was very wrong when I struggled to see our future together. That gurgling in my stomach were my instincts telling me that Niles was cheating. I knew it, but I hadn't been ready to have love ripped away from me, not when I had just lost Pru. Niles didn't support the best of who I was. It was very telling that I liked myself better when I wasn't with him. He had moments of being kind, loving and sweet, so I let myself believe he could be The One. And he had come back to me when the others hadn't, so I thought all we needed was to work through things. But it seemed what he really wanted was the good, loyal loving wife *and* his bit on the side. He was such a wanker.

My life felt like a soap opera that went something like this:

'Josie Green spent her entire life trying to be interesting, funny, clever and sexy in in the constant fear that the minute she slipped up her fiancé would be out of the door faster than speedy Gonzales. But the more she searched for 'The One,' the more 'The One' eluded her. Not even thirty years old and with four fiancés under her belt, is Josie destined to end up living alone with lots of cats? Tune in to find out.'

Ah, how embarrassing. Ok, so that's the way I *had* been, but I had also discovered the joy of my own company and was ready to take my life into my own hands. Some things were pre-determined for me, like going away to France and flying in a hot air balloon (yikes!), but the rest of it I would figure out as I went along.

'Earth to Josie, Earth to Josie.' Babs' freckled face loomed close to mine. I blinked rapidly.

'I think I've had an epiphany, Babs.'

'Oh, that sounds painful!' she wrinkled her nose up.

'From now on, my life is going to be a man-free zone.'

Babs guffawed loudly.

'I'm being serious!' I told her about my encounter with the mirror, and my poem. 'So, as it turns out, I like being single.'

'Well fuck-a-duck!' Babs exclaimed, blowing her nose. I hadn't noticed that Babs was tearing up, so rare was it to see Babs cry. 'I don't know whether to hug you or slap you. I've been trying to tell you how bloody amazing and brilliant you are all along. I'm glad you're finally acknowledging it. I guess you had to see it for yourself. But that doesn't mean that you can't dabble in a bit of pick-and-mix, you know, like in the cinema when you fancy a fizzy cola bottle and a pink bon-bon. Well you can have both: just like with dating, it doesn't mean you have to start planning a wedding. You did have fun with the salsa guy, what was his name?'

'Chris.'

'He was hot,' Babs said, her eyes shining. 'I would have. If I'd been single, of course,' she added quickly. 'Just because I'm with Jake, doesn't stop me from me being curious. The other day I was talking to this man from NatWest on the phone, he had the sexiest Scottish accent ever, made me think of highland flings and wondering what he wore under his kilt. I mean in reality he could have looked like a walrus, but still …'.

'And in real life, kilts aren't exactly in keeping with workplace attire.'

'Stop killing my fantasy,' she tutted.

'Well, I'm not interested. Man-free means man free. No romantic tussles or tangles means no broken hearts, and I get to find out who I am and what I really want.'

Oh yes, I was determined. And Babs looked deeply impressed.

'I give it two days. Two days before you start wondering whether you should give Niles another chance.'

'Not a chance.' I smiled, feeling triumphant with the way I had got the hell out of there without a second glance. 'I don't think he'll be bothering me any time soon.'

'Ok, just making sure. I'm really proud of you, Josie.' She hugged me fiercely in the manner of someone who had just graduated from the school of love fools.

There was a sharp knock on the door.

'Maybe I spoke too soon about Niles not bothering me.' Oh god.

'I'll sort him out' she said, storming to the door, her face different shades of red. She was clearly still feeling very protective over me.

'It's only the boys,' she called out. I heard hushed whispers.

'Do you want us to duff him up for you?' Dame came in wearing a long black coat and was slamming his fist into his palm.

'Yeah!' George followed up closely, fisting his palm in unison.

'No it's fine. Babs already offered,' I said, laughing at their gangster impersonations. They were hardly Phil and Grant, more like Dick and Dom, or about as threatening as George and Mildred (one of Mum's classic TV favourites).

At least I was laughing, albeit very briefly, before I started blubbing again.

'I thought you were fine, Josie, what with your epiphany and all?' said Babs, looking panicked.

'I am, but it's just that I'm so embarrassed. Sorry, you were all right and the worst thing is that I bloody well knew it … please don't say I told you so,' I said, eyeing Dame warily. But bless him, he was nothing but consoling, comforting me with a big bear hug.

'Love makes a fool of us all sometimes,' he whispered, looking down at me. 'And even if he hadn't cheated on you, he was still a slimy little shit.'

'Ain't that right!' Babs joined in, raising a glass.

'He might be a shit, or a toad or whatever, but he's still the father of my unborn child.'

Silence. Then three mouths dropped wide open.

'Bleeding Nora.' Babs spoke at last. '

'Well I figured that as we were getting married anyway … and I've always had this life plan. Get married and have my first baby at thirty, my second baby by thirty-three, and my third baby at thirty-five. I was all set to do that, as well.'

'Does Niles know you're …?' Dame pointed down at my stomach.

I couldn't contain my mirth any longer. 'Joking!' I shouted. 'I'm not Bridget Jones with her pregnancy scares. Niles was nothing if not careful. I guess he had to be if he was putting it about.' I sighed, then let out a piercing scream. I felt vaguely better and I know Ed would have approved, had he been here with us all.

'Now I'm going to do the Warrior two stance' I said, lifting my arms out and bending my knee, in the yoga pose I had looked up online. Not that easy when I had sunk the best part of a bottle of pinot and probably consumed my body weight in chocolate.

'She's in shock,' Dame announced to the room. 'You're the doctor, George. Do something!'

'No, I think it's just this epiphany. She told me it's to do with finding herself and giving men a miss for a while. I think she'll be ok,' said Babs.

'I can hear you, you know,' I said, now watching them through my legs, my head right down by my feet.

'It's normal for her to go a little bit loopy, what with all the stress she's been under. But we do need to keep an eye on her, just in case,' said George, offering his expert opinion.

'I can still hear you!' I chimed. 'And I'm fine, or at least I will be.'

I could now tick Funeral and End Relationship with Niles (another death) off the list, not that that had been on the list. What was next? Oh yes, tell Bernice that I wanted a week's annual leave at short notice. That would be interesting.

The last few days at work had become an even bigger drag, what with all the drama of late. I was restless to get away and thankfully Babs had agreed to go with me. My journey from the tube to the gallery was like walking in concrete boots, my leaden heart had sunk into my feet. The only thing at work keeping me going was my work friend Leila. She was funny and grumpy but in an amusing way.

'Josie, marriage and kids is not all it's cracked up to be,' she told me, in case I was in any doubt about my newfound man-free status. After four fiancés, I think I could definitely put marriage on the back burner. But it was still funny to hear Leila talk about the joys of wedded life. 'Seriously, when I sit cross-legged in the bath, my nipples touch my belly button, and I won't even go into my varicose veins. The grass is definitely not greener. If I was you, I would tell Bernie to stick her job and bugger off to France for a long break and forget this whole marriage business. I wish I could.' Leila had been married for fifteen years and had three children but I know she loved Sanjay and wouldn't have traded her lot in for anything.

I would have loved to tell Bernie exactly where to stick her job. If only.

When I left work, I saw that Ed had tried to call me five times. Something was very wrong.

'Josie, didn't you get my messages? You have to come down to Walsley and Barratts Solicitors on Park Lane right away,' he said without any preamble when I called him back.

I remember Ed telling me there was a reading of Pru's will today but I didn't think I was part of it. Pru had already given me a holiday in France which was beyond generous. A feeling of apprehension crept up my spine.

That feeling intensified when I arrived at the plush offices of W&B's Solicitors. The kindly receptionist motioned for me to go straight up the stairs to where the meeting had already started. I entered the room and saw that Malevolent Melvin was red-faced and in the middle of contesting something. Ed and his father were sitting quietly but looking very grim. I entered the room, saying a quick hello to everyone and then took a seat. Melvin glared at me. The solicitor spoke rapidly and at length; I wondered if he was late for his next client. From what I could make out, Ed and Melvin had both been left a decent amount of money, but Ed had also been left the flat which Melvin was not very happy about.

'The meeting is adjourned. I need to speak to you regarding a private matter, Ms. Green.' He was so formal and spoke as if we were in a court room. I watched his bearded face when he spoke and wondered if morsels of food got stuck in it. I had always wondered this, probably unfairly so about bearded men since reading 'The Twits' by Roald Dahl.

'Ms. Green?' His voice was sharp.

'Yes, I'm listening.'

The others got up to leave. Ed gave me a small smile. The strain of the last couple of weeks was etched into his face. I really wanted to catch up with him properly before my trip to France next week, hopefully I would get the opportunity.

Melvin was furious. 'Why would Gran have anything to say to her, she's not even family?' he hissed in a loud whisper that he must have known that I could hear. I could understand how upset he was, but honestly he didn't seem to possess a single redeeming quality. His father led him out of the room and gave me an apologetic smile.

'You have been awarded the sum of £25,000 pounds to be paid direct into your bank account on completion of the set task as stipulated in the letter she left you. You are to report back to this office once your mission has been completed. You will then receive another letter.'

Another letter? £25,000? What was going on? I was too stunned to speak. I wish I could ask Pru. I suddenly felt really exhausted and just wanted to be on my own. There was just too much going on for me to take it all in right now. I walked out of the office in a daze, letting the bearded solicitor know I would be in touch if I had any other questions.

***

Bernie had been back from Las Vegas for two days now and was in surprisingly good spirits when she got back. She talked excitedly about the size and scope of the hotels and casinos. Her good mood had lasted for approximately five minutes until she questioned my latest absence, expressing her insincere concern for my loss. While she was in this semi-sympathetic mood I plucked up the courage to tell her about my trip to France. She stared at me goggle eyed.

'You know these things have to be approved weeks in advance.' But it was fine for her to make a last-minute trip to Vegas, I thought bitterly.

'The answer is No and that is final.' She turned to leave, the matter closed.

'I have to go, Bernice. It was Pru's dying wish. Believe me I wanted to get out of it, but I had no choice. She's set out some pretty specific conditions, so whether I like it or not, Antibes - here I come.'

'We have a major exhibition opening next week. You can go in a couple of weeks; she's not going to know. I'm sure whatever it is can wait.'

'Actually, it can't,' I said, standing my ground. 'Look, I'm really sorry but I'm going … and I'm not coming back to work here. I quit. Effective immediately.'

'Green! Come back here, don't you dare do this!' she boomed.

I strode straight to my locker, collected my things and left. I didn't exactly tell her where to stick her job, but as good as. I passed Leila on the way out.

'You've only gone and bloody done it, haven't you?' she grinned, giving me a thumbs up.

I nodded and hastily made my way out of the building before Bernie reached me. I could hear her advancing closer. Phew! I had made it. Free at last.

Book Two
La Joie de Vivre!

Chapter 12
Up, Up & Away!!

Today was the day that I got up at an ungodly hour only so that I could plummet to my death from a hot air balloon. I know George told me NOT to watch the horrifying-but-rare YouTube video clips, but I couldn't help myself. It's like when someone tells you not to think of the colour red, or about the Bailey's cheesecake in the fridge, then it's all you can think of. Nevertheless, I tried to put thoughts of burning balloons out of my head. Not easy when I had two orange buttocks writhing in my face.

'Rise & shine, rise & shine!' Dame wiggled his posterior at me and his outfit was as bright as the weather. 'Not a wisp of cloud in the sky, perfect weather for ballooning,' he informed me with a dazzling smile.

Great, even the weather was conspiring to make this happen.

'So, how are you feeling?' Dame pointed his iPhone at me.

'Will you put that bloody thing away, otherwise I'm not coming.'

'No need to get your knickers in a knot, I just thought this incredible day should be preserved for posterity.'

'Do you mean in case I don't come back?' I sat up suddenly, the bed springs mimicking the churning in my stomach.

'Relax. You are not going to die. You've got more chance of being run over by a tractor in the field than perishing in a hot air balloon. I've read all the stats.'

Great. Now I had balloons *and* tractors to worry about.

'Fine, you can film me.' I rearranged the pillows, tilting my head to one side.

'If you are watching this, then sadly I have departed, but at least I went out with a bang.' I could see Dame's hand shaking with laughter but tried to ignore him.

'I want to thank you for all the support and love you've given me over the years. Sorry, Mum, for all the times I've been a cow. Ant. Yes, you can have my Guns & Roses T-shirt.'

'Drama-rama!' Dame rolled his eyes at me. 'You can save your speeches for your cheering patrol.'

'Cheering patrol?' I parroted. I noticed Dame's eyes were darting around the room, he clapped a hand over his mouth.

'I'm not meant to be telling you this, but you're going to have a few spectators today.' Oh God. 'Just your mum, brother, aunty, Babs, George and myself, that's it. Oh, and I think Ed might be coming too. Just don't forget to act surprised.'

'Bloody hell! I didn't expect an audience, Dame, it's going to give me stage fright.' I had a vision of myself aged five in my first school production; I nearly wet myself when I spotted my mum's bouffant bouncing up and down in the front row. 'Why do they have to be there?'

'For moral support. Because they are excited and proud of you,' Dame blinked at me, encouragingly. No pressure then.

We flew through the traffic, arriving at the Barking Mad Dog car park with over half an hour to spare, a rather apt name considering this was the craziest thing I had ever done. The flight was to take place over St. Albans in Hertfordshire, which was local for Mum, Ant and Aunty Pam. Perhaps I'd be able to see our house from up above, how great would that be? My entourage were already there when I arrived so I tried to rearrange my features to express a look of delighted surprise.

'Oh my god, I can't believe it! What on earth are you doing here ...?' I began, jumping up and down then running towards them. I'm not sure my performance was Oscar-worthy, maybe a tad OTT, but I don't think they clocked on that I knew.

Mum was dabbing tears from her eyes. 'It's incredible what you are doing darling, *being so daring*,' she added breathlessly. I guess it was touching they were here for me, almost like watching their little bird fly the nest. I told them about the whole sorry Niles saga over the phone a couple of days ago and in fairness, both Mum and Ant had been absolutely brilliant and very supportive. Mum's eyes were shining. There was something different about her. 'Mum, where did you get that scarf from? It's beautiful, looks expensive,' I said, admiring the silk fabric in striking pinks and purples.

'Lianne got it for me,' she said breezily, 'an early birthday present.' Hmm, her birthday wasn't until October and her best friend Lianne didn't strike me as the type to buy her a birthday present in advance, or to spend more than a fiver. But I chose to let it slide.

'Sometimes you've just gotta grab life by the balls,' exclaimed Aunty Pam suddenly, doing a little skip and waving her arms around like a cheerleader. It wouldn't have surprised me if she got her pom-poms out too. And no, that wasn't a euphemism for something else, although I wouldn't put anything past Aunty Pam.

'Indeed you do, Aunty Pam.'

Babs, George and Ant all hugged me tightly. Oh god, were they all thinking that I was about to die? Their squeals of delight and chattering reassured me that they were just happy for me, that's all.

I traipsed across the field where they had already begun the mammoth task of spreading the balloon out in all its brilliant glory so they could inflate it using a fan powered by a gasoline engine. I hadn't anticipated this being so much hard work, but I enjoyed it. It made me forget the fact that soon my feet wouldn't be touching the ground. We were joined by a family of four, a few couples and two elderly ladies who were relieved to have made it here at all, because they came by train and then took a taxi, but the driver got lost and they kept having to repeat 'Barking Mad Dog' car park to the bemused man. They hooted with laughter every time they said it. I think they were possibly a little bit 'Barking Mad' themselves! Still, there was a good camaraderie and spirit amongst us all and at least if we died, we'd all be together.

The basket was bigger than I thought. I suppose it had to be though, carrying sixteen passengers. Getting into the basket was harder than it looked. The side of the basket had makeshift holes which you were supposed to get your feet into, then you had to haul yourself inside. Quite easy if you were over 6ft and lanky or athletic and used to these things, but as I wasn't any of those things it was quite tricky. I watched the pilot carry the two elderly ladies on board and silently willed him to carry me on board too, but no such luck. Dame gave my bottom a big heave and finally got me inside the balloon.

I looked out of the basket at the sea of spectators, all waving and cheering us on. 'Go, Josie, go!' I heard Babs call out. Dame was recording the whole experience but he'd promised me that he wouldn't point the camera at me unless I gave him express permission. I practiced my mindful breathing: breathe in deeply, exhale fully. That's what the meditation recording had advised. A good impersonation of someone in labour minus the screaming is what it felt like. A rush of nerves and excitement hit my stomach as the basket started to rise, the ground falling away from us. George was right, I didn't feel a thing. We were floating serenely and besides the occasional blast of noisy air accompanied by the bright flickering flame, it was so quiet.

I grabbed Dame's hand. 'I can't believe we're actually doing this. This is awesome!' Dame nodded, his eyes glinting. He was being uncharacteristically quiet and had a dreamy look on his face. The old ladies were holding hands and a family who had been bickering earlier were stunned into silence, a look of absolute rapture on their faces. It was as if we were suspended in time.

I had a vision of myself smoking a large cigar with classical music playing in the background. Was that a Mozart piano concerto I could hear in the background, as we ascended slowly upwards? I sighed with deep contentment, looking out of the basket. I could see the tops of trees and fields rolling out ahead of us. A cathedral … and was that my primary school, and possibly my family home? I couldn't be sure. I could still make out the people below waving frantically up at us, then I spotted something unexpected.

'Ed, Ed!' I found myself yelling out of the basket. He was waving both of his arms, his bright green and yellow shirt flapping in the breeze. At least I thought it was Ed and hopefully not a rather peculiar and colourful shrub. I thought he was working. Damn, I really wanted to talk to him. I hadn't had a chance to catch up with him properly since seeing him at the solicitor's office, or tell him about the letter and going to France. I guess all that could wait.

I watched the world fall away beneath us. Soon the people and cars, houses and trees all looked like little Lego pieces. And the best thing was that I felt absolutely and completely safe. As the ground dropped away I felt lighter, like all my problems and fears were 'down there.' Maybe this is what Pru had intended all along; she wanted me to see life from a different perspective. 'We'll be ascending up to 5,000 feet' I heard the pilot announce. Dame asked him something but I was lost in my own thoughts.

What a year this had been. I couldn't help but smirk when I thought about Niles. There wasn't a fanny's fart that he would have done this with me. Bottled it at the last minute, more like. And to think that I'd envied him for his sense of adventure. He'd pissed off to Ireland and bonked a blonde. Not exactly adventurous or very original.

I had gone full circle and was now in quite a different place. I never thought I'd be approaching the big 3-0 in a state of being willingly single and jobless. I'm not saying that the last couple of weeks hadn't been painful. They had been, excruciatingly so. But for the first time in my life I was excited about the future, about the possibilities, about not knowing. I could never have imagined that I, Josie Green, would be floating through the sky, with a look of complete serenity and wonderment.

Suddenly I was laughing so hard, I nearly wet my pants. I gave Dame an almighty hug.

'I love you Dame, I really do!' I said, tears filling my eyes. He pointed the camera at me.

'Come here, you big softie,' he said, drawing me closer with his free arm.

I noticed we were descending down into some fields. Good job too, as I couldn't wait to pop open the champagne. One thing was certain: I was ready for the next phase of my life. Bring it on.

After a shaky landing in a muddy field, followed by an undignified exit from the balloon where I plopped onto my thankfully well-padded behind, we completed the equally arduous task of dismantling and rolling up the balloon. Champagne glasses were raised and pictures taken.

'We are still alive, aren't we? I didn't just dream this, did I?' I breathed, eyes glazed and feeling light-headed.

'Of course we are alive and this is real, you donut!' Dame gave me an affectionate squeeze. We then made our way back to the starting point where cheers could be heard. I felt a bit unworthy and embarrassed by it all, we'd hardly completed a triathlon or swum the channel but I guess in my world this was a pretty big deal. Mum, Ant and Aunty Pam swooped me up in their arms. This was also my send-off before France, another big deal, so I guess I could let myself be spoilt. I regaled everyone with how wonderful the whole experience had been.

'So now you've officially conquered the skies, I guess getting on a plane will be a walk in the park?' Babs was beaming at me.

'Well …' I began, doubtfully. 'The truth is that I'm still a bit scared but less so, knowing you'll be with me.'

I let out of a sigh of jubilation and relief. What a day, and also another thing ticked off the list. I looked around.

'Was Ed here earlier?'

'He was indeed,' said Babs, 'he looked fit to burst when he saw you take off, really wanted to stick around as well, but work called him in to do a late shift.'

There went my chances of catching up with him. My heart sank a little but I was too full of beans and excited to let that bother me now.

'We're heading off for Sunday lunch, do you fancy joining us? My treat?' Mum said. How could I refuse? Dame was helping me pack later, such was his speciality, so I could relax and have another celebratory drink or two. We all trudged off together and found a lovely country pub overlooking the hills. It wasn't often that my friends and family were together like this. After an epic day and an almost-as-epic roast dinner and pudding, I felt exhausted and very grateful that Dame was driving us back home. He also said he would stay over at the flat, to make sure I got up on time.

Dame took to the task of helping me pack like he was preparing a meticulous military operation. The list of items were about a foot long and read as such:

> *Essentials:* Passport, ticket, travel insurance, money, debit cards, mobile, some clothes, bikini, condoms, adapter, vibrator, soap, towels …

Only in Dame's world could condoms and vibrator be considered essential items. I lost interest after essential item number 34.

After all that packing I fell into bed absolutely shattered

and dreamed that I could fly. Not in a plane, or in a hot air balloon, but just by flapping my arms. I took to the sky soaring high above the clouds, feeling as light as the breeze and as free as a bird.

Chapter 13
Bon Voyage!

It was really happening. I was going to France. Today. My heart was pumping, adrenaline was coursing through my veins like someone had injected me with a huge vat of coffee. Despite having navigated the skies in a big balloon, I was still a bit nervous about getting on a plane. Maybe if I gave the inside of the kitchen drawers another seeing to? That would settle me down.

'Stop being so skittish' Dame said, lifting his head from the sofa. 'You are stressing me out.'

Getting feverish about housework was Dame's domain, so to see me dashing around cleaning things was clearly too irregular for Dame to contend with.

I sat down for a while, trying to channel my inner calm.

'Taxi will be here in one minute!' Dame announced. 'Thank god. Now come here,' he said, giving me one of his reassuring big bear hugs. 'You will have a fantastic time in France. Now GO!' he ordered, shoving me out of the door, into the lift, and waving me off as I got into the taxi.

I practiced my deep breathing in the back seat and began

to relax. Babs offered to let me stay at hers last night, but I had declined. The last time I stayed over I had been subjected to one of their legendary and deafening arguments, followed by lengthy and loud make-up sex. I blocked the memory out of my mind and began to drift off.

The taxi arrived at Victoria train station in good time, where Babs was already waiting by the Gatwick Express platform wearing a pale blue dress, chic silk scarf and huge gold-rimmed sunglasses. 'I've got the tickets – we're good to go!' she shouted loudly as she saw me approach. Any nerves I felt entirely evaporated. This was going to be an exciting adventure.

I boarded the bustling Gatwick Express with Babs and could hardly contain my excitement.

'Anyone would think we were on the Orient Express, not the Gatwick Express,' Babs said, rolling her eyes at me but grinning broadly.

'I can't believe we're doing this,' I said, not for the first time.

The only slightly irritating thing about the train ride had been a canoodling couple, right in front of us. Ok, adjacent to us, but you couldn't help but notice. His hands were continually stroking her hair and face and she was all adoring eyes and breathy sighs. '*Get a room!*' I shouted in my head. *'It won't last – just you wait.'* No-one could blame me for being cynical. Or bitter. I shuddered. That could have been Niles and I, had I not found out what a cheating scumbag he was. I shook the image out of my head. Babs made a gagging action while looking over at the couple. I smiled. Being single with Babs by my side was the best. There was no one else I would rather have gone with.

We arrived at the airport terminal, and Babs stood in front of a screen for a few seconds, quickly deducing that we had to make our way over to check in Zone H. It was early Monday afternoon and people were scurrying everywhere. I never expected it to be this busy. Zone H was teeming with people, queue after queue wound round the aisles.

We managed to find ourselves stuck in the middle of about seven Australian lads. Not a bad place to be by all accounts, but they were making a right ruckus, fuelled by a few beers I'm sure. Babs shook her head impatiently as they tried to push in. My mind had turned to what lay ahead.

'What do you think it could be, Babs?'

'What could what be?' she asked.

'The mysterious package I've got to collect.'

She shrugged her shoulders. 'It's from Pru, so it could be absolutely anything.'

'Hopefully it won't be something illegal or dangerous,' I said, half-jokingly.

Bab's ringing phone interrupted my thoughts. 'Hey Jakey, missing me already?' she began, grinning widely. Her smile rapidly faded, replaced by a look of horror.

'Oh babe, that's awful. When did it happen?' Babs stood frozen to the spot.

'Is he going to be ok? ... How are you and the family holding up?' Babs had the phone glued to her ear, worry etched into her pretty face.

I tried to gauge what was going on. An awful accident from the sound of it.

'Don't be silly, I can't go now. I'll come straight to the hospital. See you soon. Bye.'

'It's his dad,' she whispered, 'his car got hit by a lorry.

He's hurt badly, Josie, critically so.' She glanced at me apprehensively. 'I'm really sorry but I have to go, Jake needs me.' I listened silently.

'Of course, how awful. Let's go' I said, hoisting up the handle on the case.

'Josie, I don't want to ruin this for you. You go without me.' She motioned for me to stay in the queue.

'But Babs, I can't … I can't go alone, I won't know what to do, where to go, no ….'

Babs shook her head vehemently. 'You have to, Jos. It's what Pru wanted, and besides you have a package to collect.'

Babs was handing me the plane tickets, details of the accommodation, the guide book and some euros. My mind was boggling. Despite my buoyant enthusiasm earlier, the thought of flying alone filled me with utter horror. Bring it on. That's what I'd told myself in the hot air balloon, but that was with Dame by my side. What was I supposed to do now?

Babs was stroking my arm. 'You'll be fine, you'll see. It will be an adventure, yeah?' She looked at me hopefully, smiling brightly like she was trying to placate a child with a lollipop. I nodded mutely.

She checked her watch. 'I really have to go, have fun!' She hugged me briefly, her face contorted with a look of guilt - or was it worry about my ability to go it alone?

I watched as her retreating back and clack of wheels disappeared around the corner.

I stood rooted to the spot. The Australian lads breezed past me chiming 'you beauty,' as did a family with about twelve children, all loudly complaining that they wanted to go to Eurodisney instead. One of the little girls smiled up at me and said, 'Come on silly,' swinging her Peppa Pig bag past me.

I started wheeling my bag forward, my befuddled mind trying to make sense of things. Maybe I could get a later flight, maybe I could coax Dame into coming with me, maybe …?

'Can I see your passport and ticket please?' A shrill voice interrupted my thoughts.

'Umm …' I blinked my eyes in confusion; I was at the check in desk.

'Passport and ticket please,' she repeated, remaining polite but with a slight roll of the eyes.

'Yes, of course,' I said, fumbling around in my bag.

She pointed. 'I think that would be them in your hand.'

'Err right, yes …' I hesitated, wondering whether to make a run for it. With a deep sigh and a prayer, I plonked the documents down.

The woman glared at me. 'Did you pack your case yourself?'

'Yes,' I said, none-too-convincingly as I remembered the dozen or so boxes of condoms that Dame had stuffed into my bag 'just in case,' along with god knows what else.

'Are you quite sure?' She looked at me sternly, her glare intensifying.

'Yes. Yes, I'm sorry, just a bit tired.' I gave her a weak smile.

'Do you have any other items of luggage to check in?'

'No, just my hand luggage.' I pointed to my shoulder bag.

'Hallelujah. Next please!' she said, handing me my boarding pass.

A band of nervous anticipation tightened around my chest. I squinted at the departure information board. The information was flipping on the board slightly faster than my stomach. I tried to keep up, concentrating hard. There it was: 14.20 flight to Nice, Gate 101. 101? Wasn't that supposed to signify something bad, like Room 101, where you were forced to confront your worst possible fears? I gulped hard, wishing Babs hadn't badgered me into reading 1984 even though it had been a rather excellent read. Thankfully, I spotted a shop called 'World of Whiskies'. I purchased a smallish bottle of Jack Daniels to keep me company.

I made my way to the departure lounge, noticing that the leather upholstered chairs were a rather putrid peach but they looked comfortable, at least. I wondered if there were any other friendly-but-slightly-nervous solo travellers I could chat to. The few people I did see alone however were either deeply engrossed in a book or, in the case of one peroxide woman with fake tan and a tiny top, shouting loudly into her phone.

'You wouldn't believe who Tracy's going out with now …' she paused dramatically, 'only that creep in Accounts. Yeah, Mark. Yeah, I know. What is she like?' She continued, oblivious to everyone else. Listening to her made me cringe with embarrassment. I hoped that the French passengers wouldn't base their impression of the British entirely on her. A middle-aged couple looked to be sound asleep and there were harassed-looking parents trying to stop their children from tearing across the departure lounge. I gazed out at the planes on the airstrip, feeling sick.

When the tannoy announced 'Would rows 20-35 please commence boarding,' my legs started to wobble. I stood up slowly, shakily making my way to the plane. Other passengers walked past me, brisk and confident, apparently eager to get onboard. I was surprised to find myself at the plane door already. Was I not supposed to board the plane via some metal steps leading up to the aircraft? Clearly not, as there was an air stewardess with dark hair neatly tied back, beaming at me as I showed her my boarding pass. 'Good afternoon, your seat is on the right-hand side.' Her dark ponytail swished in the direction I had to go. I was sitting towards the back, next to an elderly couple.

'Did you remember to pack the jelly babies, Harold?' the silver-haired lady said, reaching over for the blue plastic carrier bag the man had on his lap.

'Of course, dear,' he said, patting her hand. 'I know how badly flying makes your ears pop. At least the weather's good, hopefully we won't be troubled by any turbulence.'

'It's not the turbulence that worries me,' she began. I didn't catch the rest of the conversation as the engines rumbled into life and a safety announcement crackled over the tannoy. I strained my ears to listen but couldn't make out much of it.

People around me were chattering, and the couple next to me had their eyes closed. Two ponytailed stewardesses were standing either side of the aisle, gesturing to the exit signs. I shot up from my seat ready to make a run for it. I took a deep breath and made a few strides towards the emergency exit.

'Are you feeling unwell?' the dark-haired stewardess was looking at me with kind and concerned eyes.

'I'm just not used to flying,' I mumbled.

'We're about to take off. If you could make your way back to your seat, I'll fetch you some water.' She paused. 'Don't worry, we're expecting a very smooth journey into France; once you're up in the air you won't feel a thing.' She smiled encouragingly at me.

Yeah, because I'm going to knock myself out with Jack Daniels, I thought to myself, retreating back to my seat.

The elderly couple were awake now, regarding me with interest.

'You can share some of my jelly babies,' the woman said, generously.

'Thank you,' I said graciously, not knowing how to tell them that it would take a lot more than jelly babies to sort me out. The engine suddenly roared into life, lurching forward and groaning loudly.

The stewardess returned with my water. 'Please keep your seat belt fastened' she said, pointing to the illuminated sign. I fumbled with my seat belt and after a few unsuccessful attempts, she leaned over me and deftly clicked the buckle in place.

'If there's anything else, just press that button overhead,' she said, pointing at an orange button above my head.

'You may regret saying that,' I laughed.

She just smiled at me in that same friendly, unflappable manner which went some way to calming me.

The plane taxied off and gathered speed. I didn't realise my hands were gripping the armrest so tightly until I saw a liver-spotted hand pat my own white-knuckled hand, and a bag of sweets was waved in front of my face. I grabbed at the jelly babies and began munching furiously. I felt my stomach plunge as the plane seemed to dip rather suddenly, my trembling fingers reached for the Jack Daniels bottle which I had placed in the seat pocket in front of me for easy access. I took a long swig and replaced the cap.

'Look at that patchwork of green and yellow,' said the lady next to me, pointing out the scene below through the window. I stole a quick glance out the window to see the plane rising away from the green and yellow crops in the fields.

I covered my face with my hands.

'Don't worry love, you're more likely to be run over by

a car, even our Harold used to be afraid of flying,' the silver haired lady said.

I looked over at Harold, who seemed a picture of complete composure.

'And now you can't stop me from getting on a plane. Love travelling, I do!' he said. 'I've been to Thailand, Japan, and even Australia.'

'I'm Joyce, by the way, and this is my husband Harold.' It was only now that I had calmed down enough to notice that they were from somewhere up north.

'I'm Josie,' I mumbled. I don't know if it was their warm northern friendliness or the combination of jelly babies and Jack Daniels but the whole story tumbled out about the Niles saga, Pru dying, the hot air balloon ride and the assignment I had been entrusted with.

'You're a brave lass,' Harold remarked when I had finished, his eyes twinkling. 'I have a feeling that things are going to work out just fine for you.'

Again, I'm not sure if it was a combination of his kindness and the Jack Daniels, or the sharp and distinct grief that erupted from my heart, but all of a sudden tears were streaming down my cheeks faster than I could wipe them away.

Memories flitted through my mind of all the good times I'd had with Pru. I longed to see her, to talk to her, to tell her about my balloon and plane ride. Another memory took hold with intense clarity. It was of my dad sitting next to me on the plane, his face crimson and blotchy, holding my little hand with his large moist one telling me that his love for me was bigger than the whole world. How I adored him. Even though Mum labelled him a useless drunk, to me he was my hero. I must have been totally lost in my thoughts because the captain had just announced that we were making our descent into Nice and the temperature was 28 degrees. I felt the stirrings of excitement around me. I leaned over the couple next to me at their invitation, catching a glimpse of distant mountains and an endless sea of blue, with dazzling white dots glinting in the sun. As the plane sank lower, I spotted brightly coloured villas with tropical-looking flowers adorning the porches. As the plane touched down I gave in to relief and pure joy. I had made it to the Cote d'Azur alive and in one piece. Joyce and Harold informed me that they were visiting family in Golfe-Juan which was the next stop along from me, so they suggested I share a taxi with them to Nice St Agustin train station.

I arrived in Juan-les-Pins at 7pm, feeling hot, sweaty and dishevelled, badly in need of a drink, a pee and a shower. My dark cotton/polyester mix trousers were clinging to me in the heat. I turned right out of the train station and walked down Avenue L'Esteral. There were shops, bars, and small hotels to the left and right of me. People were milling around the streets and outside cafés, chatting to each other in rapid French. I had expected a remote little village, or a quiet, leafy residential area.

An ice-cream parlour selling tubs and cones of the thickest and sweetest-looking ice-cream tempted me in. I went for a single vanilla cone, but regretted it when the ice-cream melted instantly, trickling over my fingers, the map becoming sticky. Fortunately it looked like I had arrived at my destination. I wheeled my suitcase into the modern apartment block and over to the lift, which thankfully was in working order. When I arrived at the apartment, I was impressed. It was very clean, functional, with laminate flooring and chrome interiors in the kitchen. It certainly made a change from the flat in

Clapham. I had the whole apartment to myself and the host had thoughtfully prepared a folder of instructions for how the TV, Wi-Fi, and air-conditioning worked, as well as restaurant recommendations and places of interest.

At 9pm I decided to familiarise myself with the area and headed straight for the sea. The streets thronged with people. On one side of the beach they were still in their swimwear. On the other side, the beach was lined with restaurants extending out on the sand, with swish white sofas and rows of neatly laid-out tables occupying space, as well as the sun loungers and parasols stretching out almost as far as the sea.

The temperature was perfect. It had cooled down with a slight breeze but was still warm enough to be in shorts and a t-shirt. I stood by the railings above Helios Place restaurant on the beach which was fronted by a gold Buddha statue. I watched well-dressed people chatting and laughing together. A stab of loneliness pierced my heart, and a longing to be back at home with Babs and Dame. Still, it was beautiful and elegant here; what Dame would call ambient chic. All the things I clearly wasn't, I observed as I looked down at my flip flops.

A few weeks earlier it would have been even more buzzing, when the town held its annual July Jazz Festival. I tried to imagine what that must have been like. Incredible and very atmospheric, I decided.

I walked along the promenade to where the road veered left from the Café de la Plage, a lovely white building with a big clock face. I reached the corner of Boulevards Boudain and Wilson and immediately the throng of people had tripled. It reminded me of a Mediterranean-style Piccadilly Circus: music blared out of bars, bright lights flashing their names, including Pam-Pam, Le Crystal, La Reserve, and people were selling fluorescent tubes to passers-by. It had gone from elegant chic to lurid in just minutes. Just as I was thinking 'all it needs now is a casino,' lo and behold, there stood a casino: the Palais des Congres.

My head started to pound, probably from the weariness of the trip and shock of actually having made it here alone and in one piece. I headed back to the apartment and sat out on the balcony for a few minutes, pouring myself a large glass of the merlot that was kindly left as a welcome by the host. People seemed to live their lives outdoors and very publicly. From my balcony I could see into my neighbour's apartment across the street; the windows and shutters were wide open and they were eating dinner. An hour later, they had finished dining but I could still see the empty table, the dining chairs and condiments on the table and the light shining brightly. It was so inviting and made me feel like I was part of the occasion in some small way. The best part was that the couple didn't appear in any way self-conscious of other people (like me) looking in. They were just naturally doing what they always do, getting on with living their lives.

The city didn't sleep here. Motorbikes continued to zoom by into the early hours; car horns were tooting, traffic thundered down the street, and on more than one occasion I awoke with a start thanks to a piercing scream, yelps of laughter, or someone singing. Despite my sleep being disturbed by the noise and the heat, I decided that there was an energy, a conviviality, a charisma about this place. So much so, I imagined it was hard to feel completely alone here. I eventually drifted off to sleep and awoke to the sunlight streaming through the shutters.

Chapter 14
Musée Picasso

The instructions in the apartment clearly laid out the bus route from Juan-les-Pins to Antibes. Before boarding the bus, I browsed in the local patisserie. The shop window was homely and inviting, and the woman greeted me with a big smile. I bought a pain au chocolat and was about to walk back to the bus stop when I heard someone call out, 'Bonjour Mademoiselle.' I turned to see a man and woman greeting each other. 'Bonjour Monsieur' she replied with a wink, as they passed each other clutching their obligatory baguettes. The greeting had a lyrical quality about it, sweet and quaint, but very 'everyday' here. Men gawped at me as I walked past, drinking their café au laits at outdoor tables. Perhaps they could sense my vulnerability and the fact that I felt so conspicuous, but despite being alone I felt a smile spread over my face. This sure as hell beat being at work. As I turned a corner I observed men standing at their balconies, grinning broadly. Oh la la! Dame would have loved all the attention.

I decided to walk to Antibes instead of taking the bus. It looked easy enough to get to on the map and I wasn't due to meet Tebor until 2pm. I'd spent many an afternoon browsing through bookstores and strolling through parks in London, so this wasn't all that different except for the abundance of patisseries, boulangeries, and Spar supermarkets. Dame would have been pleased to know that there was a pharmacy on practically every street corner, equipped with outdoor condom vending machines.

It was evident I had arrived in Antibes when I hit a square lined with trees. People sat on benches chatting animatedly, laughing and looking as if they didn't have a care in the world. Children giggled and shrieked, running through mini fountains in the middle of the square while being chased and chastised in equal measure by their parents.

The traffic hummed around all sides of the square. I was mesmerised by the fountains spraying in their individual glory, and then together in a dense mist of white water, followed a rainbow of orange, yellow and purple. There was an energy and vibrancy about this place. I imagined Pru and Bert had been here, dancing and laughing amongst the spray, not giving a hoot about how wet they got.

Armed with my map, I traversed the square and made my way up the cobbled street that was Rue de la République, linking the new town to the old. Boutiques, craft shops, more patisseries and restaurants lined both sides of the street. At the top of the street to the right was the bustling Marché provencal, a cacophony of sights, sounds and smells evocative of travels to exotic lands. It sold everything from soaps, herbs, spices, jams, cured meats, vegetables and fragrant flowers. The fruits were a rich array of oranges, greens, reds and purples and looked plump and delectable. I brought a peach for a hefty two euros; expensive but worth every cent for the taste.

I spotted a place called Meet Café, just outside the market, and I took a seat towards the edge of the market which had a large wine barrel for a table. I ordered a Perrier, becoming an observer instead of participant in the experience that was Marché provencal.

I was surprised by how well I was coping on my own. True, I was still a bit dazed and overwhelmed but that was only natural. Just then the clock from the building chimed repeatedly, marking the time at 12 noon.

A little while later, I ambled up the side of the Hotel de Ville and on to the Rue des Arceaux. I stopped to admire the picturesque Rue de l'Horage and Rue St. Esprit, with their bright flowers and small old-fashioned houses with pastel shutters and brass knockers. One of the brass knockers was crafted into the shape of a hand, the sinewy fingers poised over the knob. How unique! The shuttered houses looked fairytale-like; it made me wonder if real people lived here. Just as I was thinking this, I saw an elderly man poke his head out from one of the windows; he gave me a friendly wink and a wave.

The cathedral looked incredible against the blue backdrop of sky. What became apparent was the stunning blue coastline across the road, the water glittering majestically in the sunlight. To my left, the road wound round to expose two huge marinas which according to my map were Vieux Port and Port Vauban. Beyond these was the impressive Fort Carre, where Napolean had been famously imprisoned. I stood gawping at the rows of gleaming white yachts, sunlight bouncing off their shiny exteriors.

Rising imperially in the background, framed perfectly against the cloudless blue sky, was the grand Chateau Grimaldi - now the Musée Picasso, with the imposing large black and white poster of Picasso's face, suggestive of a steely disposition and character that I imagined had many colourful stories to tell. What was even more striking were the bronze statues perched on the castle walls. I had almost an hour to spare before meeting Tebor, so I paid the six euro admission price for the small museum, following the route to the outside of the castle.

As it turned out, Picasso only occupied the second floor with a collection of his pottery and ceramic plates, painted with smiley faces and food. My stomach rumbled. Why hadn't I eaten more than a peach earlier? I was fascinated by the black and white photos of Picasso in his studio, and captivated by the views from the windows throughout the castle. The paintings that most intrigued me were the ones depicting his deep interest in Greek mythology, where the centaur, the faun and the nymph took centre stage in the artwork. The creatures had big grins on their funny faces. They made me smile and this was best encapsulated in the wonderfully-titled 'La Joie de Vivre' painting.

At five minutes to 2pm, I quickly descended the steps of the Musée Picasso, glad that I had spent a delightful hour amongst the creations of local artists. But once I was outside, my stomach suddenly creased up. It felt like long fingers were gripping my insides, twisting them into nervous knots. I took a slow deep breath in and out, and fetched the black and white photo of Tebor out of my bag. He looked to be a distinguished and accomplished-looking man in a pinstripe suit. I surveyed the passers-by, hoping that Tebor would not keep me waiting. 'Just collect the parcel and go, how hard can that be?' I kept repeating to myself.

At a minute past 2pm I had a vague feeling of disquiet:

what if he had forgotten he was meeting me, or had been held up? I didn't have his number. An old man in a coral shirt and blue shorts walked close by – could this be him? I stared at him, he smiled and winked at me, saying 'Oh la la.' Oh great, well if nothing else I might just bag myself a sugar daddy. Distracted by the thought, I heard a deep voice from behind me.

'Josie?'

I turned around to see a tall man behind me, about 6ft in height and in his early 30s. He spoke to me again.

'Josie?' he sounded impatient, irritated.

'Umm, yes, but I was expecting … you can't be …?'

'Hardly, considering that Tebor's in his 80s.' He shot me a look to suggest he thought me dim.

'But you know I was supposed to meet him here? Where is he?' I asked sternly, not liking his impertinent manner one little bit.

'I'm Chambers, Tebor's grandson. He's currently indisposed, so he sent me instead.' He extended a hand to me. 'Anyway, pleased to meet you.'

He pumped my hand in an authoritative, business-like manner. He looked anything but pleased, his crisp black suit matching his dark mood.

As if I wasn't feeling awkward enough, his next words stunned me:

'Anyway, I'm afraid you've had a wasted journey. I don't have the package with me, and you're not getting your hands on it. It's been in the family far too long and belongs to my grandfather.'

'I have no idea what it is I'm supposed to collect; I only know that Pru gave me express instructions that I should meet with your grandfather and collect it. She wanted me to have it.'

'It's not meant for you,' his dark eyes flashed angrily at me.

'If you let me speak to Tebor, maybe we can sort this out?' I responded, trying to keep my patience in check. When he didn't speak, I continued:

'What is this precious thing anyway that's got you so hot under your heavily-starched collar?' I risked a small smile to try and break the ice between us.

He shot me a look of contempt, his dark flint eyes as unyielding as his stiff black suit.

Although I had to admit that standing there, like a cloud of thunder against the perfect blue sky, he looked just as arresting as those bronzed statues up on the castle terrace. A song came to mind from Lloyd Cole and the Commotions – something about cheek bones and having the perfect skin, and he really *did* have perfectly tanned skin with a hint of rosiness to his cheeks. Dressed in black, you would have thought that he would have at least looked hot, but no. Not a wisp of heat emanated from him. In fact, he exuded total coolness. Maybe he wasn't entirely human.

'Look, I'm sorry Josie.' His composure softened a little. 'I will explain, but not here. There's a restaurant just up near the beach that serves the freshest moules marinières in town. Let's go.'

Without waiting for a reply, he strode across the road. I quickly followed, deciding that I could endure an hour or two in this man's company if there was food and some answers available.

The location of the restaurant was amazing, overlooking the small beach and the Mediterranean. But the prices, whilst not astronomical, weren't exactly within my carefully-planned budget, considering that I would have to go home and look for a new job. The £25K that had been left to me was on the proviso that I return home with the package, which was looking unlikely by the way things were going.

'Would you mind if we went somewhere else? There were some lovely looking places around the Marché provencal?' I glanced at Chambers apprehensively.

'Don't worry, it's on me,' he said casually, moving towards the outdoor tables.

I hesitated, feeling uncomfortable. He noted my expression and rather than arguing, he surprisingly conceded.

'Cheap and cheerful it is then,' he said with a shrug.

At Marché provencal, the bustling market from before had just a few stalls left, selling jewellery and small pictures. Tables had been set up outside the restaurants, framing the square. I stopped at one that looked particularly inviting. Hearing the raucous ramblings of slightly drunk English men made me feel at home. The menu was also reasonably priced and had food that I recognised. I settled on the cheese and mushroom omelette with chips.

'So common,' Chambers coughed into his serviette, once I had placed my order.

'Excuse me?' I said.

'You come to Antibes and you are eating egg and chips. Could you be any more common?' he looked at me mockingly.

I couldn't contain my anger for another second.

'No one's told me what to eat since I was five and I didn't much listen then, so why don't you just shove a few clams in your gob and shut it?'

To my surprise he burst out laughing. 'Oh Josie, I wouldn't

dream of telling you what to eat; I was just making an observation that you might want to try something a bit more sophisticated than egg and chips while in Antibes.'

I glowered at him, folding my arms and feeling every bit like a petulant five-year-old.

'I'm glad you find me so amusing, although somewhat boring, in my choice of cuisine.'

'Egg and chips it is then,' he smirked.

But for some reason I couldn't let it drop.

'I'll have you know that I have been quite adventurous, thank you very much. In the space of two weeks I lost someone I absolutely adored then caught my fiancé boning a blonde bimbo. I quit my job, went up in a hot air balloon and flew to France completely alone to collect an unknown package from a complete stranger.'

I stopped to catch my breath.

'Wow, a lot *has* happened for you. And has anyone told you how your eyes flash an intense shade of violet when you are angry?' he said, holding his hands in front of his face in case I punched him - which was very tempting. But then he was smiling in a way (I think) was friendly.

I sighed. 'So now I'd really like to know what I'm doing here. Pru, that would be Tebor's sister in law, did ask me to collect a package. I can show you the letter if you don't believe me.'

'I do believe you.' His voice was quiet and his head lowered. I saw the little muscles clenching in his jaw. 'It's just that my grandfather has had it for more than fifty years and it would be hard for him to let it go.'

'Had what? What is it?' I held my breath.

'A painting.'

'A painting? What of?'

'Bert and Pru. She was pregnant.'

Tears pricked the back of my eyes. Pregnant. With Ed's mum. I was curious. What was so special about this painting? Was it gold-framed? Was it an unknown Picasso masterpiece? No wonder Tebor didn't want to let it go. But most perplexing of all was why had Pru sent *me* here to collect it? Surely it should have been Ed?

'But why has your grandfather got it?. Didn't it belong to Pru and Bert? It was of them, after all?'

'I've already said too much.' He stood up abruptly and handed me his business card, leaving a wad of euros on the table.

'Grandad will tell you everything, he should be fine to meet you on Thursday. Give me a ring tomorrow and we'll sort it.'

My head was reeling. 'But …'. Too late: Chambers was already striding off in the direction of the Hotel de Ville, leaving me alone with my omelette and a bottle of Becks.

I pulled out my phone and dialled Bab's number. She answered on the second ring. The whole story came tumbling out. I described the noise, the ambience, the weather, the market and - most importantly - this mysterious painting and the elusive Chambers. I could hear the glee in her voice.

'You are so going to get it on with dark and mysterious Chambers. Wait until I tell Dame!'

'Babs,' I replied, exasperated, 'Men are the last thing on my mind. Hello! Just split up with wanker fiancé?'

'Forget that twat,' she ordered. 'Maybe you need a distraction. By the way, Jake's dad is still in hospital; he's stable but Jake still needs me, so I won't be able to join you. I'm really sorry, Jos, but relax and enjoy. It sounds like you are doing ok.'

She was right. Confused and bewildered maybe. But I suppose I was doing ok-ish.

Chapter 15
Cap D'Antibes

I WOKE UP FEELING SURPRISINGLY ALERT and refreshed. The rumbling night traffic hadn't disturbed me last night and even the piercing shrieks had only woken me briefly before I fell back into a deep slumber. Once showered and dressed, I decided to make the most of the fact that I was still here.

My Riviera guide book highlighted Cap D'Antibes as being a popular haunt for the rich and famous. Well worth a look then, I reckoned. I began the walk there from Juan-les-Pins so that I could take in the stunning views. En-route I treated myself to breakfast by the beach at a reasonably-priced restaurant, Café de la Plage. A typical French breakfast consisted of a hot drink like café au lait, jus d'orange, croissants and crusty bread with butter and jam. Most delicious and a welcome break from the soggy cereal I scoffed for breakfast on a work day. Work. The thought made me smile and, more precisely, Bernice's horrified expression when I told her I was quitting my job to go to Antibes. Oh, what joy!

I strolled leisurely past the Plage Hotel Ambassador where colourful sun loungers lined the jetty and an impressive steel ship sculpture soared high into a cloudless blue sky. I sat on one of the wide stone benches, taking in the view. Men and women of a certain age were playing a very civilised game of pétanque, sporting V-necked jumpers, navy trousers, white caps and gleaming shoes. Families filled the benches, gazing out at the shoreline eating ice-cream, the occasional suited-and-booted executive striding by.

I continued on past the Hôtel Belle Rives, the huge glass windows affording me a view of the luxurious 1930s interior, as well as the velvet blue of the Mediterranean stretching out into the horizon. The hotel had been visited by none other than Picasso, Edith Piaf and a King Umberto of Italy, so my guidebook informed me. It didn't take much of a leap of the imagination to see what attracted the chic clientele to this part of the world. The glittering Mediterranean accompanied me to my right, and luxurious villas high up on a jagged cliff face to my left. Other private estates were hidden behind huge wrought-iron gates, each holding the faint promise of glitzy Gatsby-style parties, if you were ever deemed high society enough to be allowed entry. F. Scott Fitzgerald certainly had plenty to be inspired by, here in Cap D'Antibes.

The pebbled bay to my right preceded the rippled waves of the sea and I had to stop on several occasions to simply marvel at the glistening yachts bobbing along the water like satin shapes.

I walked a fair distance until I rounded a corner, carrying on uphill until I arrived at a sign saying Eden Roc. My calf muscles were suddenly feeling very weary. Thankfully there was a bus stop ahead with a seating area. I plonked myself down and looked at the timetable. A number 2 bus to Antibes was due about now; I could board that, then take another bus back to the apartment. I didn't have to wait too long before the bus pulled in. I got on and went to pay the driver, but couldn't find my purse. I searched frantically through my bag but there was nothing apart from my bottle of water, can of Coke, bag of crisps, satsuma, mobile phone and map. The bus driver saw I was distressed and starting talking to me in rapid French. He waved me onto the bus. Feeling confused and thinking I might have dropped it, I stumbled off and started looking around. After retracing my steps to the bottom of the hill I decided that it was futile to keep looking.

I couldn't bloody believe it. That purse had my money, flat keys, cards, and a photo of Niles which I had yet to throw away. I stood blinking in the sunshine, wondering what to do. The first thing to do was cancel my cards, but even if I did that, I hardly had any money to last me the day. I was loathe to do it, but felt I had no choice but to ring Chambers. He picked up straight away, sounding surprised. When he heard my tale of woe, he assured me he would get to me as soon as possible.

I stood outside the imposing gates of Hotel du Cap, Eden Roc, waiting for Chambers. The way I had been hurling that canvas bag around, I shouldn't have been surprised that something had dropped out. I was just thankful for the kindness of a woman called Linda who stopped to talk to me as I was walking around in a daze by the bus-stop. Without question, she had believed me and given me the few euros she had in her purse. I thought I had best take it in case Chambers couldn't make it for hours.

He expressed concern on the phone but I figured there would be a good amount of gloating and obnoxiousness to endure if our previous encounter was anything to go by. Still,

I was grateful that he was coming to find me. Minutes later, I saw a man approach from up the hill looking relaxed in his open white shirt and loose grey slacks. It was Chambers.

'Hey, Josie!' he called out, 'what bad luck you've had.' He sounded faintly amused.

'That was quick,' I replied.

'I own a house not far from here.'

'Oh!' I marvelled. He was a millionaire at least, then.

He gave me a brief hug, pushing up his Gucci sunglasses.

'You look a bit rough,' he said, looking me up and down. And there was the real Chambers, back again. 'You really should try being more careful. A woman on her own and everything. Have you cancelled your cards yet?' A hint of his imperious manner came shining through.

Who did he think I was, some kind of numbskull? I felt like a teenager being told off by her father.

'Of course I have!'

'Great, let's have a drink then,' he said, causally pointing at the Hotel du Roc.

'What? In there?' I said, pointing to the palatial-looking building behind me. 'Don't be so ridiculous, surely you have to be royalty to even get a sniff past the driveway?'

'Follow me,' he said, shaking his head and striding purposefully up the gravelled path as if he owned the place. 'You are right though; the Roc does get some very wealthy clientele and well-known celebrities.'

'Really?' I said, my eyes growing wide. 'Like who?'

'George Clooney, Uma Thurman, Gwyneth Paltrow …'.

'Wow!' I swooned, 'have you met any of them?'

'They're just people, Josie.'

Just people. Yeah, right. Just people who happened to hang

out at the Eden Roc where a night's stay probably cost more than my monthly salary.

'But yes, I did chance upon Clooney. It was a couple of years ago. I think it was during the Cannes Film Festival. He was with people at the next table so I didn't want to disturb him,' he said, waving his hand dismissively like it was nothing out of the ordinary.

Oh. My. God. What if he was here today? Oh boy. I hugged myself tightly, imagining the looks of envy and disbelief when I told Babs and Dame that George Clooney and I had hung out together, drinking the finest pink champagne, don't you know?

I wanted to ask Chambers more questions but he was already climbing the shiny white stairs leading to the entrance, where the door was opened promptly by a smart-looking man dressed in a sharp grey suit.

'Monsieur Chambers.'

'Marc.' They nodded at each other.

Blimey. He was as familiar with the staff as they were with him. He must have been here a good few times. I stepped inside and was dazzled by the brightly-lit marble tiled flooring, the white sofas cushioned like an opulent land of marshmallows, and cabinets gleaming with what looked like priceless jewels.

'Oh well,' I thought to myself, 'I might as well enjoy this, it would be rude not to.' The drinks were on Chambers, after all, as I had precisely seven euros to my name. If I had dropped my purse in the sandy cove I passed, or on the road, I doubt it would still be there. Still I didn't feel comfortable being indebted to Chambers and especially not in such luxuriant surroundings.

I hesitated, feeling overawed and uncomfortable. 'Look Chambers, I can't stay here. I've got no money. I should be out there looking for my purse.'

'My driver is already on it. He's just started heading back the way you came. Try and think of everywhere you've been today, from the moment you left your apartment to the moment you discovered your purse missing.'

A driver. Should have guessed. I mentally retraced my steps, which Chambers then relayed to his driver.

'Now, just relax will you?' he commanded, fixing his steely gaze on me. A slow smile spread across his face. I got the impression that he was enjoying my misfortune, only so that he could prove that he was my knight in shining armour.

He led me out onto a terraced area that simply took my breath away with crystal blue views of the coastline. The sun felt pleasant and a gentle breeze played with my hair. There were yet more white cushioned sofas and a gleaming white bar.

'Is Dom Perignon Vintage Rose ok?' Chambers asked.

Ok? I took several gulps of air.

'Yeah. That will do.' I grinned, not quite believing my feet were touching the wooden terrace floor of the appropriately-named Champagne Lounge.

The floating sensation continued as I took a tiny sip of my champagne, the bubbles fizzing pleasingly on my tongue.

'Oooh!' I giggled.

Chambers regarded me with amusement.

'So the egg and chips girl likes a bit of vintage champagne?'

'Rather!' I said, in a posh voice.

He led me onto one of the plush sofas. He looked more relaxed than when we last met; his shirt was casual and open at the neck. He leaned across the table, admiring the views.

'Chambers,' I ventured, 'I don't suppose Tebor has told you much about this painting and why Pru might want me to have it?'

His face clouded over, in sharp contrast to the clear blue sky. He said nothing for a while. He was still clearly touchy about this painting.

'I've got a yacht in Cannes. Tebor is going to be in Cannes tomorrow, so he'll meet us there.'

'Oh good,' I said, feeling relieved. Then taking in what he said, 'You own a *yacht*?' I asked incredulously.

'It's not mine. I'm only renting it for a couple of weeks.'

'Oh' I said, 'bet that didn't come cheap!'

He shrugged.

This man was clueless as to how real people lived. I thought about people struggling to get a foot on the property ladder, or even make ends meet back home.

'So, what do you do for a living?' I asked, looking around for anyone famous. Hmm. Most of the sofas were empty. There was a couple seated a few tables to my left. Both the man and lady had those neat-not-a-hair-out-of-place hairdos, smooth glowing skin and teeth that gleamed when they threw their heads back and laughed. But they were not famous. At least I didn't recognise them.

'I work in the financial sector,' he replied, not elaborating but when he noticed my quizzical expression he said, 'just think Riverian Wallstreet.'

'Interesting,' I replied, trying to sound knowledgeable. I wondered if Dame would hit it off with Chambers, what with them both being in the financial sector? I still thought Chambers was a bit stuck up and there was still something a little dark and brooding about him, but he wasn't nearly as obnoxious as when we first met. Hell, who was I to complain when I was drinking the finest of champagnes at a roof top bar with stunning sea views?

'Are you hungry?'

'No,' I said, feeling alarmed. I could not possibly eat here.

'Fine,' he said, amusement crinkling his face. His phone buzzed. 'Just a minute.'

'My driver. He's found your purse.'

'Really! Where?'

'At the Café de la Plage. You left it on the table, you careless girl!' he chastised. 'You are lucky that the waiter picked it up.'

'I am, and thank god!' I said, sighing with relief but prickling at his tone of voice. 'I just hope no-one took my keys. I don't care about the money, I only had about 20 euros in my purse. Can you ask your driver to check what's in there?'

'The purse isn't at the restaurant.'

'What? I thought you just said ...?'

'A waiter found it and handed it in to the local police, who took it to objets trouvé - basically it's like a lost property office.'

'Right, and where's that?' I asked, wondering why they hadn't just held onto my purse for a while.

'Not far from the Café. My driver is coming back to take us there.'

'Great!' I said, feeling more cheerful. Right, I just need to take a quick photo and then we can go.' I grinned like a Cheshire cat, pointing my phone at myself. Nothing like a shameless selfie in a place like this.

Chambers gave me a *you're so vain* look.

'It's for Facebook,' I told him.

'Not on Instagram?' he asked.

'No. I'm rarely even on Facebook, but this is worth putting up there.'

'Why not get in more of the azure backdrop if it's for Facebook?' he suggested, motioning for me to stand up. 'That's better,' he said, showing me.

I uploaded the images to my account with the caption: 'Day started off with me losing my purse :(... but hello! What's this? I'm now drinking vintage Dom Perignon Rosé at the Hotel du Cap, where famous people hang out :) ps ... purse has now been found. Will fill you in on my return ;)'

I sighed with satisfaction. I'd be the envy of all my friends and relatives, and even my ex-boss was my Facebook friend as I had thought her quite nice when I first started the job. I had never got around to defriending her when I found out what a bitch she was.

Chambers looked down at his phone. 'My driver is outside.'

I finished off my drink, feeling slightly tipsy but pleasantly so. I grinned at Chambers. He was beginning to grow on me, but maybe that was just the champagne talking.

His car was a very rare and exclusive Aston Martin Lagonda, he told me.

'Wow!' I exclaimed, showing that I was suitably impressed.

The ride back was smooth and pleasant, despite the speed at which the driver negotiated the bends.

We were at the objets trouvé in no time and fortunately my purse, keys and cards were all intact. The euros were missing but I wasn't going to quibble.

Unfortunately, I still only had 7 euros to my name as I had cancelled my debit card.

Chambers pulled out 500 euros from his wallet. 'Take it, Josie,' he urged when I hesitated. 'Money's no object.'

'It's too much!' I said, hating the feeling of 'owing' him.

'Fine, I'll give you 300 euros for now as long as you promise to let me know if you need more.'

'On one condition,' I said, 'you let me shout you an ice-cream!' I waved 5 euros in the air.

'Done.' We shook hands and I treated him to a coconut ice-cream which his long tongue devoured in mere seconds. 'Now I really have to run. Got some important business calls to make.'

Business calls. Yeah right. He was probably going for a dip in his oversized, outdoor pool.

'I'll text you about where to meet tomorrow.'

'Cool,' I replied, watching as he slid into the passenger side of the glimmering Aston Martin. The driver tipped his hat at me before he drove off.

Wealth and poise emanated from every aspect of his being. A man like Chambers would have intimidated me in England, I was sure of it. But maybe I wasn't quite so fearful as I believed. Maybe Pru's spirit was well and truly within me. 'Good on you, Pru!' I said to myself.

Feeling all calm and zen-like, I decided to try out a yoga class at the studio next door to the apartment. The notice read that the classes were held in English; they must get a lot of tourists. I was greeted by seven serene smiling faces. 'Good, you are just in time' the ethereal looking teacher told me.

'Please sit cross-legged and we'll begin.'

‚OHMMMMM … OHMMMMM.' The class all chanted in unison.

'Let the loving light surround you, guide your way home,' they all sang in unison.

I resisted the urge to laugh and I really wanted to fart. Maybe a yoga class after half a bottle of Dom Perignon wasn't such a good idea. I hiccupped loudly during a silent moment.

Perhaps I wasn't so zen-like after all. They all smiled indulgently at me, the class clown. Still I made it to the end of the class feeling relaxed and all stretched out.

'I hope you'll come back,' the teacher said as I was about to leave.

'Perhaps,' I said, thinking that I'd be back home soon.

Still I was glad I had given it a go. I got back to the apartment relishing the prospect of a good book, a light supper and an early night, and even feeling a little tingle of excitement by what the next day might bring.

Chapter 16
Yacht In Cannes

CHAMBERS SENT ME A BREEZY text the following morning, inviting me on board The Angelica, his hired yacht. Could that sound any more pretentious? Maybe it was for entertaining pretentious clients. I won't lie, I was kind of keen to see his yacht, but mostly I just wanted to meet Tebor, and see what all the fuss was about over this mysterious painting. He was meeting us there for a lunch of freshly caught mussels. No getting away with egg and chips for me, then.

My first impression of Cannes was that it was clean and refined. Not a drop of litter in sight. Rows of elegant and classy shops lined the streets, including Prada and Armand Thiery. I looked down at my floral dress teamed with my Karen Millen strappy heels. Not very practical, I know, but I had my flip flops in my bag just in case.

I caught a glimpse of the tree-lined promenade and rolling waves of the Mediterranean just ahead of me. La Croisette, the guide book informed me. The kind of place you could wile away the day cycling, rollerblading or simply strolling. The weather was just as it should be, hot but not stifling, with a hint of gentle breeze.

Chambers had instructed me to head to the old port just past the Palais des Festivals, where the Cannes film festival was held each May. I stopped to marvel at the handprints of the famous, including Peter Fleishman, Sharon Stone and (of course) George Clooney, amongst many others.

I spotted a row of yachts further down La Croisette. To my right I saw a clock tower, ruins, and a cluster of old-looking buildings. This had to be the old port, I mused, growing excited as I made out the swirly silver letters of The Angelica.

And there was Chambers, dressed in shorts and T-shirt, waving at me.

'Wow!' I exclaimed, 'You really know how to live it up.' I admired the shiny exterior; the yacht was bigger than I imagined. I climbed onboard.

He showed me through to the lounge and kitchen area. There was an abundance of teak and brass, with plump red velvet cushions. It was either like a very posh brothel or something out of a Barbara Cartland novel. I couldn't decide which.

'It's all I could get at short notice,' Chambers said, noticing my expression.

'It's a bit extravagant but I kind of like it,' I replied.

Chambers chattered on about how hard he had been working, and how he had hired the yacht to take out for a few days – a well-deserved break.

'Tebor should be here soon, so feel free to sunbathe for a bit, or take a dip in the sea.'

'Actually, I've got a bit of a headache. Do you mind if I lie down for a bit?'

'Sure.' He showed me through to a modestly decorated room with a comfortable-looking bed.

'Can I get you anything?' he offered.

'A Perrier, if you've got one, please.'

He poured the water in a glass for me, and left me to rest. Maybe the lack of sleep was catching up with me.

'Wake me up when Tebor arrives?'

He nodded and walked out on deck.

I awoke from my afternoon nap, limbs feeling heavy. I climbed up on deck, the fresh sea breeze reviving my spirits instantly. Chambers appeared to be looking out to sea, his tanned back glistening in the sunlight.

'Not bad, not bad at all,' I appraised, taking in the long muscular legs, the pert behind encased in black trunks and the long sweep of broad back. In fact, 'Cor!'

Whoops, I might have uttered that out loud, as he turned swiftly to me.

'How long have you been perving on me, Josie?' he said with a smile.

'Perving? I was doing no such …!'

But it was hard not to. His dark wet hair gleaming in the sun, his bronzed chest was dripping with water. My eyes inadvertently lowered and then shot up again, a fierce blush hitting my cheeks.

'It's okay. I get that all the time,' he said, towelling himself off.

Oh, so modest.

'You just surprised me, standing there …' I tailed off. 'I was half asleep.'

'How's your head now? Did the sleep help?'

'A little,' I said, still feeling a bit woozy. 'How was the water?'

'Refreshing,' he smiled.

'I may go for a swim myself … looks like a good day for it.'

I looked out at the sea: the waves were thrashing and rocking with some force. Maybe not. And just as well, as my bikini beneath my sundress was a bit on the skimpy side.

'It's a bit rough out there … but perhaps you like it rough? I could always come in with you?' He cocked his head to one side now, looking me up and down.

'No, I'll be fine,' I replied, as a sudden sense of unease swept over me.

'Suit yourself!' He looked amused. 'I'm going for a shower then.'

'What time is it?' I asked.

'Just after 5.'

'After 5?' I shouted. 'Where's Tebor? He was supposed to be meeting us for lunch?'

'He rang earlier to apologise but he had something important to attend to. He's meeting us here for breakfast tomorrow instead, and he's bringing the painting with him,' said Chambers, noticing my horrified expression.

'Why didn't you wake me up when he rang?'

'You looked so peaceful.'

'People usually do when they're asleep,' I replied angrily, feeling my migraine return with full force.

'Don't stress,' he said, shrugging his shoulders. 'You can sleep here tonight.'

I was dumbfounded, beginning to wonder if I would ever

meet this elusive Tebor, or if Chambers had set the whole thing up as a ruse to get me to spend the night with him.

'You don't need to worry, I won't bite.' He looked arrogant, smug, like he was enjoying this. 'Come on, Josie. It's not like you've got anything better to do, so grab some food and soak up some sun. You must be famished.'

With that, he headed off to shower.

I looked out at the turbulent sea. Chambers must have sailed a fair distance while I was asleep, we were some way from land. I was in the middle of nowhere with Chambers. A complete stranger to me until a couple of days ago. I wanted to go back to Juan-les-Pins. No, I wanted to go back home, to England, but would he let me go? A horrible realisation was starting to take form. What if Chambers was part of the French Mafia? What if this painting was so precious that he would do anything to stop me getting my hands on it? What if he had engineered this whole thing to have his way with me? What if he had psychopathic tendencies and his plan was to throw me overboard?

I couldn't believe I agreed to meet him on his yacht. I had read countless stories of young women being lured by men on holiday, then drugged and raped, or worse. Old Josie would never have agreed to it. England Josie was safe and sensible. What had I let myself in for? I retrieved my mobile from my pocket. No signal. Great. Not a soul knew where I was. A sudden jolt of fear and panic cut through my veins like an icicle.

I clasped my hands together. 'God, if you are listening, please tell me what to do. Please god. PLEASE!'

'Josie?'

'Ahh!' I screamed, almost falling overboard.

'What are you doing?' Chambers was standing behind me in a pair of tight shorts.

'Isn't it obvious?' I said, my heart beating faster than a drum.

'It looked like you were praying.' He began walking towards me.

I pushed myself against the railings, my mind racing.

'You are trembling.' He sounded concerned. 'You don't look well at all. Maybe you should lie down some more?' He moved closer towards me.

'Get AWAY from ME!' I shouted.

He stopped in his tracks.

'What is wrong with you?' He sounded cross.

'You set this up didn't you? Tebor's not coming, is he? How do I know you're even Tebor's grandson? And I want to go home. Let me off this yacht at once!'

He didn't say anything for a while. 'You really don't trust me, do you?'

'Why should I?'

'I suppose you are right,' he conceded, sighing. 'I'll ring Tebor right now and get him to explain everything. Would that help?'

'Yes, I think it might.'

Chambers pulled out his iPhone from his shorts pocket. At least some networks had reception. I really would have to invest in a new phone when I got home.

Thankfully he got through to Tebor almost immediately. 'Grandad, I know you are busy but Josie really needs to talk to you.' He paused, listening. 'I'll just put her on.'

'Hello?' My voice was shaky. A resonant, well-spoken voice spoke back with a French twang. 'Josie, I am très désolé. I let you down. Twice now. The first time I guess old age and ill health is to blame, now I've had some family business to attend to urgently. I do hope Chambers has been treating you well.'

I was still alive so I guess that was something. 'He has,' I confirmed.

'I wanted to give the painting to you in person, I wanted to explain what it meant to me. Pru wanted me to explain things.'

'I don't understand what there is to explain?' I faltered.

'If you could be patient just once more and I promise everything will make sense.'

'So you are definitely coming tomorrow morning?'

'Yes. At nine in the morning. I will bring breakfast and the painting.'

We talked for a few more minutes. He told me how he had moved to the South of France after his mum had met and fallen in love with a Frenchman.

'Bertrand and I loved it here. The schools were good, the climate was favourable and the girls were charming, but no one stole his heart until Pru. She was holidaying in Antibes with some friends. Bert knew instantly that she was The One. He moved to England to be with her. They came back sometimes, but then no more.' His voice tailed off. 'Anyway,' he concluded brightly, 'We'll catch up tomorrow and … don't worry, I will be there.'

I don't know how good my instincts were or if I trusted them, but I had a good feeling about Tebor. I believed him.

'By the way, I know Chambers is a bit of a rogue, he has how do you say an eye for the ladies, but I promise you that you are safe with him.' He hung up.

I guess I had no choice but to trust Chambers. I could always go back to the apartment and come back tomorrow, but after my initial terror of being with Chambers, I felt somewhat reassured. Talking to Tebor had helped. Maybe I should try to get to know him better. I decided to quiz him a bit over supper.

'Have you ever been married, Chambers?'

'Why would I want to do that?' He looked genuinely puzzled. 'Women are more trouble than they're worth.'

'Have you had your heart broken?' I asked.

'No. Not particularly. I've dated a few women over the years, but I'm too busy to settle down, and women are far too complicated and temperamental for my liking.' I had a feeling that he was directing that comment at me, but that was hardly fair, considering we'd only just met.

'So, you are more the heartbreaker?'

'No, not really.' He shrugged his shoulders in a non-committal fashion.

'What's *your* story, Josie?' he asked, deflecting the attention away from himself.

I regaled him with the whole sorry Niles saga, as well some of my other disastrous relationship tales.

'Forget relationships or marriage and just have some fun for a change,' was his advice.

'I've already decided that I'm better off man-free,' I quipped.

He then spoke a lot about his younger sister Grace who was abroad in New York, studying fashion. It was clear that he was really protective towards her, a bit like Ant was towards me. He loved living in the South of France, it was the only life he knew after all, yet his French was only 'mediocre'.

'Our clients are mostly English and Japanese so I haven't had much reason to converse in French,' he explained. He also mentioned that he sometimes flew to New York or London for business.

Chambers opened a bottle of wine and put on some music, a compilation CD by the sounds of it. We continued talking about our respective lives. It was clear that the mood had shifted.

'Are you having a good time, Josie?' His dark penetrating eyes searched mine while fingering the rim of his wine glass. He drained some more of the dark red liquid, licking his lips, his stare intensifying. I squirmed in my seat, suddenly feeling an irrepressible need to giggle. I clapped a hand over my mouth but couldn't contain it any longer, peels of laughter erupted from me and once I started I couldn't stop.

'I'm glad you find me so amusing.' Chambers lips set hard in a line.

God, he was so serious! Sexy and seductive, damn hot in his Speedos, but so very serious with it that somehow I found it hard to take him seriously. I tried contorting my face into a picture of sternness, but this only made me laugh harder.

Chambers eyes were flashing angrily at me. 'You are the most infuriating creature I have ever come across!' he hissed.

Creature. He really was something out of Dynasty or Downton Abbey.

Laughter contained, I looked at Chambers with curiosity. He was a striking man with his jet-black hair and coal eyes, and very charming with it. Most definitely a catch for any discerning woman. I'm sure he had flocks of women throwing themselves at him and wasn't in the habit of getting turned down too frequently, yet I had no desire to impress him in any way. It dawned on me in wonderment that I had achieved what I had wanted since my split with Niles. Oblivion. I didn't need Chambers to love me, or even fancy me. It was one thing to tell everyone I was on a man-break, but to actually be putting it into practice was something else. With that I sprang off my seat.

'Let's dance, Chambers! I love this song!' The hum of Artic Monkeys filled the room.

I bounced around the room with joy, gleeful liberation suffusing every cell in my body.

Chambers shuffled his feet awkwardly.

'Just let go, let the rhythm move you,' I shouted above the music.

'I've not consumed nearly enough alcohol for that, Josie,' he said, falling back on the sofa.

'You don't need alcohol!' I tried pulling him back up. 'Look at me! I'm drunk on life!' I chorused, flinging my arms and legs around with abandon

'Clearly.'

'Come on, you're the one who said I should be having fun. What about you?' I encouraged, trying to get him to throw his hair back a bit. 'Now that I've got over thinking you're a murderer or rapist, I am kind of enjoying myself,' I laughed.

'Are you sure I can be trusted?' he leaned into me.

'I don't know for sure, but I'm not afraid to knee you in the nuts should you try anything inappropriate,' I said confidently.

'Oh, and by the way. The reason I didn't get my bikini on earlier was that it's like the Amazon jungle down there,' I said, pointing to my lady parts. 'Haven't bothered with a Brazilian in weeks. And when I bend over my stomach rolls over my thighs.' I patted my slightly protruding belly.

Chambers frowned.

This was so much fun. Chambers was beginning to view me in the most unflattering light possible and I was on a roll.

'This morning, actually on most mornings, I shave my chin hairs off with my Bic razor. It's really quick,' I said enthusiastically. 'And …' pausing dramatically for effect, 'I'd take a cup of Earl Grey and a chocolate Hobnob over a bonk on most days.'

Oooh, I was having so much fun! Too much fun to listen to that tiny voice telling me that I might fancy him just a little.

'Feel better for that, do you?' Chambers regarded me impassively. 'You only had to say if you didn't want to sleep with me.'

'But everything I said was true!' I said earnestly.

'Just for the record, you can have biscuits AND bonk, it doesn't have to be one or the other,' he said. 'I'm going to bed.' He paused, I think still half hoping that I would join him. 'Your door has a lock on it, so don't worry. You really are safe from me.'

'Good night, Chambers.'

'Go knock yourself out with tea and biscuits then,' he said, sloping off to bed.

Yeah!' I said, punching the air, thinking about the film 'How To Lose A Guy in 10 Days'. 'How to lose a guy in 10 minutes' more like, I thought to myself with a certain amount of pride and satisfaction.

***

Just as Josie was drifting off feeling pleased with herself, a few miles away Tebor was feeling anything but. He had tried to prepare himself for this meeting and imagined what he might say, but his mind was blank.

His wife spoke:

'Don't worry, things will work themselves out. You've punished yourself for far too long.'

'I know,' he smiled sadly. 'I'm so lucky that I found you and I'm blessed with beautiful children and grandchildren, but every time I tried to forget about her I couldn't. Now she's gone and I never got the chance with Emilie.'

Tebor let out a huge sigh, his shoulders sagging downwards. The past had caught up with him. So many thoughts and memories consumed his mind. He felt as if his heart was breaking all over again. He didn't know how he was going to explain himself.

Chapter 17
Secrets Revealed

MEANWHILE ED WAS ALSO IN a reflective mood. He read the letter once more:

14 April 2013

Dear Ed,

If you are reading this letter then it means, well, you know what it means. Hopefully I've died peacefully in my sleep as I always imagined and not in a crumpled, morbid mess. I know you are going to be feeling sad and shocked, but If truth be told, I've been dreaming of Bert for the past 6 weeks. His skin is translucent, his hair all wild and he's beckoning me into a flower-filled field. That's where I want you to imagine me, Ed.

Maybe I have been having a few aches and pains and feeling more tired of late, but I didn't want to worry you. I just put it down to age, my rich diet and indulgent lifestyle. How many 87-year olds do you know who party with their bingo friends into the early hours?

Ed – I love you so much. You have made me so happy. Getting to know you again in these last few months has brought me greater joy than you will ever know.

But there is something I haven't told you; I should have told you sooner but I didn't know how.

A long time ago I went to Antibes in the South of France. It's where I met Bert. It really was love at first sight. He moved to England to be with me, and every year we went back to the South of France to visit his family. One time we decided to stay in Antibes for almost a year, living with his brother Tebor. Both brothers couldn't have been more different. Bert, as you know, was gregarious and outgoing. Tebor was a bit of a recluse, a brooding local artist. Everything was great to begin with, but then Bert seemed to change overnight. He was subdued one minute, volatile the next. I just couldn't understand it and felt hurt every time he pushed me away. I didn't know it as the time, but Bert had been getting terrible migraines and he thought it might be something serious. He later found out through tests and scans that it was a benign cyst which they treated, but I wish he had shared what he was going through with me, but you know your grandad, stubborn and proud.

Things changed when I became pregnant with your mum. Bert was overjoyed and cheerful again. He asked

Tebor to paint the three of us, the burgeoning family he called us. I couldn't continue with a lie after that, because the truth was that I had slept with Tebor and fallen pregnant. I knew it was his because the dates fitted, and Bert and I had been trying for a baby for the previous two years with no success. I could say that Tebor took advantage and seduced me when I was vulnerable, he even tried to convince me that Bert was the one having an affair, but I shouldn't have been so weak. I regretted it instantly. It must have killed Tebor too, because he went into a kind of delirium after that. He didn't quite cut off his ear (like Van Gogh) but I think he was heading that way.

Bert was distraught, but he was willing to forgive me and give our relationship a go back in England, and raise Emilie together. He assured Tebor that when the time was right she would be told the truth. Tebor, however, became demented. He didn't understand that I loved Bert and that our brief encounter had been a mistake, at least for me.

I tried to include him in Emilie's life. I sent him updates, said he could come and visit. He did visit a couple of times, and she knew him as her 'uncle Teb' but he seemed so consumed with pain that he stopped getting in touch. Emilie never found out the truth. And then it was too late. I do regret that. It was sad they never really got to know each other.

Tebor did turn his life around though, and he is doing well now. He still lives in Antibes. I know you are going to think this strange, but I'd like you to visit him, get to know him. He did wrong, but he's not all bad. There is also something I'd like you to collect from him, he will tell you what you have to do with it.

I have enclosed an air ticket in a separate envelope. I hope you are not too angry with me, Ed. I was young and foolish, but Bert and I were soulmates. The funny thing is that our relationship grew stronger after my indiscretion. We were there for each other until his final days. And now we will be together forever more.

May your life be long and happy.

All my love, always
Granny Pru xxxx

Ed folded up the letter, his body racked with huge sobs, his mind reeling. He couldn't believe that she had carried these secrets around with her. Had she shared them with anyone else? Definitely not with his mum, who never knew the truth about her father. It was something of a shock, to say the least.

'Indiscretion.' That's what Gran had called it. He couldn't imagine Gran using that word, let alone committing an 'indiscretion.' The whole tone of the letter didn't seem like her, yet it was. It was as if she was being guarded, careful, scared of being judged. But who was he to judge? Going off the rails after his mum died hadn't been part of his master plan. He pictured his mum: beautiful, fair haired, gentle and proud of him. Her eyes shone when she told her friends that her son was going to university and that he could do anything he set his mind to.

Why did she have to die? She had been hit by a drunk driver one night after her waitressing shift. The speed he was going at, she never stood a chance. Yet he lived and she died.

Getting shit-faced on drugs was his response to his mum's death. His dad hauled him off to an Australian bootcamp detox that turned his life around, but at what price? Hadn't he abandoned his gran when she needed him the most? He had stayed in Australia because he couldn't face coming back home.

Ed also thought about his grandad who, in his heart and mind, was Bert. He was the one who had been there for him, growing up. He came to visit him in Australia five years ago. Maybe the travel and exhaustion had completely done him in, because he died of a massive heart attack two weeks into his trip. Gran had warned him not to go as he had already had a scare and the cardiac doctors told him to take it easy, to cut out the rich food and get some exercise. But did he listen? No-one could have stopped him getting on that plane. Stubborn as a goat, she told him. Still, it laid heavily on Ed's heart.

Ed shuddered at the memory. Losing people he loved didn't get any easier.

And what was he going to do about his 'real' grandad in France? Pru wanted them to meet, so he figured he should go. But he was hardly relishing the prospect of meeting this stranger. A man who by the sounds of it had lied and deceived to get his own way. Maybe it was a good thing that he wasn't involved in Mum's life, he sounded like a bit of a nut job in all honesty. And what was this about collecting something from him? Why was Gran being so cryptic?

Ed got through his gran's funeral somehow and her desire to have people dancing as was her way. (She enclosed a separate letter with her funeral instructions). Ed learned that Pru had filled his brother in on all of the secrets and lies too. Melvin had no interest though in getting to know his 'real' grandad; he scarcely had time for the grandad he grew up with. All Melvin seemed interested in was how little he was left with in the will. Even though Gran had left Melvin more money than Ed, Ed had been given the flat which made Melvin more bitter than if he'd been sucking a bowl full of lemons.

'Everything should have been split evenly,' he fumed at the time, but then discovering that his son had been left a rather generous trust fund made things suddenly more palatable.

***

Back at home, Josie's mum, Dixie Green, opened her front door humming to herself. She spotted a black box. She picked it up and took it inside, carefully lifting the lid open. Wrapped in pink tissue paper was a small wooden Japanese doll dressed in a red kimono. She'd always wanted to go to Japan. They had been meaning to go, but then work got in the way, then the kids came along. They never had found the time to go.

***

Three weeks after his gran's funeral Ed found himself in the South of France, nervous at the prospect of meeting Tebor. What would he say to him? It pained him to think of the suffering that his gran had endured over the years because of what she had done with Tebor. He had taken advantage of her vulnerability and had betrayed his own brother. He had spoken with Tebor on the phone a week ago to confirm that he was coming out to France; the man had broken down in tears when Ed told him that Gran had passed away. He said it confirmed what he had been expecting, because he too had received a letter. She had said her goodbyes and wrote that she felt the time for her to go was close.

Now he found himself sitting opposite Tebor in his hotel lobby bar in Cannes. Tebor was nervously folding his hands in his lap, sweating slightly, which was understandable considering the heat. He was very tanned with a head of silver-grey hair and looked younger than his age, which must have been around the eighty-five mark.

When he spoke it was in quiet, well-spoken tones with a hint of a French accent, asking if he could get Ed a drink. He was not what Ed had expected at all. He'd expected someone arrogant and cocky, who he would hate on first sight, but the man looked a little frail with a slight stoop, something he only noticed when he walked over to the bar.

He certainly looked very different to his grandad Bert, who was robust, hearty, loud and a bit bonkers.

'Gran told me everything,' Ed said when Tebor returned with the drinks.

Tebor sighed. 'You must detest me.' Ed said nothing.

'Bert had everything going for him. Good at school, good at sports, great with the girls. He also had the sort of personality that made people take notice: funny, charming and kind. I was jealous. Bitterly jealous. I tried not to be, but I was.'

'So you slept with his wife?'

'I fell in love immediately. She was Oh la la, but Bert saw her too and naturally she went for him. I didn't intend to get between them but when I saw that they were having troubles, I was angry with him for disappointing her. I wanted to be there for Pru.'

'You made her think he was having an affair, and you manipulated her. That was despicable.' Ed spat the words out.

'I felt so ashamed of myself, but I couldn't help it. I took any chance I could to be with Pru. I'm not proud of what I did, Ed.'

Hearing about their 'affair' turned Ed's stomach. He made it sound more significant than the 'indiscretion' described in Gran's letter. He gulped down his beer, hoping to get this meeting over with and return to England as soon as possible.

'She mentioned something I have to collect?'

'I did love her, I swear,' Tebor said, his eyes misting over. He reached his hand over to Ed's.

'It wasn't easy knowing that I had lost Pru. Knowing that I could never really be part of Pru's and my daughter's life, not in the way that I truly wanted. That destroyed me. I couldn't bear it, so yes, I did go a little crazy but at least now, finally, I've been able to meet you. One part of a family that I thought I'd lost forever.'

Ed thought about his mum and felt a lump fill his throat and chest. He looked at the man in front of him, his grandad.

'I can't pretend that this is going to be happy families. This has all been a huge shock to me, so maybe for now if I collect whatever it is Gran wanted me to collect and we'll see after that. Gran said that you would instruct me on what to do next.'

Tebor nodded solemnly and for a while they both sat in silence, drinking their beers.

He then took out a clean white handkerchief from his pocket and laid it on the table.

He carefully unwrapped it to reveal a necklace. Now Ed was more confused than ever. He looked at the purple-blue stone that hung on the silver chain. He held it up to the light, marvelling at the intensity of colours and the different greens - and even black - that shone when he held it up to the light.

'It was your Gran's. A tanzanite pendant. I gave it to her as a present, but she left it behind.'

The jewel was dazzling. He could imagine Gran looking absolutely divine with this glittering number adorning one of those evening dresses she had so loved to wear. But he couldn't understand what he was supposed to do with it.

'This is for me?' Ed asked.

'She wants you to give it to someone.'

'What?' Ed thought he hadn't heard correctly.

'That's right. You are meeting them tomorrow at 7pm in Cess Café in Monaco. The address is in this envelope. He handed Ed a faded cream envelope.

'Who am I meeting?' Ed asked.

'That will be made clear when you get there.'

'I don't see how. Did she give you a description of this person? And why would she send me all the way here to pick up a necklace to give to someone else?' Ed's brows were furrowed in confusion.

'Just be patient, Ed. All will make sense soon enough.' With that, he patted Ed's hand and stood up. 'If you don't mind, I need to retire for the night. I've taken the liberty of booking you a room here for the night. If you would like to meet for lunch tomorrow, this is my card.'

Tebor handed Ed a white card with his name printed in small neat typeface, along with his his contact number.

He excused himself and left Ed to brood. What had his gran been thinking?

Ed continued staring at the necklace. Could he trust Tebor? It looked like he hadn't much choice. Gran had made it clear in the letter that Tebor would tell him what to do next.

Ed slept badly that night, despite lying on a comfortable

double bed topped with the softest of duvets in a room that was well air-conditioned. He was hoping to talk to Tebor over an early continental breakfast but could hardly touch his cheese and ham croissant. He looked up in nervous anticipation every time someone entered the breakfast room. He wanted to know about Tebor's life since he had last seen Gran. Had he gone on to marry? Did he have children? Grandchildren? Was he really repentant about what happened with Gran? By the time the last breakfaster had left the dining area, Ed wasn't sure if he did want to know. Perhaps it was just best that he just meet whoever he was supposed to meet, and then go home. That didn't stop him enquiring after Tebor with the hotel receptionist, only to discover that he had already checked out. Ed looked at his watch. 10am. He tried Tebor's mobile phone but it went straight to voicemail.

***

The moment had arrived. I spotted him approaching, a dapper-looking man with white hair slicked back with hair oil, I presumed. He had a slight crook to his spine but looked healthy and tanned, holding a black cane in one hand and a large canvas bag in the other.

'Grandad!' Chambers called out, grinning broadly.

I could see a slight resemblance in their smiles. I wondered if Tebor had also been a rogue in his time. Although Chambers, to his credit, had been the perfect gentleman last night.

'Josie, Josie, Josie, enchanté!' Tebor greeted me like I was a long-lost friend, hugging me to his chest and kissing me on both cheeks.

'I was beginning to wonder if I would ever get to meet you,' I smiled up at him.

'Again, my apologies. I did want to meet you in Antibes, but had the most terrible cough, my health isn't what it used to be,' he said, clearing his chest to illustrate the point. 'Then a little business cropped up yesterday. Anyway, I have breakfast as promised,' he said, waving the bag. 'Ham, cheese, croissants and the most perfect pastries.'

'I also have the painting,' he said, noting my expectant expression. 'But breakfast first, if you don't mind.'

I had waited this long, so a few more minutes wouldn't do any harm. We breakfasted out on deck. The weather was perfect as always, but I had a feeling that it was going to be a roasting hot day, come midday.

'I trust you slept well,' Tebor asked, his eyes twinkling as he looked at me and Chambers. I couldn't help blushing at the implication, even though nothing had happened.

'Like a log,' I said.

'You know me, Grandad. I do everything I can to ensure my guests are comfortable,' Chambers added with a smile.

'About the painting,' I said, changing the subject. 'I'm really surprised that Pru would leave it to me. Can you shed any light on that?'

Tebor laid back in his chair, tilting his face up to the sunlight and remained silent for a while.

I sure hoped he was wearing sufficient sun protection factor otherwise he might wind up looking like a lobster.

'Before I show you the painting there's something you should know.' Tebor let out a long deep sigh and his shoulders slumped over; he suddenly seemed to age fifteen years.

'No. On second thoughts I'll show you the painting first and then explain ....'

The painting was roughly the same size as my bathroom

mirror, wrapped in brown paper with white string. He delicately unwrapped the painting and laid it on the table.

It was an oil painting of Bert and Pru in front of a cypress tree that Antibes was famous for, with a hint of blue sea behind them. Bert had one arm around Pru's shoulders and the other hand placed protectively on her slightly-protruding stomach. The painting was clearer than the faded photos Pru had showed me of the two of them. There was a fixed intensity in their gaze which the painter had captured well. Pru was wearing a beautiful long blue dress, which I imagined was made of velvet. She wore the most striking necklace which caught the sunlight. Bert was wearing a pale suit and looked strong and handsome. I took a deep breath. The painting was exquisite.

'It's stunning!' I said. 'You said you would explain?'

Tebor's face grew visibly distressed, and he began:

'I painted this. I painted them but it should have been me with her,' he said sadly, delicately traced the outline of Pru's stomach in the painting. 'That baby was mine.' With that revelation he broke down, crying. Chambers cradled him.

I waited with baited breath.

When he didn't continue after a while, I spoke again.

'You were with Pru before she met Bert?' I asked, confused.

'We had an affair.' He spoke so softly I almost didn't hear him.

'But that can't be?' I said. 'She was devoted to Bert, they were married for fifty-five long happy years. She told me herself,' I said, incredulously.

That's all true,' replied Tebor, fatigue etched into his face. 'But we had a moment, more than a moment, when I made her believe that Bert was having an affair. She turned to me for comfort. I took advantage, but I loved her. I really did.'

Silence.

'She left this painting behind. It tormented her, knowing that she had deceived Bert when the picture was painted. I've treasured it ever since, even though it made me feel bad. I loved seeing the swell of my child in her belly.'

'Then keep it. I don't want the painting,' I whispered, upset.

'It was important to her that you have it. That you knew the truth, that she wasn't perfect. That love wasn't always easy.'

He shook his head smiling fondly. 'Reality was too hard for her, and it was for me also.'

I shook my head, unable to reconcile the Pru that I knew and loved with what I had just heard. My heart suddenly felt frozen.

She had been my love inspiration. I had wanted a relationship just like hers, but the truth was she had cheated. Just like Niles had, just like my previous fiancé had, just like my dad probably had.

Tears were swimming in front of my eyes. I bolted the yacht as fast as I could.

Let him keep the damn painting. I didn't care about the £25K waiting for me at home.

I heard both Chambers and Tebor call out to me, but my brain was numb with shock. I needed to get away. Ideally, far away from everyone.

Chapter 18

Cess Café at 7pm, Monaco

I WALKED ALONG THE PROMENADE, MY head spinning like I had just come off a waltzer at a fair. All of my life I had been with someone.

My first boyfriend was David Jenkins. We were both six years old; he was short for his age so had to jump up to kiss me. He was only too pleased when I asked him to carry my satchel, coat, and anything else that needed carrying. It made him happy, so who was I to argue? But I soon got tired of his dog-like devotion, so I dumped him for James, who was seven years old. He was strong and tall for his age, but it all went wrong after that. Instead of being the dumper, I became the dumpee - right up until my final dumping by Niles. I guess I technically dumped him after finding him in that compromising position I couldn't bear to think about. That hurt. That hurt like hell. Yesterday I didn't think about him. Yesterday I actually felt good about being on my own. Now I felt hurt and betrayed by Pru too. Why set me these challenges that had me facing my fears and feeling good about myself, only to knock me down? I was finding it hard to believe she had sent me to France just for this.

Pru had told me how Bert made her laugh, dance, and skip with joy; they were soul-mates, she'd said. If that was the case, how could she have believed Tebor and given in to temptation so easily?

Despite everything, it seemed that Bert had forgiven her. Or had he punished her in some way? How difficult must it have been to raise his brother's child? Yet Pru spoke about their love like it had been a fairytale. Maybe that's what she had to believe to get through it. Maybe in her last years all she could remember were the good times. I smiled as I remembered the misty morning a few months ago when I saw her dancing the foxtrot with an imaginary Bert; she looked so dreamy. Now I would never get the opportunity to ask her about her life with Bert.

I wondered if Ed knew. Is that what Pru's letter to him had been about? If he knew, would he want to come here and meet his grandad? Suddenly I wished that I could talk to him. Have him here with me, to help make sense of it all.

***

Ed paced around the promenade mindlessly. Granted it was beautiful, but he felt restless. He forced himself to sit on a bench and people-watch. Glamour and wealth permeated the streets, from the little pooches on silver-studded leads to their owners who bore an uncanny resemblance to their pets. Tebor had called, inviting him to lunch back at the hotel. The terrace views were spectacular and the food delicious, he'd added. Ed's stomach churned. He wasn't sure if he could hold anything down. He considered going to the Matisse museum, but knew that wouldn't stop the obtrusive thoughts running through his head. Namely, why had Gran *really* sent him all the way here, if only to give this damn necklace to someone else? Had she really wanted him to get to know his biological grandad?

Ed wasn't sure how he felt about that, getting to know his 'new' grandad. A little before 2pm he headed back to the hotel. Tebor had sounded a bit strange on the phone. The air-conditioning was a welcome relief when he stepped in to the cool hotel lobby. Tebor was already there, looking dapper with a black cane and slicked back hair.

He grinned at Ed, showing off pearly white teeth. 'I hope you slept well and had a good morning, Ed.'.

'I had too much on my mind to sleep well. Still I can't complain, it's amazing here,' replied Ed, gesturing around the lobby.

Tebor smiled, but he looked on edge.

They went up to the terrace for lunch and the views were as spectacular as Tebor had promised. Ed gazed out towards the beach, not really knowing what to say. 'So, I think Gran wanted me to get to know you …' he began.

'And what do you want?' Tebor regarded him thoughtfully.

'I suppose it would help to know a bit about you, about your life.'

'Well, I married Jacqueline a few years after Pru left. She's a wonderful woman; I love her dearly. I was lucky to find her after Pru. I don't deserve her, I suppose,' he said, sighing. 'Anyway, I went on to have a family of my own: my daughter, Beth, and my son, Luc. Beth is sadly unable to have children, but Luc has two, Chambers and Grace, so I have been blessed.'

He took out a handkerchief, wiping his forehead. 'I never

forgot about Pru or my daughter. Pru included me in Emilie's life; she sent me photos and updates and I visited her a few times but she only ever knew me as her uncle. It killed me not to say anything, or see her more often. I kind of went mad, to be honest. She absolutely worshipped Bert, and he was a great dad to her.'

Tebor looked down at the floor.

'And then it was too late to get to know her because she was gone.' He said this gesticulating with his hands as if she had just vanished in a puff of smoke.

'She was an angel,' Ed said, thinking of the sweet forgiving woman that had been his mother. 'An angel who was killed mindlessly and needlessly.'

Tebor broke down in a stream of tears, years of anguish pouring out of him. Ed felt awkward and didn't know what to do. He settled for placing his hand on Tebor's hand which was laying on the table.

They sat in silence for a few minutes as Tebor wiped away his tears.

'I last saw Pru at Bert's funeral, but she hardly acknowledged me. I ruined everything with everyone.' He looked completely broken. Ed looked at him. The poor bastard had suffered enough.

'I'm here,' Ed said. 'You've got your family - and I'm here, too.'

Tebor smiled at him gratefully, still wiping away his tears.

Tebor placed a brown parcel on the table, gently unwrapping what was inside. It was the painting Gran had told him about.

Ed gasped. 'Is that …?'

'Pru and Bert, and my daughter. Your mum,' he said, gesturing to Pru's bump.

Ed stared in wonderment, delicately touching the swollen stomach in the painting

'It's incredible,' he breathed.

'I'm not sure Josie felt quite the same way about it.'

'How do you know …?' asked Ed in amazement.

'She's here. I met her, earlier today. Pru wanted her to have the painting, but actually I think she intended you both to have it.' He was smiling now. 'She was always so mischievous.'

'What are you talking about?'

'I shouldn't really be telling you this, Pru would be so cross, but it's Josie who you are meeting at Cess Café tonight. My grandson Chambers will make sure she gets there. You are going to give her the tanzanite necklace,' he said, as if it all made perfect sense.

Meeting Josie … Cess Café? Tanzanite necklace? 'Wait, isn't that the same necklace that Gran was wearing in the painting?'

Tebor nodded, laughing now.

'That Pru is a crafty woman, she's got her plans for you … for the both of you.' He raised his glass of red to the air. 'To Pru, you mischievous minx.'

***

Chambers was striding towards me and didn't look best pleased. Oh god, I really wasn't in the mood.

'Why did you run off like that?' he asked.

'Maybe I'm in shock,' I said, feeling annoyed that he couldn't just let me be.

'Wouldn't you be, after hearing all that?'

He shrugged his shoulders in that infuriating way he seemed to have.

'Grandad's a good bloke.'

'You would say that. I don't want the stupid painting! Let him keep it. Like he said, it's all he has left of her.'

I stopped in my tracks suddenly, turned to face the beach and plonked myself in the sand unceremoniously.

'Did he really love Pru? It clearly didn't take him too long to move on, get married, have children.'

'What other choice did he have?' Chambers replied. 'Pru wanted to be with Bert and Grandad felt horribly guilty for the grief he put everyone through.'

I sat hugging my knees.

'Him feeling bad doesn't make things alright,' I said harshly. 'I really want to be on my own, if you don't mind.'

He sat beside me on the sand, not understanding the concept of me wanting to be on my own. I said nothing. He said nothing. We just sat.

'You've been through a lot, Josie,' he said eventually. 'With your ex, your job and your life, not knowing what to do next. It's not surprising this is all a bit much.'

'I guess I've never known what to do next,' I said. 'Even being here was decided by Pru. I used to think that I had it all figured out. Get married, have a family, live a happy life. You know, that kind of thing.'

'The thing with life is that sometimes it's full of twists and turns, falling in the mud then getting back up again. It's not knowing what happens next that makes life interesting. Just look at Pru and Bert, and Grandad.' He paused, perhaps thinking this wasn't the best example to illustrate his point.

'A lot of mistakes were made and believe me, Grandad is

sorry, more than you'll ever know. Despite his love for all of us, this has eaten him up inside, but it's time he let go of the past.'

I let his words wash over me, feeling a little more comforted. Finding out about Pru made me feel like I was going backwards, but then I remembered being up in that hot air balloon, having that different perspective of letting life unfold without trying to control it. Exactly what Chambers was alluding to. He was actually quite wise when he wasn't being such a grumpy git.

'Thanks Chambers.' I smiled warmly at him.

'Pru *did* want you to have that painting and my grandad is ready to let it go.'

'Guess I should go get it from him then and get back to my life back home,' I said, getting up off the sand.

'I spoke to Grandad earlier. I think he's a bit shaken up by this, can you collect the painting from him tomorrow?'

'So, what am I supposed to do today?'

'Let me drive you to Monaco?'

'Monaco?' I said, bewildered. 'Why?'

'Because it's really cool there. Full of glitz and glamour like you've never seen before. I've made us a dinner reservation at Cess Café for 7pm.'

'Why would you do that?' My nerves jangled. I know he just said something about life not being straightforward but why couldn't anyone in his family be straightforward?

'I can't go, I've got nothing to wear for starters.'

'Tebor's fixed that. Do you remember the dress Pru was wearing in the painting? Well, she wanted you to have it. Tebor left it back on the yacht. I think it will fit perfectly!' he grinned, looking me up and down.

'I don't know if I would feel right wearing that dress. Besides, wouldn't it be all old and moth-eaten by now?'

After a moment, I stood up abruptly. 'No. It's not going to work,' I said.

'What's not going to work?'

'This whole Monaco seduction routine. You lucked out with me last night, so you want another go.'

'Will you get over yourself?' he said, a familiar arrogance creeping in to his voice. 'If I had really wanted to seduce you, you wouldn't stand a chance.' He looked at me smugly.

'Come on,' he commanded, 'back to the yacht.'

I thought about storming off in the opposite direction but within seconds I meekly followed him. I didn't want to admit it to anyone but he exuded a powerful masculine presence that hadn't affected me (much) last night, but now I was finding it disturbingly sexy. Maybe I was just rattled after finding out about Pru and Bert? How could I believe in love again? Maybe a harmless flirtation was just what I needed. I shook away the thought and decided that a catnap on the yacht would do me wonders.

I slept as soon as my head hit the pillow. The shock of what I heard today had clearly exhausted me. I woke up a few hours later feeling perkier and grabbed a Perrier from the fridge. Pru's dress was hanging up behind the door. Midnight blue velvet: it was exquisite. Despite feeling odd about wearing Pru's dress I slipped it on. It hugged my body like a glove. With any luck I might actually be able to do the zipper up. I struggled to reach round the back, arms all over the place, trying to reach for the zip.

'Let me help with that.' Chambers stood in the doorway. I gasped, not knowing how long he had been standing there.

He walked over to me slowly, pausing before he delicately pulled up the zip. He seemed to be taking his time. I felt my spine tingle as his fingers brushed onto my skin.

I turned around to face him.

'Breathtaking,' he whispered, looking down at me in awe. His dark eyes burned into mine. Despite my downright defiance and resolve last night, I felt myself weakening. He moved closer to me, placing his hands either side of my waist, stroking the soft velvet fabric. Last night I had been totally immune to his charms but now, as he stood opposite me in his charcoal suit, touching me in that way, I felt my insides liquidising. His eyes took on a raw hunger matching my own but suddenly he pulled away from me.

'Damn,' he said, looking furious. 'I have to get you to Monaco.'

'We could always do something else?' I suggested, mildly alarmed by his sudden change in temperament.

'No!' he said adamantly. 'We can't. We have dinner reservations and they must be kept.'

He stormed out on deck and then stormed back in, eyeing me again in a way that told me exactly what he was thinking. But again, he seemed to be battling some kind of inner turmoil.

'If you stand there like that I will be forced to ravish you and that won't do.' He looked furious again, and stormed back out on deck. I really didn't know what to make of this spectacle. Who did he think he was? Frigging Christian Grey from the book 'Fifty Shades of Grey'? He was certainly fifty shades of something for sure, or shadier than the real Slim Shady.

I continued to get myself ready and by the time I stepped out on deck he had cooled down, calmly escorting me to the pier. His driver was going to drive us to Monaco. I slid into the cool leather seats of the shiny silver Aston Martin. We were certainly going to arrive in style.

Chambers mixed a vodka martini for me. Of course he did, because now he thought he was frigging James Bond, that's why! He chatted away animatedly and was quite cheery, considering how dark and menacing he had been just a few moments earlier.

He told me that Monaco was, in fact, a separate country from France, although it was easily accessible due to being on the same train tracks that ran through Cannes and Nice. I learned that Monaco was the second smallest country in the world and that only the Vatican City was smaller.

Vatican City was a country? I didn't even know where Vatican City was. I thought it was a made-up place.

'Have you been?' His eyes shone as he spoke.

I didn't want to admit that this was the first time I had left the country since I was almost five.

I shook my head, saying nothing.

'Monaco is the most densely populated country for its size so you better stick close to me. I don't want to lose you in the crowd when we get there.' He raised a perfectly shaped eyebrow at me. 'Monte Carlo is the newer part of the district, famed for its wealth and glamour … and its casino, opera and ballet-loving citizens. Anyway, I should stop rambling on,' he said, noticing my over-awed expression.

It was just as well, as my mind had begun to drift back to our semi-steamy encounter on the yacht. Blimey, I couldn't believe how quickly my man-free resolve had slipped away. I was finding it hard to concentrate. Thankfully he refrained from regaling me with any more history or geography, seeming happy to sit in companionable silence for the rest of the journey, listening to something classical on the in-car sound system. I sipped my martini - shaken not stirred - and looked out of the window as we sped along. The sun was fading and the sky was pastel, blue streaked with orange rays. I smiled to myself, my eyes feeling a little heavy.

I was jolted back to life by the sight of a marina with row upon row upon row of gleaming white yachts, each one boasting enormous wealth and extravagance.

'Welcome to Monaco!' Chambers smiled at me.

I was sure glad I was wearing Pru's dress now. My floral summer dress and cheap sandals definitely wouldn't have fitted in well here. Thankfully I had packed my Karen Millen heels. I continued peering out the car window at the colourful houses rising out from the rocks. They looked like little doll houses perched high up in the cliffs.

The driver stopped the car and I got out a little unsteady on my feet. Maybe that second martini hadn't been such a good idea. As it was so hilly and steep, I really had no choice but to hold on tight to Chambers and the thought made my cheeks warm slightly. If bringing me to Monaco was some grand gesture to impress me then he really shouldn't have. I was already beyond impressed. Still, I might as well enjoy a nice meal out.

I teetered along in my delicate heels, clinging on to Chambers who, in turn, supported me masterfully. We walked near the beachfront and came to a small promenade lined with kid's amusements, merry-go-rounds, hot-dog stands, slides and rides. In all honesty, this part of Monaco was a bit like Brighton. A sharp contrast to the shiny and magnificent yachts all lined up on the harbour. Maybe this part was to cater for the non-billionaire contingent of Monaco.

Chambers made a call to his driver, asking him to drive us to Cess Café instead of taking a five minute stroll up the hill. It was a good call; my calf muscles were already aching because of the heels. Maybe I could enjoy the sights on the way down instead? When we arrived at Cess Café a little before 7pm, a waiter showed us to an outdoor table.

My first impressions of the place was that it had a unique atmosphere. Impeccably-dressed women exuded class and extravagance, dripping in real jewellery rather than faux bling, and the men were kitted out in high-end fashion. I felt a bit of an imposter, despite wearing a beautiful dress and shoes. I glanced at the menu: the food was as expensive as I had imagined, but not outrageously so. Maybe a little bit over-the-top for a girl who usually opted for a cheeky takeaway or a Marks & Spencer's ready meal for one. There was a divine range of fancy-sounding dishes which I mostly didn't understand and ... ohhhh ... there was also a good steak option on the menu. That would go down nicely with a bottle of red.

'I'm just nipping to the loo ... ahem, to the ladies restroom,' I corrected myself, trying to sound refined.

'I'll order the steak for you, shall I? Cooked medium, with a bottle of the finest Merlot?' He was a bit unnerving, the way he seemed to know what I was thinking, what I wanted ... mmm ... I wonder if that applied in the bedroom, too? 'Stop it, Josie!' I told my raging hormones.

I headed inside to find the Ladies room. I noticed some rather cute guys smoking near the doorway; they were looking over at a pair of well-dressed ladies wearing killer heels, perfectly polished lips and not much else.

There was something about them though, I couldn't quite put my finger on it. I went inside the cafe and saw much of the same. Men and women conversing, a discreet exchange of cash, then they left together with a simple nod and smile. High class hookers! Why had Chambers brought me here, of all places?

If that hadn't been enough of a shock for me, then there was more to come. I hurried back to our table after doing my business in the high-class loo, only to find Chambers deep in conversation with another man. As I got closer, I found myself staring at them both for a moment.

'Ed!' I must have screamed because the posh diners all turned suddenly, turned back to their food after giving me a look of total disgust. Ed stood up and gave me a hug.

'What the hell are you doing here?' I was so happy, pleased to see his familiar face. I then glanced over at Chambers who was looking somewhat shifty.

'I was just thinking about you today, wishing you were here. You know, don't you? About Pru and Tebor. That's why you are here?'

'I got a letter. It was painfully honest,' Ed said with a big sigh. He still looked like he was in shock and his face had reddened in the hot sun.

'I didn't find out until today. I was shocked, too.' However hard this was for me, it must have been a million times harder for Ed. He had a grandad he hadn't known anything about.

'Did you meet Tebor?'

'Yeah, I thought I would hate him instantly but he actually seems quite nice. I can't get over how selfish he was though, and how he could do that to his own brother. Grandad Bert must have gone through hell when he found out.' Ed stared straight at Chambers who was fiddling with his linen napkin. Ed sighed deeply, putting his head in his hands. 'It's all a bit surreal, to be honest.'

'I know,' I said, because I didn't know what else to say. 'I still can't believe you are here. How crazy is that?'

'I'll leave you two to catch up,' Chambers said quietly, slipping off into the shadows.

Chapter 19

Back On The Yacht & Beyond

'So Ed,' I asked tentatively, 'honestly, how are you holding up?' He looked serious and a little shaky, so far removed from the jolly carefree Ed I had met only a few months ago. Poor thing had been through so much.

'Losing Gran has been like losing Mum all over again. It has hit me like a flaming truck.'

'Me too,' I said, reaching out to take one of his hands that were placed awkwardly on the table. I could see he was fighting back tears. 'I really wanted to be there for you, make sure you were ok, but you scarpered off after the balloon ride.'

'Yeah, sorry about that. Two of the waiters called in sick, so they asked if I could cover, but I wish I'd said no. Well done you though, for conquering your fears and for flying here solo. I knew you would. You are pretty damn amazing, except you don't know it most of the time.'

He peered at me from behind his straying fringe. My stomach did a little flip as his piercing blue eyes sought mine.

'Babs told me about Niles too. What an utter fool.'

An unbidden image surfaced of Niles in bed with she-who-should-not-be-named (or, in fact, couldn't be named as I didn't think to stop and ask the trollop her name).

I shrugged my shoulders. 'I've moved on. I'm the new, improved Josie who takes to the skies and definitely does not entertain any would-be wanker fiancés.'

'Glad to hear it. Great dress by the way.'

It's Pru's.'

'The one from the painting?' Ed asked.

I nodded.

'Incredible,' he breathed, then checked himself as if that remark had slipped out unwittingly.

I shook my head, batting away the compliment. My skin prickled with heat as his gaze travelled up and down the length of my body.

He looked up suddenly, reddening in his characteristic way.

This dress made me irresistible to men. That was a fact. I'd had quite an impact on Chambers earlier, and now it was having an effect on Ed. Good on you, Pru! I gave her a mental thumbs-up.

The waiter came over with our bottle of Merlot and two glasses. Chambers hadn't returned, possibly due to the fact that he was being entertained by one or more of the high-class hookers outside. I wouldn't put it past him.

'I have something for you,' said Ed. 'Close your eyes and hold out your hand.' I hated it when people said that to me, I always thought they were going to put a great big hairy spider in my hand. Babs once held a tarantula at an exotic creatures exhibition in Earl's Court, she said it actually felt quite nice and not scary at all. That's because it had just sat there, but I bet if I held it, it would have run up my arm and all over my face.

'I think you'll like it.'

That sounded reassuring, couldn't be a big hairy spider then.

I closed my eyes and held out my hand. Ed placed something cool, possibly metallic, into my outstretched hand. I opened my eyes, staring at the most intense blue stone I had ever seen in my life, which was attached to a gleaming silver chain.

'Ed, this is your grans!' I said, instantly recognising it as the one she wore in the painting.

'I know, and she wanted me to give it to you,' he said, his blue eyes shining. 'Here, let me,' and already he had taken the necklace from my hand, sliding the chain around my neck, deftly doing up the clasp.

Truth be told, I was a bit overwhelmed. Wasn't it slightly odd that I was sitting here wearing Pru's dress and now her sure-to-be-expensive necklace? But on the plus side, I was now wearing a piece of real jewellery just like my fellow diners. I shivered, goosebumps popping up all over my skin like a nasty rash. It was as if Pru was here, breathing on me, and I wasn't quite sure what to make of it.

'Why? Why would Pru want me to have her jewellery, her dress? In fact, why did she send me here at all? That painting should belong to you.' I felt a weight pressing on my chest and I was struggling to breathe.

'It was all part of her plan,' he smiled happily. 'She wanted us to meet here and be captivated by the magic of the place. I believe Gran and Grandad celebrated their first wedding anniversary here.'

He stopped and looked at me with tenderness, smoothing back a strand of hair that had fallen on to my face.

'There is something special about us being here together, don't you think?' His expression was full of longing.

Oh god! I looked down at my dress, felt the weight of the chain around my neck. Was Ed about to propose, I wondered? Was there a similar Tanzanite ring in the offing? Ed was my flatmate who I'd only known a few months, who I felt comfortable with, who I thought expected nothing from me. Was he being pushed to propose on the wishes of his dead gran?

'Ed, you're not thinking straight,' I said, trying to sound calm. My heart was beating wildly in contrast to my even tone. Finally, I was starting to embrace the single, and even slightly gutsy Josie who did things her own way. But there was something about what Ed was saying that rattled me, that got under my skin. The one person who I knew I was safe with, who didn't appeal to me in that way, what with his ridiculous tufts of hair and his peculiar dress sense. Then why was I starting to feel myself being pulled into the magic as if I were under some spell? It was just the setting, the ambience I told myself. I'd just been getting it on with Chambers for god's sake, no wonder my head was spinning.

'I know you're right for me,' he said confidently. 'Gran thought so too.'

'She's a fine one to be dishing out love advice,' I burst out. 'She cheated on her husband and withheld the truth from her daughter.'

His face went from puce to purple in a split second, a tumultuous mix of expressions crossed his face from anger to disbelief to grief to sadness, but he said nothing.

'What do you want from me, Ed? You know that I've just

broken up with my fiancé, do you really think I'm ready for any of this?' My voice was trembling. I tried to ignore the fury that was beating inside my chest like a wild bird that had been caged.

'I'm really sorry about Pru, Ed, truly I am, but she sent us both a letter to try and orchestrate our lives. Well I'm tired of other people thinking they know what's best for me. I've always tried to please people, and I've practically bent over backwards with my head up my arse to please the men in my life and I'm telling you, Ed. I. Am. Sick. Of. It. My life is a joke.' I sat fuming.

Ed nodded silently, his face resembling a beetroot. He looked at me with an expression I couldn't read, but there was definitely huge disappointment in the mix. But I didn't care, I had to get out of there.

I got up and fled from the restaurant, my heels clacking nosily on the concrete. Once I was safely outside, I rang Chambers.

He picked up the phone immediately.

'Chambers, take me back to the yacht please.'

'I'll be there in two minutes.'

The silver Aston Martin pulled up beside me in less than 30 seconds. Relieved, I got in and slammed the door shut. The driver sped away. Chambers watched me quizzically but said nothing. I wasn't in the mood for small talk anyhow. He moved closer to me and embraced me. I put my face into his chest and took huge breaths.

'Thanks,' I said in a small voice.

'Anytime,' he said, murmuring into my hair. Once I had calmed down a little, I sat back up and opened the window. I took in huge gulps of air.

'I'm sick of people trying to run my life,' I said forcefully. 'My mum, my boss, my mate Dame who moved out of his flat and brought in Ed to live with me, and now Pru. I'm pretty sure she wants me to marry her grandson, it's absurd.' I shook my head.

'Ridiculous.' I shook my head harder. 'From now on, I make my own plans and do what I want.'

'You should absolutely only do what is right for you,' Chambers agreed with me.

'What I need right now,' I said, feeling impulsive and reckless and sliding closer to him, 'is this.' I leaned over and kissed him. I had never done that before. I had never initiated the first kiss. His mouth opened to receive mine.

'Oh god,' I heard him groan, deep in his throat. He was kissing me back slowly at first but then with complete abandon. I grabbed his thick dark hair and pulled this head hard towards me. He seemed to enjoy it, his eyes glinting in the moonlight, his chest heaving up and down.

I felt powerful, exhilarated. The breeze blew my hair behind me and the car picked up speed, as if the driver sensed our urgency.

I placed my hand gently on his knee, tracing my fingers up to his thigh and paused, a wicked smile playing on my lips. I delicately touched the visible bulge in his pants, and the bulge jerked to life as if a jolt of electricity had careered through it. He groaned deeper.

'Josie, please.'

'Please, what?'

'Don't stop,' he replied desperately.

I removed my hand. 'I don't want your driver to have an accident,' I whispered, noting his intent gaze in the mirror. I giggled feeling every inch the naughty schoolgirl and thinking how rude and impersonal it had been of me to never have asked the driver his name. But now was hardly the time. A devilish instinct made me want to tease Chambers and the driver a little. The driver couldn't have been more than in his early 40s and was quite handsome from what I could see. I jutted my breasts out, crossed my legs and gently pulled my dress up to reveal a silky-smooth olive tanned leg. I murmured in pleasure as I stroked my leg up and down. I don't know what had got into me, so much for not wanting to cause an accident. At home Josie would never behave in such a way, except for the time with Chris in the Salsa bar closet, of course. If only I had shagged Chris instead of running back to Niles like the pathetic wimp that I was. *Was* being the operative word. There was a new Josie in town and she wasn't taking any prisoners.

'You're behaving very badly, Ms. Green. I think you deserve a spanking,' Chambers hoarse voice interrupted my thoughts.

'Uh-uh,' I wagged a finger at him, 'maybe you deserve a good spanking.' I always seemed to behave correctly, in and out of bed, always trying to please and moan in the right places, whether I was getting any satisfaction or not. Well screw that. I straightened down my dress demurely and sat back in my seat, like butter wouldn't melt.

He grabbed my hand as we approached Cannes Promenade and with a hasty thanks and goodbye to the driver, we bolted from the car. I was tingling, fizzing with excitement. Unless Chambers had a sudden change of heart, I was pretty sure I was in for some pretty amazing rumpy-pumpy.

I was ready to leap on him as soon as we got into the yacht, but he grabbed my hands to halt me.

'Are you sure Josie?'

'Yes, I'm sure,' I said, feeling slightly irritated.

He continued staring at me with a worried expression. Uh-oh, I thought, not again.

'It's just that I'm not your knight in shining armour. I have no intention of proposing.' He looked at me cautiously.

'Well thank fuck for that!' I pushed away an image of Ed who most definitely looked like he was about to propose, and kissed Chambers again before he could say another word to completely kill the mood.

His lips were soft and sensuous, his tongue teasing and probing. The way he explored inside my mouth sent a riot of sensations throughout my entire body. I was dizzy with delight.

'Not so worried about your lady forest or bulging belly then?' he said, poking me in the ribs. 'Sure I can't interest you in a cup of tea and a Hobnob instead?' I threw my head back and laughed, looking him right in the eye. 'There's only one knob I'm interested in tonight.'

Oh god, now I sounded like Dame.

'Last night you weren't remotely interested, now Iook at you.' He looked smugly into my eyes, my pupils no doubt dilated with desire, my cheeks rosy.

'I've decided that I may find you mildly attractive after all …' I began, then gasped as he traced his finger tip around my right nipple. His touch was delicate through the soft velvet fabric. I sighed. Maybe I should try to play it cool, not show how much I wanted him, but there was no denying the effect he was having on my nipples straining through the velvet fabric. I couldn't take this much longer.

Launching myself at him I grabbed his chest, working furiously at his buttons. He swept me up in his arms as if I were light as a feather, carrying me into the bedroom. He threw me onto the bed and continued teasing me through my dress. He turned me over and finally unzipped me.

'Me Tarzan, you Jane.'

I giggled. Serious, imperious Chambers coming out with that line was too funny.

'No, me spanking queen,' I said, squeezing and slapping his bum. I'd been dying to do that since I'd seen him in his Speedos. I was just about to unbuckle his trousers, when I felt a buzzing and saw a light illuminating from his pocket. The force of the vibration made his phone fall out on the bed. A picture of a lady appeared on the screen with her red lips wrapped around a banana.

I'm guessing that wasn't his sister. The phone buzzed again insistently.

'I'm busy,' he said, speaking into the phone. No hello or anything. 'I told you before, I'll call you when I can.' He sighed. I watched the little muscles tighten in his jaw, his voice was cold. It was like a draught had entered the room. He jabbed the phone off.

'Now, where were we?' He continued trailing kisses down my neck, but my mind was a whirl of thoughts that I couldn't really connect to. The moment had been lost.

I jumped off the bed and headed for the bathroom. 'Josie, that was no-one, really.'

I shut the door on him and looked in the mirror. My hair was tousled, my make-up smudged, but I'd never looked so hot and fierce. I knew he was no angel, but that blatant image of banana lady didn't really do it for me. All I wanted to do now was leave, but it was a bit awkward considering it was late and I had no way of getting back home. Still I couldn't stay in the bathroom all night.

I unlocked the door and came out to find Chambers standing stark naked, donning an erection that nearly poked my eye out.

Unbelievable. I frowned. 'Come on, Josie, we were enjoying ourselves.'

'Yes, we were, but funnily enough I'm not in the mood now.'

He sighed. 'That bloody phone.'

But was it just the phone thing? I didn't feel angry or upset, just jolted out of my lustful reverie. I had sobered up pretty sharpish and there was only thing I fancied.

'Tea and biscuits,' Chambers said, reading my mind and pulling on some clothes.

I grinned and nodded. 'Thank you.' My stomach grumbled in anticipation, as I hadn't got to eat my steak at the restaurant. The restaurant. Suddenly all I could think about was Ed. Ed. Oh god. I'd had bust-ups with Babs and Dame before, but that was different. I'd known them ages, they were like family to me. But Ed was a different kettle of fish. He had totally freaked me out by the way he had declared his feelings so unexpectedly. After the Pru and Tebor bombshell, how did he expect me to react?

I sipped my tea, lost in my thoughts. 'Josie, what are you thinking? You're not upset?' Chamber's voice brought me back to reality.

'No. I was just thinking about earlier at the restaurant,' I shook my head. 'Come here,' he pulled me into his arms and stroked my hair. A flicker of unexpected desire shot through me as I felt his biceps rippling through his t-shirt. He was like something straight out of a romantic novel, his body was contoured to perfection, his face chiselled just the right amount and he was a charming so-and-so when he wanted to be. But he also had a cold and cruel side that unnerved me.

'Are you ready for bed?' His voice had a seductive edge to it.

'Yes,' my voice croaked as I tore myself away from his hypnotic gaze. 'Alone. I'm going to bed alone.'

'You know where I'll be if you need me,' he smiled. I couldn't blame him for trying.

'Goodnight Chambers.'

'Goodnight Josie.'

I stumbled to my room feeling exhausted all of sudden, and I was out like a light as soon as my head hit the pillow. It was a deep sleep but then I started to toss and turn as Chambers and Ed swam side by side, limbs extended both powering through the water in a race to get to the other side. There was a loud thump as Ed hit his head on the side of the pool and blacked out. I gasped and started running towards him but my legs stopped working, and all around me I heard cheering as Chambers brandished a trophy. I woke with a start and for a minute couldn't place where I was.

The smell of coffee and eggs wafted through the air. I went to investigate and found Chambers seated at the table, drinking coffee and reading a newspaper. He looked composed in his crisply tailored business suit.

'Oh good, you're up. I've got to go.' He looked at his watch. 'Business to attend to. I've made you breakfast.' He smiled at me and hugged me tightly. 'Anyway, stay as long as you want, I should be back by tomorrow morning.' He blew me a kiss. Damn that man, if he thought I was going to still be here when he got back, he was seriously deluded.

'Bye Chambers,' I called out cheerily as he left.

He did make pretty decent coffee though. I wolfed down the eggs and toast, taking my coffee out on deck. It looked to be another glorious day.

Chapter 20
It Takes Two To Tango

I FINALLY GOT ROUND TO CALLING Ed and was relieved when he picked up on the second ring. I stuttered something stupid, hoping that my conciliatory tone would put him at ease. He sounded quiet and hesitant but agreed to meet me for an ice-cream on the promenade. We had separate flights home tomorrow so if it all went to pot, at least we wouldn't be bumping into each other at the airport.

I grinned as I looked back at the The Angelica. This yachting lifestyle was something I could get rather used to if Chambers ever decided to invite me back. Now wearing my sensible flats, I headed back to the promenade. Heels were hardly appropriate when there was no one around to make sure that you didn't fall into the water.

'Hi Ed,' I said, taking a deep breath when I spotted him, his shoulders hunched over and hands thrust deep into his pockets.

'Josie.' He eyed me warily.

'I'm so sorry,' 'I was a total prat.'

We both spoke together. He gave me a small smile.

'So, you're sorry that I was a total prat,' he said.

'You weren't a total prat …'.

'Just a partial prat then?' His smile widened with his usual boyishness.

'You weren't even remotely prat-like. If anything, I was the prat.'

'We could stand here debating our prat-like qualities, or we could just kiss and make up?' He raised an eyebrow.

I hugged him tightly, feeling happy again. He smelled fresh and spicy, like one of those cologne adverts. The effect was stirring up something inside me. Oh god, it must be all those pheromones still swilling around my system. I gave him a hasty kiss on the cheek.

He reciprocated by kissing me on both cheeks. 'When in France and all that.'

I smiled, marvelling at how at ease I felt with him. This is how things were meant to be between us. How could it have gone so wrong last night?

'About last night …' I began

He looked embarrassed. 'Yeah I shouldn't have been so full-on. Especially with you being so cut up over Niles.'

I had a guilty flashback of my frolicking with Chambers. Yeah. Really cut up.

'I'm sorry for running out on you.'

'I did feel a bit of a twat when the waiter came over to ask how our food was and saw you had disappeared. He was nice enough not to charge for your meal though. Think he felt a bit sorry for me.'

'I should have stayed and listened to you,' I said, remembering how angry I had felt. 'But you kind of threw me somewhat.' I smiled to myself. I could be quite fierce when I wanted to be.

'It's probably best you didn't,' he replied. 'My ego was a bit bruised, but I'm over it now,' he said, shrugging nonchalantly.

His fine hair kept flying into his face like an unruly bird's nest. I resisted the urge to brush his hair away.

'Ed, do you think love is ever for real?' I asked abruptly.

'I'd like to think so, Josie.' His face was impassive as he looked out at the expanse of sea. 'No-one's perfect. Not even granny Pru.' He smiled broadly and nodded his head. 'In fact, I'm sure she loved Grandpa Bert; they loved each other very much.'

'But do you trust Tebor?'

He shrugged. 'I think he's sorry. And he reminds me of Mum. They have the same smile.'

His turquoise eyes were shining brightly. A look of blissful peace crossed his face. We sat on a bench, eating our ice-cream and looking out at the Med. I stroked his arm, the tufts of hair feeling surprisingly soft.

'I was really worried about you last night Ed,' I said, biting my lip. 'Are you okay and are *we* good?'

'I lost the plot for a bit,' he said, stroking his chin thoughtfully. 'I guess you never really get used to losing someone but yeah, I think I'll be ok. And I'm happy that we are still friends.' He gave my arm a squeeze back. 'Don't worry about me, I've got a little black book full of numbers back at home. All I have to do is click my fingers and they come running, I've just been so busy with work and everything of late …'. He rubbed his peeling nose.

Little Black Book, mmm! I thought, trying to stop my

sarcastic eyebrow raise. I'd never heard him talk about girls except that one he left behind.

'Ed, you mentioned someone in Australia, what happened?' He'd never really explained, and I'd never asked him directly.

'Sarah. Her name was, and still probably is, Sarah. She jilted me at the altar in front of about fifty people after choosing that exact moment to confess she'd been having it away with a work colleague. She begged me to forgive her after humiliating me like that. And the stupid thing is that I tried. I really tried, but I couldn't stop feeling sad about it.'

'Ed. I'm so sorry. What a shitty thing to do.' Oh god, and he still believed in love?

'The ironic thing is that she sent me an e-card telling me that she'd married the colleague. I received the notification the day after I found Gran. The funny thing was that it really didn't bother me. Nothing like death to put things into perspective.' He laughed a small, hollow laugh.

I swallowed back tears and hugged him close.

'Anyway, besides Gran's half-baked plans to get us together, she did get something very right though.'

'What's that?'

'That I am destined to be a world class chef. She's only gone and booked me an exclusive three-day cookery class at the Epicurean School in Venice's classiest Hotel, the Gritti Palace.' His eyes bulged with excitement and he looked at me like I should be really impressed.

'Oh wow. That's amazing, Ed!'

'It's really famous,' he gushed. 'Greta Garbo, Clark Gable, Ernest Hemingway … they were all regulars. I'm going to learn a whole range of Venetian cicchetti.'

'Huh?'

'Little dishes, like Venetian tapas. It's all the rage right now,' he continued 'Spider crab, cuttlefish, samphire ....'

'Of course,' I said, thinking how my culinary expertise didn't really extend much further than beans on toast. Definitely more 'never dine with me' than 'come dine with me' which, of course, was Ed's favourite programme. He should go on it, or maybe he could go on that programme 'Dinner Date' and impress the ladies with his Venetian concetti, or whatever it was called.

'So, when are you leaving?' I asked.

'Friday, next week. The course is only three days, but Gran said that she has rented an apartment for me just a couple of minutes from St. Mark's Square. I'll be there a couple of weeks. I can practice and perfect my skills.' His eyes shone brightly. It was good to see him looking happy.

'That's fantastic, Ed.' I smiled at him but felt a bit sick at the thought of being in the flat alone. What if Niles showed up? Maybe I could convince Dame or Babs to move in while Ed was away? No, no, I would be just fine on my own. After all I had been through, being alone was the last of my worries.

'Your gran got more than one thing right,' I said. 'If it wasn't for her, there is no way I would have got up in a hot air balloon or flown here alone. She inspired me and believed that I could do it. It made me believe in me, too.'

'I'm glad,' said Ed, beaming at me. 'So, as it's our last night here, I was wondering if you were up for an outdoor Tango lesson?'

'Tango lesson? With you?' I said, laughing.

'Are you mocking me, Ms. Green? Don't you think these

hips have got rhythm?' he said, sashaying across the sand, his shorts flapping in the breeze.

'I'm impressed,' I said, even though he looked a bit of a dork.

'I told Tebor we would go.'

'Tebor tangos?' I asked. Was there nothing that wouldn't surprise me about that family?

'He's the teacher. Been teaching for 25 years. Locals, tourists, right in the square in Antibes. Have you ever been to a class?'

'No, but I've been meaning to. I've done Salsa.' I had a flash back of Chris in that closet.

I smiled. 'So what time is it?'

'7pm. Wear your heels.'

With that, he handed me a flyer. 'I'll catch you later, things to do.' He waved goodbye before I could say anything. I was transfixed by the flyer. Tebor with his pearly whites and too-tight trousers, clutching a sensuous heavily made-up elderly lady. Oh. Dear. God.

I blew 75 euros on a pink satin dress with sequins in the hem. Well, I needed something to wear to this dance ... plus they went really well with my heels. I thought Ed might suggest we go there together, but he seemed preoccupied when he left and he hadn't called me since, so I made my own way there in a taxi. Maybe I was overdressed but the flyer looked glossy and extravagant, so I thought the people would be too.

I arrived just before 7pm and there was quite a mixed crowd of old and young, dolled up *and* dressed down, and thankfully a good handful of men. Not quite a 50/50 ratio but enough so I wouldn't have to lead. Thankfully Ed, being a man after all, would be leading. I searched the crowd for him. Where was he? I tried his mobile but it was switched off. Great. Just Great.

'Josie!' Tebor was waving frantically at me. 'So glad you could make it.' He walked gracefully across the square. I could hardly believe that a man in his 80s could still be teaching a class, but it seemed to be keeping him young.

Earlier I had noticed him stooping a little when he walked and holding a cane, but now there was no cane and no stoop, seemed like tango worked wonders for him. Maybe he did the whole cane-and-stoop routine to get a seat on the bus or something.

He greeted me enthusiastically kissing me on both cheeks. 'You look beautiful, so elegant.'

'Thank you,' I said giving, him a little bow.

'Have you seen Ed?'

'No, but don't worry, he's coming. I'll wait a few minutes for any other latecomers before I begin.' With that he was swept away in the crowd and cornered by some twirling woman trying to grab his attention. He managed to prise himself away and clapped his hands together theatrically.

'Right, I can see you are all eager to begin, so let's begin at the beginning. Let me see you walk.' Everyone looked at everyone else with bemused expressions, except the few that had clearly been before and were already sauntering around the square in a determined fashion. I tried to copy their upright posture, arms held out as if with a partner and tried to make my feet flow. After a minute or so my arms felt really heavy and I felt I was dragging myself around. I promptly crashed into a hefty bloke which sent me flying, but he barely seemed to notice.

'And try not to bash into each other,' Tebor had spotted

me. 'Very good everyone, tango is about walking and moving with confidence, with precision.' He demonstrated his 'tango walk' which did look kind of impressive; some of the older ladies swooned.

'Now for the 8-step basic. Ladies, watch me first.' They didn't need to be told twice. It looked simple enough. It consisted of moving forward, side, back and side. The men mirrored our moves so when we went forward, they went back.

'Let's try it with a partner now.' Squeals of excitement and looks of anticipation rippled around the room. Heaven help me, it was like being on a group first date. Where the hell was Ed? I decided to try a few of the moves on my own before I braved it with a complete stranger.

'It does take two to tango, you know,' a husky voice behind me said. I swung around.

'Chambers! Aren't you supposed to be doing an important business deal?' I couldn't help feel a little frisson of excitement.

'I finished up early, didn't want to miss the fun.' He looked exceptionally handsome in his bluish grey two-piece. I looked him up and down and met his dark penetrating eyes. I flushed. He grabbed me by the waist and pulled me towards him, my heart did a little gallop, my feet got all flustered. How was I supposed to remember the steps now?

'You haven't been paying attention, have you? You naughty girl.' Chambers' lips brushed my ear. He was back on form and didn't look like he'd be taking any prisoners.

Chambers started moving with ease and confidence to the music that now played.

'I thought you couldn't dance,' I said.

'Only tango. Grandad makes me come to the classes. He

says it encourages the ladies.' He smirked at me, raising an eyebrow. A image of the blatant banana lady entered my mind.

I tried pulling away from him, suddenly feeling a bit giddy. He held me closer.

'Tango is a dance for lovers,' he purred. 'It's only a matter of time, Josie. The chemistry between us last night was undeniable.'

He twirled me around. I didn't have a clue what I was meant to be doing.

'You're really good,' I said.

'You should see my gancho!'

'I believe I got a pretty good eyeful of your 'gancho' last night,' I said empathically.

He looked amused and sent me spinning. Oh god, was I seeing things or was that Ed standing in the background, wearing a look of utter fury, dressed up like a Christmas turkey complete with ruffles?

I quickly disentangled myself from Chambers and ran over to Ed, almost tripping over myself.

'Holy Guacamole,' I heard myself say, something I heard on a night out once. It was the first thing that had popped into my head. 'You are really late,' I said, trying to look cross.

'But I see you didn't waste any time.' He looked down, blinking his eyes rapidly.

Chambers chose that precise moment to stride over.

'Everything okay here?'

Ed gave him a lingering dirty look and turned away. 'Enjoy the rest of your night, I'm sure you will.'

'What's eating him?'

'He saw us.'

'So?'

'So! He likes me. He said he was fine with us being friends, but clearly not.'

'Yeah, all because Granny Pru wants you to be together. Last night you said you weren't going to follow anyone's plans, so forget about him.'

'He's still my friend. I should see if he's ok.'

'What? And just piss him off some more? Bad idea. Come with me. My car's over there, we can be back on the yacht in twenty minutes.' He kissed me hard, his tongue possessing mine.

I managed to extract myself from his mouth. 'No, Chambers. I have to go and ...'

He continued to hold me tight. 'No,' he persisted, 'You are coming with me right now, or you face some very serious punishment.' Mmm, he was getting all Fifty Shades on me and obviously wasn't used to women saying no to him. In fact, he was more used to women wrapping their lips around his banana. Well, tough raspberries to that.

'I am going to speak to Ed, and not you or anyone can tell me that I can't.' I shook him off and started to walk away.

'Tease!' he called out. He was a prick, after all. I didn't dignify him with a response.

'Ed,' I screamed out loud, above the clatter of feet and music. He hadn't managed to walk too far in his too-tight trousers, but he was flapping his arms around plenty to compensate.

'Ed!' I said, drawing level with him. I noticed he was holding a package wrapped in silk with a red bow.'

'It's yours,' he said, thrusting it into my arms. 'I got it framed this afternoon. It's what Gran sent you here for after all.'

'Ed, I don't know what to say.'

'Save it. For Chambers, maybe. I'm not stupid Josie, I could see what was happening between you two.'

Tears sprang to my eyes. I wanted to protest, tell him that it wasn't like that. That even if it was, I was single. The look he gave me stopped me from saying anything else.

'What happened? Were you seduced by his shiny yacht and bulging bank balance?'

He didn't wait for an answer. My heart sank as he strode off as fast as his tight trousers would allow.

What a great last night this had turned out to be.

I headed back to the apartment in Juan-les-Pins and poured myself a hefty glass of Merlot. It felt good being 'back home'. I sat out on the balcony and looked over at my neighbour's window, hoping to catch a glimpse of their nocturnal activities. Their shutters were closed, not even a hint of light glimmered from their windows. The streets were unusually quiet and everything was still, which only increased my feelings of desolation.

Why had I come here? Why had Pru been so insistent that I come? Now everything was more messed up than ever. I downed the glass of wine almost in one. Ed's words reverberated around my brain like bloodthirsty mosquitoes, taking a pinch here and there. The look on his face had been cold enough to freeze blood. I shivered, despite the humidity of the night. The last couple of days had certainly been very revealing. How could we go on being flatmates now? The situation seemed untenable and irreversible.

The thought of going home now filled me with dread. The reality was that I had no job, no fiancé and my flatmate most likely despised me. Good going, Jos! While total freedom had felt like an adventure less than a week ago, it now weighed heavily on my heart. Why couldn't I have remained suspended in time up in that hot air balloon when everything seemed simple? I looked in the mirror, remembering my poem and all that I had learnt. Trust. That's all I had to do. Trust that everything would be ok.

I gulped down the rest of the bottle. I couldn't be bothered to pack, that could wait until morning. I was looking forward to seeing Babs and Dame and getting into my own bed. Some very loud and merry people suddenly started singing under my balcony. There went my quiet, peaceful night's sleep.

Thoughts of Ed also poked me back into wakefulness. Bloody Ed, why couldn't I get his flustered face and blinking eyes out of my mind? What right did he have to be upset about me getting it on with Chambers? He said he was cool with us being just friends, but evidently not. I tossed and turned some more, punching my pillow. Why did I care what Ed thought anyway? The opinion of Mr. Ed Bloody Chancellor was of no importance, I decided, and promptly fell asleep.

Chapter 21
Surprise, Surprise!

I WOKE UP FEELING DISORIENTATED AND the room was swirling. For a minute I thought I was back on the yacht doing the tango. The sound of a scooter and a scream reminded me that I was in the noisy Juan-les-Pins apartment, and today was the day that I flew home.

I stumbled out of bed; the rocking feeling had subsided but I was parched. I gulped down a glass of water trying not to think about the disaster that was last night. The glittering sequinned dress and the strappy shoes served as a reminder. I started throwing my things in my suitcase and was almost done when I heard a car horn bleat repeatedly. Not that unusual but it seemed to be directly below my window. I stepped out on the balcony and saw the silver Aston Martin. Chambers! What was he doing here?

My heartbeat quickened. I waited for him to emerge in slow motion with a dozen red roses between his teeth, climbing his way up to the top floor of the apartment to rescue me from my lonely life, just like Richard Gere had done in 'Pretty Woman'. Even as I thought this, my brain was like 'yeah, whatever, real life does not work like that.' The truth is that even if Chambers had been there I would have told him to sling his hook. We had chemistry and a prelude to what could have been a steamy one-nighter but that's all it had amounted to.

Instead the driver got out. No Chambers.

'Master Chambers sent me,' he called up to the window. 'I have some of your things,' he said, holding up a bag. My dress, flip flops, and a lipstick I had carelessly left behind. 'Master Chambers wishes you a safe and pleasant journey back home, he wanted to come himself but had some important business to take care of.' Of course he had, 'entertaining' some other lucky lady no doubt.

I finished packing my things with a heavy heart. A week earlier all I had wanted to do was collect that damn package and be gone. But for the first time in my life I had experienced something and somewhere out of the ordinary. And I liked it.

The final item to be packed was the painting. I unwrapped the silk cover and saw it had a lovely gold frame around it. I gently eased the painting out from the cover. It was exquisite: the cypress tree and hint of Mediterranean provided the perfect backdrop. Pru held a protective hand over her stomach, a gentle smile playing on her lips. On closer observation, her dark eyes looked slightly fraught, and the more I looked at the painting, the more disturbed she seemed. Bert, clearly oblivious to the ensuing revelation, was happily beaming and looking every bit as proud as an expectant father would be.

It made sense now. Pru wanted me to see that love wasn't perfect, that life was about taking chances. Her plan was to get me away from my humdrum life and have me fall head over heels in love with Ed. Well that hadn't exactly worked out, had it?

I made my way to the plane without incident. It took off without incident and I slept for most of the flight with the aid of my miniature bottle of Jack Daniels from the good ol' World of Whiskies airport shop.

There was one other thing I didn't want to face, aside from Niles, Ed, my mum, brother, and the barrage of questions from Babs and Dame.

My birthday. My great, big sodding birthday. Thirty. Today. I had tried my utmost to forget about it. I thought if I evaded it, it might just sneak off into the sunset. I texted Babs to let her know not to make a fuss. She claimed to have forgotten about it and said we could have a 'quiet drink,' just me, her and Dame. She was being far too compliant. I wasn't sure I could trust anything she said or did after the whole blind date debacle. If need be I would lock myself in my room with my whisky.

Back in London, I squeezed myself onto a crowded tube which was running late, thanks to severe delays. Some poor sod had ended up under a train. I momentarily considered joining him. We were packed like cattle, my belly was pressed into the protruding buttocks of a tall, broadly built man. I tried to manoeuvre myself but found I was completely stuck. I got the giggles and felt my heaving stomach vibrate onto his bum cheeks which only made me laugh harder. Thank god I was getting off at the next stop. The man resolutely ignored our bum-to-belly connection.

Stepping out into the late afternoon sunshine it did feel good to be back and at least Ed wasn't home until a bit later, by which time I would be safely tucked up in bed. Bed. Now that was a comforting thought. I was looking forward to a nice long shower and then flopping onto my bed. Just me and total tranquility, something I hadn't had in amongst the noise and bustle in Juan-les-Pins.

Just like everything in my life, things didn't go according to plan. As I lugged my suitcase up the five flights of stairs, due to the fact that the lift was temporarily on the blink yet again, I had the growing sensation that something wasn't quite right. I scrambled for my keys and opened my door. I was greeted by the sweet sound of silence for about five seconds and then there was an almighty crash and an 'Oh Fuck.' Oh Fuck Indeed. An intruder was in my flat. My heart was hammering. I thought about running back out, but something drew me inside. This time I was greeted by a huge 'SURPRISE!' and a sea of at least twenty beaming faces. Bloody Babs and Dame, my mum, brother, Aunty Pam, various cousins, Layla from the gallery, and a couple of friends I hadn't seen in years.

A bloody surprise party, just what I didn't want! There were balloons and party poppers strewn across the flat, as well as a gigantic cake in the centre of the room. As if my heart wasn't already in a state of shock. But just as I was gawping at the cake, WTF…! It suddenly burst open and a man jumped out wearing nothing but what looked like PVC leopardskin hotpants, shouting 'SURPRISE!' Everyone raised glasses of champagne and started singing Happy Birthday at the top of their voices. Someone shoved a glass in my hand. I gulped down the fizzy liquid gratefully and looked back at the man. Oh. My. God. It was Chris from the mop cupboard in the salsa club. What was going on? Had I just walked into the Twilight Zone? Music started blaring out from somewhere,

80s disco by the sounds of it, and everyone started jumping up and down.

Before I had time to react or respond to what was in front of me, Babs almost knocked me over with an enthusiastic hug. She had the decency to look at least a little bit guilty while whispering out of the corner of her mouth, 'Sorry about the whole *'surprise birthday'* thing, I know you told me not to but …' She looked at me all Bambi eyes and bouncing curls, 'Oh, and about Chris. Well it's actually a really funny story. Dame spotted his card on the floor by the sofa when he was cleaning up and thought it would be kind of cool to ring him. Anyway, it turns out he's a strip-a-gram and was totally on board with surprising you.'

'Ah,' I said, because I didn't know what else to say from behind my forced smile and with the feel of several expectant eyes on me. 'What a surprise!' Somehow I managed to stay composed.

'Happy Birthday, Josie darling!' Mum said, rushing over to hug me and planting noisy kisses all over my face. 'I've missed you so much.' She almost squeezed the life out of me.

'Only been gone a few days,' I said, embarrassed, trying to brush her away.

'I know, but I was worried about you being on your own and so much has happened since you've been away.'

Out of the corner of my eye I saw something rather alarming. Oh. Dear. God. Aunty Pam was doing what looked like the lambada with Chris, copping a good feel of his buttocks in the process.

'Anyway, there's something I need to tell you,' Mum continued.

'Can it wait?' I asked distractedly, as Babs was waving her arms in my direction.

'Well yes, this isn't really the right …'. We were interrupted by Aunty Pam making her way over with Chris, trying to encourage Mum to dance.

I tried to avert my eyes but couldn't stop my mouth twitching. He looked like he wanted to talk to me, but other than a hasty 'Happy Birthday,' he didn't get much chance.

Babs marched over to me, tugging my arm urgently.

'There's something I need to tell you and it can't wait.' She looked like she was about to explode.

'I'm drinking sparkling apple juice,' she whispered, bundling me into a corner.

'Right …' I said slowly, wondering why she felt the need to share that bit of 'vital' information with me. She continued staring at me, clearly trying to communicate something important.

'Oh!' I said, comprehension dawning on me. 'Oh! Oh Fuck!' There could only be one reason why Babs would be drinking apple juice in place of champagne.

'You're not?' I said, grinning madly.

'I bloody well am!' She looked ecstatic.

I didn't have time to say anything else as it was Dame's turn to come bounding over to me, stopping only to give Chris a thumbs up. He was ensconced between my mum and Aunty Pam in a disturbing threesome dance routine. Aunty Pam's behaviour was no surprise and it seemed that Mum, under the influence of alcohol and Aunty Pam, was just as bad. Chris managed to dart me a desperate 'please rescue me' look but I simply shrugged my shoulders and tried not to laugh *too* loud.

'Dame,' I shrieked, 'WTF made you invite Chris to my party?'

'If that's all the gratitude I get then you should have stayed in bloody France,' he said mock-moodily. 'Come here you cheeky bitch,' he said, beckoning me over a second later. 'I've really missed you. I need someone to keep '*Miss can't keep her knickers on*' in check.'

'Yes, about that, how did that all happen? When? I mean I've been gone literally a week and I didn't even know you were trying.'

'We weren't exactly, but we got a bit careless during a drunken pinot shag a couple of months ago' she continued airily, 'and I totally forgot about it.'

'Does Jake know?' I asked.

'He should do, he was quite actively involved,' she smirked.

'No. I mean does he know you're pregnant?' I said that louder than I intended to, worried that she was taking it all too casually. I searched the room for him, concerned he may have heard.

'He couldn't make it as his dad just got out of hospital today, but yes, he's thrilled.'

'Are you sure?'

'He couldn't be happier. I think this thing with his dad has made him realise how short life can be.'

'No, I mean are you sure you are pregnant?' I asked.

'Yes, it's all been confirmed by the doctor. I know this wasn't exactly planned but we are so excited!'

I felt happy but rather shocked and overwhelmed by all the revelations of this evening. What a welcome back.

'This is turning out to be one hell of a birthday,' I said, raising my glass.

'I can make it even better,' said a voice behind me. Mr. PVC-Chris-Leopardskin-Hotpants.

He went in to kiss me full on the mouth, but I turned away just in time. I felt my face get hot and must have blushed furiously.

'This is no time to play shy, Josie. Maybe I could be your private dancer?' His sensual lips that I remembered so fondly were curling up in a smile. Dame and Babs nodded enthusiastically, encouraging me into the bedroom.

Thankfully I was saved by Layla from the art gallery wanting to hear all my gossip from France. My cousins crowded around, not believing that I had actually gone further afield than Sheffield. Friends who I hadn't seen in ages remarked how well I looked. Despite feeling tired and wanting a night to myself, it was really nice to see everyone. I felt a lump in my throat, sad that Pru couldn't be here too.

Meanwhile Mum was acting even more peculiar than usual. One minute she was all over me, the next minute she couldn't even make eye contact when I tried to talk to her. I shoved some cheesy Wotsits in my mouth and excused myself from the others. Oh God, I hope she wasn't pregnant too, but considering she was nearly sixty and drinking worrying amounts of wine that seemed hardly likely. (Her proclamation to remain sober hadn't lasted very long.) Anyway, I already knew what it was. My mum had a new man. That had to be it. She said a lot had happened since I'd been gone.

I strode over to where she was standing. She looked jittery and started folding a paper napkin into a tiny square.

'It's alright, Mum. I already know.'

She looked aghast, comically so.

'It's pretty obvious. You are glowing. You are all over the place, a bit twitchy. I'd say it's got to be a new man.'

She hesitated a fraction too long before denying it.

'It's okay, Mum,' I said gently. 'You *are* allowed to be happy. It's been a long time since Dad, so if you've met someone else ....'

A strangled sound came out of her mouth. She looked like she wanted to cry. Something wasn't right. A bubble of unease gurgled in the pit of my stomach.

'Well?' I waited. 'You can tell me.' I stroked her arm reassuringly.

The silence was heavy.

'Excuse me a second,' she said, fanning her face and scuttling off to the bathroom.

Strange. Very strange.

Ant sauntered over. 'Have you noticed that Mum's being a bit weird?' he mouthed through his upturned collar.

'Even more so than usual,' I confirmed.

'She's been getting mysterious gifts.' Now he had my interest.

'Gifts? From like a secret admirer, you mean?'

'Could be,' he whispered. Something was delivered the other day in a black box. She took it straight up to her room.'

'Go on,' I urged, wondering what it was about gifts and secrets. I'd had enough of those of late.

'I tried to ask her about it, but she was being all evasive.'

That was it. I wanted to know what was going on right now.

'Mum,' I called. 'Mum!' I checked the bathroom and kitchen.

'Aunty Pam, have you seen Mum?' I asked, spying my wayward aunty copping another feel of Chris in his hotpants.

'She said something about not feeling well. She did look a bit pale, probably gone to sleep it off.'

I couldn't believe it. Mum had sloped off without telling us. All this fuss over a new man; they really weren't worth it half the time.

Talking of men, I noticed that Ed had returned from France and was engaged in an animated conversation with Babs and Dame. Ed. Oh God, that's all I needed. I'd half expected him to stay at his Gran's. The flat did belong to him now, after all. He looked relaxed in a baby blue t-shirt and black jeans. He threw his head back and laughed at something Babs was saying. How could he stand there pretending all was hunkydory after what had happened between us?

He certainly looked like he was having a good time. Still I couldn't help feeling nervous; he might look happy now, but what if he turned into a fire-breathing dragon the second he spotted me?

I took a deep breath and slowly made my way over to where they were standing in the kitchen, stopping to pick up a handful of popcorn, downing a whisky and coke for courage. It was only then that I noticed a petite blonde was clasped on to Ed's arm, howling with mirth, her blonde ringlets cascading down her back. Who was she? Maybe she was one of the many women from his little black book? Another round of laughter erupted from the group; Dame looked like he had just wet himself. It looked like they were having a jolly good time without me. I couldn't help but feel left out and annoyed, especially when the blonde stroked her fingers up Ed's arm. I wanted to turn and run like my mum had done, but Dame called over to me.

'Josie, come join us. Why you being such a party pooper?' I could have killed him. Why couldn't I just sit in a corner and inconspicuously down a few whisky and cokes? Oh yeah, because I was at my surprise thirtieth birthday party which I *really* could have done without.

'Hi!' I said brightly, with a big smile. 'Thanks for this, I'm having a blast!' I couldn't have sounded more insincere. Babs gave me a look of concern. There was an awkward silence. The blonde gave a tinkling little laugh and said 'Happy Birthday, Josie.'

'Thanks,' I mumbled, giving Ed a pensive stare. He held up his champagne glass.

'May all your wishes come true, Josie.' He clinked his glass with mine, his face impassive. What was he even doing here, I wondered, thinking it was about 7pm. A quick glance at my watch told me it was well after 10pm.

'Are you going to introduce me to your *friend?'* I asked.

'Josie, meet Madeline. She's just started waitressing at Café Rouge.'

'And you've been such a good mentor, Ed. I don't know how I would have managed without you,' she breathed.

'Nice to meet you,' I said through gritted teeth.

'So, what was up with your mum?' Dame asked.

I sighed. 'Something strange is going on with Mum. I think she's got a boyfriend.'

'Ohh ...' Babs and Dame both chorused.

'But there's something not quite right. One minute she couldn't wait to tell me all about him, now she's disappeared.'

'She's not dated anyone for ages, Jos, she's probably just

worried what you'll think. She'll tell you when she's ready,' Babs affirmed, nodding her head.

I smiled, feeling a bit better. 'I'll just say bye to people,' I said, noticing some of my guests were getting up to make a move.

An hour later I was alone nursing a milky hot chocolate, feeling thankful that everyone had finally left.

Ed's door creaked open. He padded over to the sink.

'Thought I heard you,' he said, pouring himself a glass of water.

'Sorry, did I wake you?'

'No, I was just lying in bed, thinking.'

'Oh?' Oh god, he was going to have a go at me.

'Umm Josie,' he raked his hand through his bedroom hair, 'I seem to be making a habit of it. Acting like a giant tit, I mean.' I shrugged my shoulders but secretly I think he had a point.

'It's up to you what you do with your life, or who you do it with. I shouldn't have interfered. I had no right. Josie, you are incredible. Funny and strong, feisty and kind, and …'.

'And?'

'And so unequivocally beautiful. Inside and out.' He sighed.

I took a sip of the hot chocolate and a little bubble of pleasure floated up inside me. *Unequivocally beautiful, inside and out* … that sounded quite poetic.

'Anyway, I managed to get an earlier flight to that cooking school in Italy. I leave tomorrow. Might be gone a while.' He mumbled the words in a hurry.

'Tomorrow! How long for?' My heart contracted, the bubbles of pleasure popping loudly.

'A couple of months, maybe more.'

A couple of weeks, he'd told me earlier. 'It's all a bit sudden. What about work?'

'I quit. Called my manager as soon as I got off the flight. Now that Maddy's got the hang of things, she'll take over some of my shifts.'

'Maddy?'

'Madeline, I introduced you to her earlier. I've been training her up.'

'I hate that you are leaving, Ed. The fact that you're going so suddenly and for so long.'

This should have been the perfect solution. I had decided after all that our living situation had become difficult, but my heart thudded painfully. I felt responsible for messing things up between us.

'I need to do this for me, Josie, and maybe some time away will do us both good.'

I nodded but my head was screaming *Noooooo!* Ed was wonderful and warm and honest and silly and dorky … and I liked him. I was startled by the realisation that I might actually *really like him.* Did I? How had that even happened? I wanted to tell him, but the words got stuck in my throat. Maybe he was right, we'd both been through so much. A bit of time and space might be just what we needed.

'You'll be fine. The way you've been handling your life and having adventures, you'll probably be flying a helicopter or abseiling down the Shard by the time I get back.'

Ed gave me an affectionate hug but still I couldn't speak. At least he said he was coming back.

He poured himself a hot chocolate and squirted a huge

dollop of whipped cream on top. Next in went the mini marshmallows, followed by crumbled flake. Nice.

A new emotion took hold of me as I watched him. A timidity, a tenderness, a gentle heat better than any hot chocolate flooded me.

Ed held my gaze and before we knew it, our creamy, foamy hot chocolate mouths collided. It was warm and messy, and his hands were in my hair pulling me close. A fuzzy, tingling sensation erupted inside me, sending waves of pleasure in places I didn't even think about, like the backs of my knees and the tips of my toes. We could have been kissing for five minutes or an hour, I had no idea, but suddenly Ed pulled away.

'Oh shit. I'm a tit. A giant tit. I've only gone and done it again.'

I stared at him glassy-eyed, still in a state of swoon.

He scarpered off into his room before I had the chance to say anything.

Why did things always have to be so complicated?

Chapter 22
The Final Chapter

I TOSSED AND TURNED, FINALLY DRIFTING off into a fitful sleep where dreams of Ed's enlarged face oozing fresh cream plagued me. I woke up with a start. This was ridiculous! I flung off the bedsheet and proceeded to creep over to the door and into the corridor. I don't know why I hesitated, as I had already decided to wake Ed and discuss our predicament like the mature, rational adults that we were.

I stood outside his door taking a few breaths, knocking gently on his door. Without waiting for a response, I quickly turned the handle and walked in before I lost my nerve. Ed was fast asleep, a shaft of light through the curtains illuminated his frame. Okay, so he liked to sleep in the buff, with no top sheet. I know I should have got out of there pretty sharpish, but my legs didn't seem to move. I watched the gentle rise and fall of his chest; his hair was matted and a small smile played on his lips. Maybe he was having sweet dreams. My eyes drifted to his lower body, I moved a fraction closer. As if sensing someone was watching him, he started to wriggle around. Oh god. What was I going to do?

His eyes flicked open. 'Josie?' he said, sounding understandably alarmed.

'Hi,' I breathed.

'What the fuck …? He scrambled to the chair to pull on a t-shirt and some boxers.

I turned as he got up, my cheeks flaming. Oh. Dear.

'Is everything okay?' He sat on the bed and switched on the bedside lamp.

'Umm, I just wanted to talk about things.' To say that I felt like a moron was an understatement. Oh well, he said that he felt like a total tit earlier, so I guess we were even. Kind of.

'Things are weird between us. I didn't expect …' I began.

'Neither did I. Look I'm sorry, it won't happen again. I'm leaving in the morning, for fuck's sake.' I was taken back by his fury but then again, I had just scared the shit out of him.

'I didn't come in here to have a go.' I said, my fingers instinctively brushing my lips, remembering how soft his had felt, but maybe that was on account of all the whipped cream.

'It kind of took me by surprise, the kiss and … how much I enjoyed it.' I blurted out.

'What about Chambers? Did you enjoy kissing him too?' There was no anger in his voice, just a slight edge to it.

Shit. Chambers. The truth is that he had clean gone out of my head.

'I did,' I replied honestly, 'but it didn't mean anything.' Even as I said it, it sounded like such a cliché.

'Sorry. Like I said, it's your life and I have no place telling you what to do, or who to do it with.'

'My life's been something of a rollercoaster, what with four fiancés and a funeral.' I sat beside him.

'And then some,' Ed said, giving me a wry smile. The light made his skin glow.

'Well, mine's not been much different. I haven't had four fiancés, but I did almost have a wedding, if we're making comparisons. And I'm none too keen on getting my heart ripped out again.' I didn't blame him for doubting me. Niles, Chris, Niles again, then Chambers. Like a game of romantic ping-pong, but my feelings for Ed had caught me unawares.

I gently placed my hand on his, hoping he wouldn't pull it away. I hated that I had caused him pain. He looked down at my hand.

'And I realise you're not ready to be with anyone, Josie, and I get it. I really do.'

I nodded in agreement, even though part of me wanted to snog him senseless.

'I guess I do need time to figure out what I want from life, post-thirty. I've done things I never dreamed I would, and half the time I've felt brave and the other half terrified.'

'That's like most of us, Josie. But the difference is that you've triumphed despite the turbulence and become stronger for it. You are remarkable.' Remarkable. I let the word settle in my mind. It was true that I wasn't going to be the sort of person to shy away from challenges. Not anymore.

'I think it's time for a new list, but this time it's going to be my list and I'm only putting things on it that will make my heart sing and have me throwing my hair back with joy.'

Ed laughed, 'Good for you. Sorry, it's just that you reminded me of Gran then. She knew how to have fun. I loved her for that.'

'Me too. She certainly had a way of dancing with life, even

at her funeral, but I don't think Melvin was too impressed. He looked like he was going to have a fit.'

'Yeah, that was classic.' He was wiping tears from his eyes. We sat in silence for a while, reminiscing. He pulled me into his arms and held me. It felt like the most natural - and the only - place I wanted to be. Heat flooded my body as his fingertips traced a line up the nape of my neck and into my hair.

'I should go,' I croaked eventually. 'Your flight leaves in 6 hours.' But I was finding it hard to pull away.

He blinked at me. 'Buona notte, Josie.' He kissed me on the forehead.

No matter what happened next, I felt close to Ed. We'd shared laughter, wine, tears and a few fuck-a-doodle-do's (from 'Four Weddings and a Funeral') over the months.

I closed the door softly behind me as I left. I lay awake for a while wondering whether to go back to him, or whether he'd come to me. That typical dilemma that you always have in romantic movies or books. But this was real life, and I knew that now wasn't the right time. I squeezed my eyes shut and fell asleep.

By the time I got up, Ed had left. I found milk in the fridge and pancakes on the table. Where he'd found time to buy provisions, cook and tidy away the remnants of last night's party, I had no idea. I noisily swallowed the lump in my throat.

The whole day stretched ahead of me, and rather gloriously so. The sunlight was streaming through the window and making pretty patterns on the wall. I found a heart-shaped piece of card under the stack of pancakes. In the middle of the stack was written: 'A reminder to do whatever makes your heart sing!' Ah!

With a spring in my step and a smile on my face, I grabbed my keys, the half bottle of champagne still in the fridge, and a plate of pancakes with strawberries. I ran down the stairs and out into the communal gardens. The feel of grass underneath my bare feet was amazing. I scrunched up my toes revelling in the sensations. Then I attempted to do something I hadn't done since I was seven years old. A cartwheel. Whoops, nearly knocked the champagne over. Couldn't have that. I know I looked a bit bonkers, especially when I exposed my stripy knickers mid-air. I sat on the grass, gulping the champagne and stuffing my face. Let the neighbours peep at me through their blinds, I didn't care.

'I will be more playful,' I affirmed out loud. Worry and fear had been my companions for as long as I could remember. Fear that I would never find anyone. Worry that I wouldn't be able to keep anyone interested for long. But sitting here now, I felt relaxed and joyful. I hugged my knees to my chest.

I looked up; a plane flew overhead. I watched its journey across the sky. That could be Ed up there following his dreams, making things happen. My heart swelled.

All of a sudden, I was hiccupping and couldn't stop. That's what champagne did to me. I'd also sunk quite a few whisky and cokes last night. Maybe I'd just lie down for a bit.

I woke up on the grass with a start, the wind blowing my nightdress up. How long had I been here? Luckily my keys were still by my side. I grabbed my things and headed back to the flat.

I pinned the red heart up on my fridge and wrote 'find a fun course' in felt tip pen. I hadn't studied since my uni days, but that had hardly been fun. But before I planned anything else, I needed a shower and a chat with Mum.

I picked up my phone. I'd had a missed call and someone had left a message. It was Mum!

'Josie, I got myself a mobile, fancy that! Well this is my number. Listen, can we meet? I want to explain things. Sorry about last night. Bye.'

I was about to call her back, when a text appeared.

> *'Have just learnt to text! How exciting darling. Meet me for lunch if you can. 2pm at Carluccio's in South Ken. Bye. Mum :)'*

I smiled. That just proved it. It was never too late to learn.

> *'So glad you've got a phone, Mum! Don't worry about last night. Looking forward to seeing you for lunch. Josie xx'*

I wondered if Mum would be bringing her 'man-friend' along. I was kind of hoping that she did. At least I'd be able to suss him out for myself.

I arrived at Carluccio's a little early and grabbed a table by the window. She strode in a few minutes later, wearing killer heels and a little black dress, a bright silk scarf hung loosely around her neck. Wow, she looked stunning but where was her boyfriend? 'Be still, eager mind!' I told myself.

'So how are you, Mum?' I asked as she sat herself down.

'Good, really good.' Her eyes flicked over the menu. 'What shall I have? Mmm.'

I browsed my menu. The waiter came over. Dark, Italian.

'Buongiorno, bellissima donne! What can I get you? You are sisters, non?' Typical roguish charmer.

'No, this is my daughter. She turned thirty yesterday.'

'Non!' he gasped in horror. 'You don't look old enough to have such a daughter!'

'Two glasses of champagne on the house,' he said, snapping his fingers.

I hadn't been planning on more champagne, but it would have been rude to refuse.

Once we had ordered our food, Mum spoke. 'So about last night. I know I was acting a bit strange.' This was it, the big reveal.

'Your Dad's been in contact.' Not what I was expecting, to say the least.

'In contact? Dad? As in you've seen him?' My heart started hammering. He'd barely communicated since he left, with only the odd word to let us know that he was still alive.

'No, but he's been sending gifts in the post.'

'Really …?' I was on the edge of my seat, champagne poised to my lips.

'The first thing I received was this …' her eyes lit up as she placed a postcard on the table. It was a bird with bright purple feathers nestled on a bush. Ok, so I could see the resemblance. Mum was colourful and striking, rather like the bird but still, it seemed a strange choice of postcard. I turned the card over. 'Graceful and floating free, this bird captivates with its beauty and elegance.'

'The hummingbird relates to a time when we were in the garden on a warm summer's day and this bright bird came swooping down out of nowhere and landed next to me. I didn't know that it was a hummingbird at the time, but your dad told me. That's the day he proposed.' Her face was radiant, her smile bright. Her fingers moved up to stroke the silk scarf around her neck.

'Did Dad give you that too?' I was in a state of slight shock.

'Yes, it was sent with a note that read, 'Because you're worth it!' He always liked to indulge my penchant for silk scarves.'

'Was there anything else?'

'A Japanese doll.'

'A Japanese doll?' I echoed.

'Because we always talked about going to Japan, but never got to go.'

'Right,' I said feeling perplexed. 'Anything else?'

'Just a cinema stub to 'ET.''

'ET? As in that alien thing.'

'Extra Terrestrial. We had quite a meaningful encounter in the back row.'

La, la, la, la, la. I really didn't need to know that.

'Why send those things … and why now?'

'I think he's ready to come home.'

'Really? And how do you feel about that?' I felt kind of numb. Had he stopped to think about Ant and me in all of this?

'Do you know where he is? Did he tell you?'

'No, but I'm sure he will. I feel him close by. I know this is a huge shock, Josie, and believe me, I have a million questions I want to ask him. But I am glad he's been in touch. I never stopped loving him. No one has ever come close to replacing him.'

I didn't know what to say. I'd waited twenty-five years for news of his return and now it seemed imminent and all rather surreal.

'You will tell me when he gets in touch again?'

'Of course. He's your dad and he's coming home.'

'Do you mind if I skip dessert. I need some time to process everything, some time alone.'

'Sure. Call me, darling. If you want to.' Mum's eyes were full of concern as I fled the restaurant.

I headed in the direction of the museums and just kept on walking. It was nice that Mum was so happy. Clearly she was, but was Dad just teasing us with these gifts? I don't think I could actually fully believe that Dad was coming home until I saw him in the flesh. It seemed I'd been thinking a lot about him these past few months. But what if he upped and left again? Unfortunately, I'd had rather a lot of experience of men leaving. Ant was too young to remember him, being only a few months old when he disappeared.

I tried to push thoughts of Dad out of my mind. I'd had enough shocks and surprises in the last few weeks. Was it too much to want a bit of quiet time? A touch of the mundane would be quite welcome right now. More than anything I wanted to pick up the phone and talk to Ed, but he'd only just left and we were meant to be having space and time away from each other. I flopped onto the sofa and enjoyed a quiet night in front of the TV. Calm at last.

That night I slept for ten hours straight and felt somewhat refreshed and restored for it. I turned on my phone which then beeped at me several times.

Seven text messages from Babs. Shit! Babs! I'd forgotten all about her, what with everything else.

> *'Had to get up five times in the bloody middle of the night to bloody pee.'*

> *'Feeling queasy. Just the smell of Jake's sausages makes me want to puke.'*

'Just been sick, is horrible. I hate being pregnant!'

'Ooh, I could murder a deep fat fried banana smothered in peanut butter.' Now that was just weird.

'I'm soo horny, not sure Jake can manage round three, though.' Really? Did I need to know that?

'Will you be my birthing partner, pleeeaasee xx'

Oh god, now I felt a bit queasy. Wasn't that supposed to be Jake's job, I wondered? But then I remembered her telling me he'd passed out twice when visiting his dad in hospital. He'd discovered an almost pathological fear of blood, guts and other dodgy bodily fluids. It's a good thing that Babs had been there for him.

'I love you xxx' Ah!

I was just about to call her when another message came through.

'So tired, having a nap. Call you later xx'

I wondered how I was going to get through seven months of Babs being hormonal and wine-deprived. I made a mental note to order 'What to expect when you're expecting' from Amazon. I'd need to be prepared too, especially if I was going to be her birthing partner. Gulp.

I googled 'fun short courses in London,' wondering if it would find me a course on how to be a good birthing partner, or how to talk to your dad after twenty-five years. It didn't throw up any matches, but maybe that's because those things didn't exactly fit into the category of a short fun course. It did throw up plenty of other things though, including guitar and singing lessons, cake decorating, dress-making, how to make bridal bouquets, etc.

I think I'd give that one a big fat miss, thank you very much, as well as something that sounded particularly intriguing: 'how to please yourself.' Indeed. A course in masturbation, perhaps? Perfectly fine, but I wouldn't want to do it or discuss it in front of anyone else. I read on. Phew, it said something about self-expression through movement and sound. There was a taster day coming up. I signed up before I could change my mind.

I spent the rest of the day reading and thinking. One thing I realised about life was that I couldn't stop it throwing things at me, so I just had to deal with life as best as I bloody well could.

I caught up with Babs and Dame the next day. We all got foot rubs and facials, followed by a very indulgent cream tea. Babs had the excuse of mad hormonal cravings, and Dame and I had no choice but to scoff our faces to keep her company. I told them about France, Chambers, Ed, and my dad.

'Blimey, Josie, and your life used to be so boring,' Dame retorted.

'I know! And I've started having these imaginary banal conversations with Dad. About the weather, washing-up, what to wear ... sometimes we're laughing, sometimes I'm shouting at him and wondering how the hell he could have ducked out of our lives. Maybe if he'd let us support him, he would never have had a bloody break-down in the first place.'

'It's perfectly normal to feel all those things, Josie.' Dame stroked my arm. A cigarette would have been welcome about now, but a) we were indoors in quite a posh tea establishment, and b) Babs was pregnant. Two compelling reasons not to light up.

'So, what *are* you going to do?' Babs asked, picking up her third slice of chocolate hazelnut cake.

'For now, I've booked a few days in the Peak District, give myself a chance to think through things without any added dramas.'

'Do you want me to come?' Dame asked.

'No, I'd prefer to go alone, just me and a few sheep,' I smiled. I kept my new 'Heart List' to myself, as it was my list after all, and I was just making it up as I went along which felt like the right thing to do - for now.

'If I didn't know you better - and the fact that you have without a shadow of a doubt changed - I'd say that you've hooked up with someone new, or maybe slinked back to Niles?'

'No way!' Babs said it for me. 'Josie rocks. She'd never go back there.'

She was right.

'Seriously guys, I'm going alone. If I can do foreign travel, I can certainly do the Peak District. Give me a chance to dust off my walking boots.'

'Walking boots?!' You own about thirty pairs of totally inappropriate footwear, all high heels or shiny, and maybe one pair of manky trainers!' Trust Dame to pay particular attention to my shoe collection.

'That's where you're wrong, Damian. I have a pair of walking boots.' I just needed to find them, that's all. They were still in a box somewhere from about five years ago.

'You will be back in time for the birth, won't you?'

'I'm only going for a few days, Babs. There is no way I would not be there. I am your birthing partner, after all.'

She looked happy again. 'You love Ed, don't you?'

That had come out of the blue.

'You do, don't you?' she squealed. 'You want to kiss him, you want to love him, you want to marry him.' Oh god, a pregnant Babs was so annoying.

'Maybe she loves Chambers. He had her writhing in sexual bliss, clearly wanting more if it hadn't been for that banana lady.'

'I do not love Chambers.'

'So you *do* love Ed!' Babs was positively beaming.

'Maybe I love me. I am still man-free. My dalliance with Chambers doesn't count.'

'And you only snogged Ed once, so that doesn't count either.' Dame smirked at me.

'Exactly. What will be will be.'

The next day I received a phone call from the solicitor asking when I'd be available to come down to their offices, and to bring the painting with me. Well there was no time like the present.

The same hairy-faced solicitor greeted me at the office. Not that I had anything against hairy faces, it's just that an abundance of hair and bushy eyebrows seemed to make me nervous, I don't know why. On the plus side, he seemed altogether more pleasant and not so stern this time.

He coughed and cleared his throat. 'I think it best if I give you a few minutes alone, Ms. Green.'

With that, he looked at the painting and seemingly satisfied, he asked me to sign a document. After that he handed me a letter and excused himself.

I opened the letter, my heart pounding.

'Dear Josie,

I trust you've had the most amazing Journey. Hopefully you are not too cross with me. I expect you know all about my affair all those years ago by now, but I'm only human and have made a right hash of things in my time so forgive me and also for my meddling and matchmaking. It's not like me to try and control things!

I had to smile at that one.

'But I just wanted you to see that there's more to life than you thought, so now you've fulfilled your task, I've enclosed your cheque for £25,000. Enjoy it, you deserve it!

I hope, dear, that you will also find a path that you're passionate about, as that little gallery is far too limiting for you.

I've enclosed two extra gifts, I hope you don't mind ...

The first is an open ticket to Thailand, and a place called the Elephant Nature Park in Chiang Mai. It's a wonderful elephant rescue & rehabilitation centre I came across about 10 years ago, they really look after the orphaned elephants. You'll love it.

The second is a separate cheque for £20,000. I hope you will use it towards your wedding fund. I know it's been your life's desire to get married and a girl needs a pretty dress and nice shoes and a decent venue and they don't come cheap. So imagine me there but Josie, don't rush getting married. You will know when you meet the right one. I will be applauding you all the way. Even if it's not with my Ed ;)

Have a wonderful life. Be brave, be bold.

All my love always.
Pru xxxx

I sat for a while, remembering when we watched together a programme about orphaned elephants a few months back. Such striking, social creatures who loved and protected their family members. She hadn't told me that she visited an elephant sanctuary. There was so much she hadn't told me, but I guess I had been pretty self-absorbed, wallowing in my own pain. I wish I had the chance to get to know her all over again. I hugged the letter to my chest, silent tears falling. She had really noticed me, seen things in me that I hadn't even acknowledged myself.

Her kindness and love were abundant, her spirit burned bright. I had a duty to carry on her legacy of being brave and bold, as she had wanted.

There was no going back now. Shortly afterwards I left the stuffy office and basked in the afternoon sun, coming to rest underneath a huge oak tree. When I returned to the flat I took the painting out from its wrapping. I didn't want Pru, Bert and her baby to be a secret or hidden anymore. I dug about in one of the kitchen drawers to find a picture hook, and hung up the painting.

Next, I pulled out the jewellery box from under my bed and opened it up, watching the ballerina twirl. I took out the tanzanite necklace and held it in my hand, enjoying the coolness of the stone, its colours seeming to change every few seconds. I dug out my walking boots and packed a small case. I included the red heart from the side of my fridge. I'm sure I'd find inspiration to add a few things to my list amongst the hills, the trees, and the sheep. I was really looking forward to my little trip.

So. There you have it. My year before turning thirty had been pretty epic. I can't imagine anything topping it, but that's the funny thing about life. You never know what's coming next.

Epilogue
One Year Later

I LOOKED OUT AT THE CRASHING waves, magnificent and powerful, yet soothing at the same time. The moonlight shone on the water, making it luminous. This place was magical, especially now that Ed and I were the proud owners of the Hummingbird Café in Boscombe Bay.

Ed had completed his chef training in Italy, then gone on to Paris. The world could quite literally have been his oyster, but he told me Pru and Bert had taken him and his brother to Boscombe on many a balmy summer, and he had fallen in love with the place. Bournemouth was beautiful and lively but Boscombe, just down the road, had stolen his heart.

Speaking of hearts, after Ed left I spent three utterly divine months doing exactly as I pleased, having gained inspiration on the 'how to please yourself' course. Things on my heart list included painting the flat in neutral colours, comedy acting, burlesque taster sessions and - wait for it - taking a helicopter flying lesson. Admittedly I'd had to squeeze the pilot's bulging biceps really hard when the helicopter took a sudden nose dive, but it was all part of the course.

The bravest thing I did though was fall in love again … with Ed. I surprised him by showing up in Venice. I loved watching him at work. His hands were so deft at creating culinary delights that pleased all the senses. Luckily, I hadn't put him off his game and that's when I knew it was *amore*. He was the one. 'The One.' I cringed when I thought about the countless times I had convinced myself I had found 'The One.' But this time it was for real. I gave him my heart list and told him that my heart wouldn't be complete without him in it. He whooped and cheered and nearly tipped me off the gondola and into the Grand Canal.

When we returned to England, Ed told me about his Boscombe Bay dreams. I fell in love with the place almost as much as I fell in love with Ed. We found the café within two weeks of being in Boscombe. The flat above the café was delightful and I used some of the money Pru had given me to fix up the place to make it really homely. I liked getting to know the locals and promoting the business. The college had courses in social media and web design, running a business and bookkeeping, and I found that despite a few teething problems, I was actually quite good at it. Maybe my degree hadn't been such a waste of time after all.

Soon enough we were able to employ two part-time staff and we used some of our wall space to exhibit local artists. We also ran a supper soup club for rough sleepers twice a week. The memory of that man in the park had never left me and now I was in a position to help the homeless in a more practical way. Our trip to the elephant sanctuary in Thailand was booked for the middle of January. I was super excited about going. I had caught the travel bug at last!

As for my friends … well, I'm pleased to say that I made it

down the aisle to stand proudly beside the girl of my dreams. Yes, that's right. The girl of my dreams. Bridesmaid to the beautiful Babs, best friends forever. Mum had dabbed a handkerchief to her eyes during the ceremony and whispered to me not to worry, that it would be my turn soon. But I wasn't worried, I was surprisingly content not to be planning my wedding for a change. As for Babs, I was in awe of her, especially after watching her bloom through pregnancy and give birth to baby Zoe. And I'll have you know that I was a rather good and supportive birthing partner, despite needing a few gin and tonic's to get me through it all.

Jake had been there too, overcoming his fears to give her support when she most needed it. He had settled down into the role of loving husband and doting dad. He currently had a small but significant part in the Globe theatre performance of Hamlet. Dame and George were blissfully happy in their Hampstead home. I'd put money on them being engaged, if not married, by this time next year. And I was finally living the life I was meant to be living, not life according to my mum, or my boss, or my insecure younger self. Not even Pru was telling me what to do anymore, although she would forever be guiding me in my heart.

The biggest shift in the last year had been having my dad back in our lives. After twenty-five years of wondering if I would ever see him again, or what he looked like, or what I would say to him, I finally met him. After a few weeks of us stumbling around each other trying to pick up the pieces of the past, we began to talk really honestly. I'd found out that drugs had hugely contributed to his breakdown and that he'd lost himself, as well as his family, for all those years. But he seemed well enough now, determined to be there for the three of us.

He had spent a lot of time helping us decorate the café and was good at fixing shelves, sorting out lighting and all the sorts of things that Ed and I were generally lousy at. Granted he was more of a friend than a dad, but I was enjoying getting to know him and found that I quite liked him. He became good friends with Mum as well. Not lovers, Mum assured me. I wasn't sure if she was trying to convince me or herself, but I trusted that she would do what was right for her.

Ant was so similar to Dad and could turn his hand to anything: labouring, plumbing, electrics, travelling. Ant was currently in Bali with his new girlfriend. They had backpacked around Singapore, Malaysia, and Indonesia, so he hadn't been around to see the grand opening of Hummingbird Café, but that was fine. I had enough to keep me occupied.

Ed visited Tebor again, getting to know him slowly. He isn't all bad, Ed conceded. However, his feelings towards Chambers remained frosty. To say that they were not at all enamoured with each other was an understatement. In fact, I was pretty sure Ed hated Chambers. Meanwhile, I guessed Chambers regarded Ed with little more than disdain. Ed said he saw him schmoozing up to another girl, no doubt seducing her with talk of his yacht and billionaire lifestyle. Ed looked at me a little insecurely from under his floppy fringe to see if any jealously registered on my face, but I wasn't in the slightest bit interested. What we had had been a brief encounter. He could shag a thousand girls for all I cared. I had my Ed.

Ed, who puffed out his chest and got all cross that Chambers had got to me first. It was kind of cute.

I smiled to myself thinking about the scene in Bridget

Jones's Diary when she had Mark Darcy and Daniel Cleaver fighting over her. Mmm, that might have been rather hot although I suspected Ed would have ended up with multiple injuries and in casualty, while Chambers would have breezed back to his yacht, not a hair out of place. So maybe not …

Niles had barely entered my thoughts either. My guess was that he was crying into his coffee and booking an appointment with a counsellor, wondering how his love life could have gone so horribly wrong, how he could have been so stupid to cheat on me. At least that's what I liked to think. If he was still with his Irish blonde bit of fluff then good luck to him. I had my own gorgeous bit of fluff to play with.

On a rare quiet midweek afternoon Ed suggested that we close early.

'Are you sure?' I asked, as Ed was devoted to the business.

'It's a lovely afternoon and I'd like to take my favourite girl out on a picnic.'

'Wasn't she free?' I joked. Ed tickled me under my ribs and pulled me in tight.

'You're my girl, my only girl,' he whispered thickly into my ear.

Joy rippled through my heart. Ed was full of sweetness and I never got sick of it.

He laid out the picnic, complete with salmon, strawberries, champagne, crusty bread … yum.

I relaxed on the blanket after lunch. Ed ran off towards the waves saying something had caught his eye. I watched him go around picking up shells. Was he thinking of making me a shell necklace, I wondered? Honestly that boy was as balmy as a box of frogs, but I loved him.

He bounded over to me. 'Look at these shells, aren't they amazing?' he was saying, looking at them in awe.

'Very pretty,' I replied, smiling up at him. He held out his hand, gesturing me to stand up. I admired the shells, turning them over. Then he handed me one, asking me to close my eyes first, saying this one was particularly amazing. I opened my eyes and saw the shell but there was something in it. Something shiny was glittering up at me. I gasped and then sobbed, throwing my arms around Ed. I nearly dropped the shell in my excitement but managed to recover it just in time. I took out the ring with the gorgeous blue stone. I was shaking, still not able to speak.

'Will you?' Ed gave me a crooked smile, looking a little nervous.

'Of course I will, I do!' I shouted, for all the seagulls to hear.

I guess I, Josie Green, was getting married after all.

Ed whooped and lifted me in his arms, swinging me round. Something twinkled up in the sky as if it were winking down at me, but there were no stars in the sky at this time of day. There could only be one explanation. Pru was toasting us from up above.

Good on you, Pru!!

The End

About the Author

Priya has led a life filled with challenge and adventure from trekking the Himalayas, to shaving all her hair off for charity (it grew back!), to witnessing the magical Aurora Borealis, the Northern Lights in Reykjavik. Her most recent journey took her to the beaches of Goa, completing her yoga teacher training course.

Her writing journey began almost 20 years ago. She wrote the first three chapters of this book, before stuffing them in a drawer to gather dust. Finally, she decided to finish what she started, the result being her debut novel, 'Josie's Upturned World.'

Priya can often be found doing yoga in her garden or dancing like a crazy thing, not caring if anyone's watching! She also has a love for certain foods beginning with 'C' – cake, chocolate, cookies, cheese, crisps, and chips to name a few.

Visit her website to find out more:
www.priyapopat.co.uk
Instagram: @priyapopwriter
Twitter: @priyapopwriter

Acknowledgements

Thank you to my long-suffering family members, Sheena & Mili Popat for providing endless support and encouragement in the completion of this project. Couldn't have done it without all your read-throughs and sensible suggestions.

Thank you to my dear friend Kevin who is an amazing volunteer at Paul's Cancer Support Centre. He took the time and trouble to read through and help edit an earlier draft of this book, despite this really not being his genre at all!

I also want to give a big shout out to all my friends & family who have believed in me and kept me going. I'm so lucky to have you in my life.

And a MASSIVE thanks to the amazing & inspirational Callie who helped edit my final draft and make this book a reality.

A big shout out to Streetlight Graphics for producing an awesome cover design and interiors.

Most importantly, a huge thanks to my readers. I really hope you enjoy reading my debut novel. May your lives be filled with joy, challenge and inspiration. I've made it my mission to take on new challenges like Josie and lead a life of purpose and passion.

To find out more visit me at

www.priyapopat.co.uk

29231027R00180

Printed in Great Britain
by Amazon